Sierra Nevada Trail of Murder

JENNIFER QUASHNICK

South Lake Tahoe, CA
www.mountaingirlmysteries.com

ISBN: 978-0-9906750-0-6

Library of Congress Control Number: 2014915473
Cover Design: Vicky Shea, www.ponderosapinedesign.com
Cover Photo: Moya Sanders
Copy Editor: Mary Cook

Orders, inquiries, and correspondence should be addressed to:

Mountaingirl Mysteries
PO Box 550145
South Lake Tahoe, CA 96155
www.mountaingirlmysteries.com

To all who passionately fight
for the protection of our environment

Keep close to Nature's heart . . . and break clear away, once in a while, and climb a mountain or spend a week in the woods. Wash your spirit clean.

—*John Muir*

ACKNOWLEDGMENTS

This book would never have gone beyond my own computer if not for the extensive help, support, encouragement, advice, hard work, and passion of so many others in my life. I am deeply thankful to the following people, without whom I would not have been able to write this book:

My parents, Carol and Terry, provided me with the best childhood a girl could ask for and the means to develop confidence and trust in myself. They have continued to support and encourage me every single day—probably far more than they expected to at this point.

Moya Sanders, an amazing friend and inspirational person, gets as much credit for this book as I do. She has been a shoulder to cry on, an artistic adviser, an amazing photographer, and she has set up the world's best unofficial dog park.

Diana Sanders, who read the first draft, flaws and all, and encouraged me to keep going.

My Aunt Linda, who came back into my life right when I needed her, reminded me how important it is to be yourself and to always play outdoors, and whose editing helped keep Rachel in line.

Kim Wyatt, owner of Bona Fide Books, an amazing woman who does more in a week then most of us do in a year, still manages to take the time to support local writers, and whose innocent question "What's MgM stand for?" got this whole thing rolling.

Randy Mundt, an excellent editor, writer, and strategic user of red ink.

Tamara Wallace, editor extraordinaire, gave me the confidence to know when the write words—I mean right words—were being used.

Local author Janet Marlborough's quick review and honest insights were invaluable.

i

The warm welcome given to all aspiring writers by the members of Tahoe Writers Works encouraged me to keep moving forward; their honest insights were exactly what I needed, and I have been lucky to continue to learn from them.

Todd Borg, local Lake Tahoe author of the Owen McKenna mystery thrillers, gave a complete stranger the right advice when she needed it.

Other friends and family helped by reviewing, editing, and encouraging this book, including Dr. Karen Borges, Jared Manninen, Angela Olson, Angela Paul, Mary Richardson, my grandmother Evelyn Warddrip, and my sister Shelley Whittaker, who also unknowingly took my favorite picture with Bella (followed up by my favorite picture with my sister).

I am grateful to those who have dedicated their lives to protecting Lake Tahoe and from whom I have had the immense pleasure and amazing luck to learn lessons in life, work, advocacy, humor, and adventure: Laurel Ames, Michael Donahoe, Susan Gearhart, Craig Thomas, Judi Tornese, Ellie Waller, Ann Nichols, Dave McClure, and countless others fighting the good fight in the Sierra Nevada and beyond.

And last, but not least, I am indebted to my sweet Bella, who brought positive energy into my life when I needed it, whose antics inspired me to start writing this book, and who has kept me laughing and smiling ever since.

AUTHOR'S NOTES

Those familiar with Hope Valley and this particular trail off Luther Pass may notice I took some topographical liberties with the actual "Trail of Murder." I hope you can forgive me (pun intended), but the actual trail is far too welcoming, and accessible, for such a plot.

If you are looking for the amazing companionship a dog can provide, I urge you to do some research into breed characteristics with your lifestyle in mind. After that, if you decide to add a dog to your family, please first consider adoption/rescue. It won't be long before you find yourself asking exactly who rescued whom. Learn more at http://www.humanesociety.org/.

As for Bella's breed, Border collies are high-energy herding dogs; they are wonderful dogs but only with enough exercise, attention, and mental stimulation from their owners. We regularly hike, snowshoe, play games, do tricks, and have play dates with canine friends. Like me, when she doesn't get enough exercise and outdoor time, she's not a happy girl. Please visit http://www.bcrescue.org/bcwarning.html for more information on Border collies.

PROLOGUE

"Man, you should've just let it go," he said, pulling the trigger, surprised he'd actually done it. His nervousness was reflected in the barely perceptible tremor of the gun, but the bullet still struck as he'd intended, killing the other man instantly as it seared through his brain. He watched the body crumple to the ground, with only the slightest drip of blood from the small hole on his victim's forehead. Strangely the trickle of blood stopped well before it could drip onto the pine-needle-covered forest floor.

As Spencer stared at the lifeless form in front of him, he replayed the past few minutes in his mind. To an observer, the two of them would appear to be friends out hiking for a day. David, about fifteen years his senior, had no idea this would be his last hike. In fact, he'd even expressed his appreciation for Spencer's help carrying the extra weight of the ice packs needed to keep the water samples cool as they ascended the hiking trail. David was, no doubt, the more experienced hiker, wearing a well-used day-hiking pack that comfortably carried the weight of the contents on his waist. Spencer struggled to keep up, out of breath from regular lack of exercise and clearly not dressed for hiking. The best he'd been able to do was pull an old pair of tennis shoes from his car, along with the double-handled dark-green gym bag with the gun and silencer inside. He'd played the city kid with the stubborn pride, refusing to take the more comfortable backpack David had offered.

Less than five minutes before, Spencer had done what David had probably been expecting the entire time—he stopped, gasping for air, and said he needed to catch his breath. The older man had chuckled.

"I'll get the bottles ready for more samples." Spencer had watched, trying to hide the tension that ran through his entire body, as David removed his pack and walked a few feet to the side of the path, setting it on a fallen tree. He did some digging in his pack, first removing a new pair of disposable laboratory gloves Spencer recognized after seeing a pair at the last sample site and setting them next to the pack while continuing to look in his bag, head down with his back to his assassin. Next the man removed a small ice box and continued digging. Spencer quickly grabbed the gun and had it positioned squarely at David's head just before David turned back toward him, a small water sample bottle in one hand, a permanent marker in the other, saying, "I'll go ahead and note the . . . ," before going mute after his eyes registered the barrel of the gun aimed at his head five feet away. "What the . . . ?" was the last thing he'd said before Spencer pulled the trigger.

Now, his mind struggling to return to the present, Spencer realized he was still staring at David's lifeless body, wasting precious time he couldn't assume he had. He removed the silencer from the gun and fit it into David's backpack, grabbed the marker and bottle David had been holding, and began stuffing his own bag inside the pack, planning to wear it back down the forest trail. As he leaned over to rearrange the contents inside, he looked in the direction the bullet had gone. It had left David's body and lodged in a fallen tree, surrounded by a few sprayed drops of blood. Strange, he thought. Even though his boss had said this type of gun would yield a "clean shot," presuming he aimed it right, Spencer had expected more of a mess. Still working on an adrenaline high, trying not to think about what had just transpired, Spencer noted he would have to dig out part of the tree to retrieve the bullet and try to make the damaged bark look like natural "wear and tear"—not hard as this was a diverse forest, with trees ranging from a few feet to several hundred feet tall, and various decaying fallen trees along the way, all with their own unique shapes and markings. As he was ready to grab the disposable gloves from where David had set them on the log, he heard an unexpected whistling sound coming from the other side of the trail bend that lay a few hundred feet ahead. He froze. The sound of a woman's voice echoed through the trees. Spencer grabbed the bag, inadvertently knocking the gloves to the ground next to the body. Walking as lightly as he could and wanting to hide as soon as possible, he started down his own path parallel to the hiking trail. He'd only gone a few feet when to his side Spencer noticed a thicket of dense pine trees that he could easily hide behind. He hoped the body was hidden well enough that the person or people would simply pass on by. It had taken all of his courage to kill David. He knew he wasn't prepared, emotionally or otherwise, to add innocent bystanders to his list.

~

"Bella, come here girl!" Rachel called out as she continued along the narrow, rock-lined dirt path, wondering what "gift" her one-year-old dog, Bella, would find for her this time as she followed an undetermined radius around the hiking trail, nose to the ground. Rachel had to laugh. Bella, a black Border collie mix Rachel adopted from a rescue agency six months ago, had a knack for finding various items along the trails and presenting them to her in comical "look-what-I-found-for-you" ceremonies. Typical treasures included pinecones, branches, a few rocks, and, on rare occasion, other less desirable remnants left behind by horses or coyotes.

3

Bella was taking longer than usual to catch up. Sometimes the canine found a special scent trail and wandered a bit longer, so Rachel kept calling as she continued walking up the trail. She loved being here, roaming through the granite-laden Sierra Nevada mountain range and watching Bella discover unseen trails time and time again. Today was even more beautiful because the weather had finally reached sixty-five degrees, and she enjoyed the warmth of the sun on her winter-white bare legs. She hiked just about everywhere she could, but this trail—the Yova-Pioneer Trail—was one of her favorites. Although a bit outside of the Lake Tahoe Basin where she lived, it was rarely used and, therefore, a great trail for training Bella off leash. Better yet, no mountain bikers. She'd had a "run-in" last summer with a reckless cyclist, and, although she knew he was the exception, not the rule, she was still upset when she thought about it. There she had been, lying on the side of the trail, covered in dust, and scratched by the rocks she'd landed on when she'd barely had time to jump to the side as the biker raced down the path. His reaction? A distant "sorry" as he continued to speed down the trail.

"OK, Bella, let's go!" she called out again and was relieved when she finally heard the clinking sounds of Bella's identification tags approaching. She laughed and reached into her treat bag for a dog biscuit, curious about what Bella had found while praying she wouldn't discover some live animal or "horse apple" in the dog's jaws. Leaning over to trade the dog treat for the special "find," Rachel softly asked, "All right, sweet girl, find your mom some old buried treasure she can sell to pay for your special treats?" This had become a long-standing joke among her friends—that she paid more for Bella's food than her own.

In response to the word "treat," Bella dropped the object she'd carried and sat patiently waiting for the small biscuit in Rachel's hand. Absently holding it out for the dog, Rachel leaned down further, curious about what Bella had found. It was a large disposable glove, like the kind she wore when collecting water samples for work. Finding lost items like spare clothing on the trails was common enough, so although this was a bit odd, Rachel didn't think much of it at first. She gave Bella a rub and pulled a plastic doggie pickup bag from her pocket, planning to retrieve the glove using the bag and stow the littered item in her pack. However, just as she reached for it, a shiny red smear on the glove caught her eye. It looked like fresh blood.

"Oh no, you didn't cut yourself on something, did you?" she asked, reaching for Bella. It wouldn't be the first time—for a dog that picked up sharp-edged pinecones and pulled branches from piles of brush, she was lucky Bella hadn't yet required stitches around her muzzle. After checking Bella for wounds she stood up and looked around. Fresh blood in the forest could easily be explained by wildlife activities, but fresh blood on someone's disposable glove? Maybe someone was hurt?

"Show me where you found it, girl," she said, waving her hand in the direction Bella had just come. The pup eventually caught on, turned, and began retracing her path. About a hundred feet later, Bella stopped and sat, looking expectantly at Rachel. She gave the pup's ears a rub as she looked around. There was a bit of a break in the layer of pine needles that covered most of the area, but bare spots rustled by wildlife weren't uncommon. A feeling of unease settled over Rachel, and although some instinct told her silence might be a good idea, she still heard herself tentatively call out, "Hello? Is anyone there?"

Without thinking, one hand reached for the cell phone in the side pocket on her cargo shorts while the other held Bella's collar. As expected, no cell service here. She still held the phone in her hand, not sure why, but it seemed to provide an odd sense of security. Wanting to retreat yet kept from doing so by the image of some poor graduate student out alone collecting field samples, injured and laying helplessly nearby, she made herself take a few steps forward and peered around the enormous dirt-filled root system of a large Jeffrey pine, long ago weakened by age and eventually knocked down by a windstorm. Her eyes went right to a large beige-colored hiking boot. One more step forward and she saw that it wasn't just one of the strange lone shoes or socks she'd come across before, always begging the question why someone would walk out of the forest with one bare foot. This one hadn't been "lost" by a previous hiker.

The owner of the boot, a tan male appearing to be in his forties, was lying perfectly still with a small yet distinct bullet wound in his forehead. The barely perceptible oozing of blood below the hole was the only movement Rachel detected. Below his forehead, lifeless hazel eyes remained open, staring up into the sky. Nausea then panic set in. She'd never seen a dead body up close and personal. Tears unexpectedly filled her eyes as she wondered who this man was. Her reverie was broken when, as if from a distance, her own voice roared in her head. *This was no accident.* This was fresh. Recent. Before the implications could fully register and send the right signals to flee from Rachel's brain to her feet, she saw movement to her side. Bella shifted, perking up her ears to respond to something foreign she had heard or scented. Someone is watching us, Rachel thought. The person who just did this.

"Bella, let's hike!" she whispered as she began stepping back and waving in the direction they'd just come from. As Rachel took off at a sprinter's pace, Bella thankfully dashed forward well in front of her. Rachel realized she still carried the glove in her bag-lined hand. Good, she thought. Maybe it could help identify the man. Caught up in her thoughts and emotions, it was just a few steps later when Rachel tripped over a small pile of granite rocks about the size of her fist. Falling face first, she tumbled in a half somersault that ended in an abrupt stop. It only took a few seconds to dust off and sprint forward once again. Rachel had covered another hundred feet before she realized her hands were empty. She'd dropped the glove out of her bag-lined hand. They had miles to go to get back to the relative safety of her pickup. She couldn't turn back now. Continuing, she found herself constantly peering over her shoulder as they rushed down the trail, breathing a sigh of relief when, with each step down the hill and each glance back, she saw no one—and no bullets came flying by.

~

Spencer quietly observed the brunette-haired woman and her dog through the intermittent view from his hiding place. She appeared to be a bit younger than his thirty-two years yet much like a slightly older version of Lori, his "friend with benefits." Her presence had completely rattled his already strung nerves. So far as he knew, hardly anyone ever hiked this trail, let alone on a weekday. Of all the days! Not only did he get talked into doing this, or rather half threatened, but the location and timing had also been specifically chosen by his boss. He sure hadn't wanted to come out here in the middle of nowhere. At least they left. Spencer didn't know what he would have done if she'd seen him or her dog had caught his scent. He hadn't been able to see much more than a black tail from where he was hiding, but the woman's discovery of David's body had been in full view. Walking back toward the body minutes after the pair had run off, he realized there was just one glove next to the log. *Oh no.* Looking for its match, he continued to expand his search from the body, following the general area the woman had run, and finally he saw it. Spencer let out a deep breath he hadn't realized he'd been holding. As luck would have it, she'd dropped the glove. He could still clean it all up, chip the bullet and blood spatters out of the tree, and get David's body down the hill. He wasn't looking forward to that, but he'd brought along some items in his bag to help. Spencer had less than a mile to go, thankfully in the opposite direction from the woman, and the steep descending slope of the trail worked in his favor. He'd planned to retrace his steps and wipe out any shoe prints. Better yet, the storm clouds forming in the distance just might be the second stroke of luck he would have today.

Spencer used a combination of ropes and tarps to help transport the body back to his vehicle. Perhaps if he hadn't been so nervous, he would have stopped David much sooner, not only cutting down the distance he now had to half carry, half drag the body, but he'd also have likely avoided encountering the woman and her dog. *Well, too late now.*

It took him quite a while, stopping every so often to use various limbs and branches to sweep out his shoe prints and scatter loose pine needles over the trail. If someone were looking for evidence of something, chances were they could find it. He did his best, although there was no way to mimic the original "natural look" of a trail barely used. But with the thunderclouds forming overhead, he thought maybe the weather would do the work for him. If not, his boss could probably make sure someone didn't look too hard.

Spencer was not in shape in the slightest, and as the adrenaline wore off, the exhaustion and throbbing muscle pain of his activities began to set in. Finally, he arrived where David had parked his Jeep earlier that day. Spencer's accomplice, who had spent the morning digging a hole in a remote location about twenty miles away, opened the back door and helped him load the body into the back. "So you actually followed through. I'm impressed," the other man smirked.

"I told you I'd take care of it, and I did. Let's get going." Spencer knew better than to mention the woman and her dog to his partner.

They each drove separately toward the highway. About a quarter mile from the main road, Spencer parked off the rutted dirt path and climbed into the vehicle with his partner. After a wordless drive to the freshly dug hole in the ground, they buried the body then returned to the parked vehicle. They drove back to the Carson Valley separately, ten minutes apart. David's Jeep would be wiped down and disassembled well before anyone even realized he had disappeared.

~

"Let me get this straight. Not only did you leave a witness, but you are just now telling me about it?" yelled Mike, Spencer's boss of almost seven years and part-time father figure. The outrage in Mike's voice surprised Spencer, even though it wasn't the first time he'd heard his boss's rage. It had just never been directed at him. In fact, lately Mike and his "new partner" seemed to have been going out of their way to be nice to Spencer, encouraging him to do a few extra favors "off the books." They'd mostly been petty crimes, which was fine for Spencer. He was, after all, involved in the plan and was certainly no angel. Plus, Mike had taken him under his wing after his grandfather abandoned him, leaving Spencer with no one else. Over time Mike helped him become more confident and aggressive, helping him to earn more money than the pathetic "salary" his grandfather had always pushed for. Things were going to get even better, and only three people knew about the true details of their most recent plan. That was until one of their subcontractors, David Payton, walked into Mike's office one day, interrupting a meeting between Mike and Spencer to express concern over some water samples he'd gathered that didn't look right. They made it through the afternoon playing the concerned businessmen, deciding they would investigate the problem starting the next morning. However, that night Mike made two phone calls, and by the next day Spencer was accompanying David to help him take what would turn out to be his last sample while Mike's new partner was digging the grave.

"No, she did *not* see me. I heard her dog's tags in time to hide. Sure, she saw the glove but dropped it as they ran off. She has nothing. Trust me, we're fine."

"Then why did I just learn that based on some woman's report they sent two officers out there to investigate this afternoon?" The anger in Mike's tone hadn't lessened.

"Well, maybe she got scared and reported it. I suppose the police would have to follow up on something like that, but trust me, there was nothing left to find. I took care of it, just like we discussed." Almost as an afterthought he added, "It also rained there about an hour afterward. Summer thunderstorms. We're fine." Spencer watched as Mike paused for a few moments then sat back down and poured a hefty portion of his favorite scotch into two ice-filled glasses, pushing one across his desk to Spencer.

"OK, I suppose if we can avoid any more . . . situations, that would be better. But I'm going to have some friends keep an eye on this woman, and if she causes any more trouble, *you* are going to have to take care of it. We can't risk anyone looking into this. Got it?" In a gesture Mike did so often that his hair seemed to be thinner on the sides of his head than the top, Spencer watched silently as he flattened his hands on his head just above his ears and moved them back, presumably smoothing out the grey and black hairs that grew in untamed directions. Spencer nodded then reached for his drink, emptying the burning liquid in one large gulp. He hoped the woman would just leave well enough alone.

CHAPTER ONE

Two weeks later, Rachel stood in the police station frustrated and scared, although she tried her best to hide the latter. Once again she found herself asking law enforcement to help her, only to be disappointed by their inability to do so. Given the circumstances were nothing at all like years ago when she found herself seeking out help from law enforcement for a different reason, and perhaps with some new staff now in play, she had hoped that maybe they would help this time. She hadn't taken the decision to report what she saw lightly, having avoided anything that might require her to rely on, or even trust, law enforcement for several years following her last experience. Captain Ron Taylor, a tall broad man in his fifties who boasted a 1980's Tom Selleck mustache, had agreed to meet with her again. Unfortunately, it appeared to her that she was on her own, just like before, and she had to admit it didn't surprise her.

"I'm sorry, Ms. Winters, but we found no trace of a body or any indication of an altercation. You were there with the officers. You know they completed a thorough search. I can't explain what you think you saw, but without a body or any evidence to suggest there was one, there is simply no crime to investigate. I suggest you go home and try to move on."

"I don't *think* I saw him; I did see him." She still kicked herself for dropping that glove. When the two officers went back with her, not only had the brief thunderstorm covered the landscape with large raindrops, but the glove was gone. Although she had never felt significant gender discrimination in her job—in fact it seemed more women worked in the environmental science world than men sometimes—she had still developed a sensitivity to men treating women like they were helpless, overemotional girls who needed to be "put in their place by the big strong man." Perhaps even more so because as a child, she'd matched her brothers at everything they'd done—searching for tadpoles in ditches, building forts along creeks, riding horses for miles and miles, and coming home covered in dirt just about every night. Rachel did not react well to being placated. But she tried to remain calm now. They may refuse to help her, but it would be smart to avoid alienating law enforcement. Plus, she knew there was already a perception among several officers in the department that she was just a local nutcase who spent one too many days in the sun. Although any officer who had been involved a few years ago in her "situation," as they'd called it, knew damn well she hadn't made *that* up.

"I know my drawing skills leave much to be desired, Captain Taylor, but would it hurt to at least keep checking for missing people fitting the general description I gave you? What's the harm?"

"Look, Rachel, we've been out there twice. And there were some thunderstorms out there last week that flooded the area out. Frankly, we've given the investigation of your report more time than we can afford. Our force is down by half compared to a few years ago, most of us are balancing more cases than we can handle, and there is simply nothing there to investigate. I spoke with the chief, and he directed me to move on. I'm really sorry." The sympathy on his face, although probably well intentioned, just upset her more.

Seeing the man's lifeless body had rocked Rachel to the core, but after she was back in her pickup with Bella curled up next to her in the passenger seat, she couldn't stop her mind from running through how she felt in that split second when she'd realized the murderer was still there. Watching. Making matters worse, after filing a police report that afternoon, she had started to observe additional traffic driving by her house—very noticeable on a side street that rarely harbored many vehicles beyond the few residents in the area. Strange sounds on her phone calls began occurring a few days later.

"So, Captain Taylor, are you sure there are no missing persons reports for the man I *saw*, perhaps from other departments?" It was a redundant question she'd been asking every day for two weeks.

"No, nothing."

"OK. And to confirm, because there is no evidence of a crime, you believe that I must be . . . what, making up the drive-bys and phone calls as well?" It was becoming harder to remain calm, and she knew her voice portrayed the anger and sarcasm of the statement. Although she lived at the south end of Lake Tahoe, a large mountain area visited by millions of people each year, her own small neighborhood outside of city limits was comprised of more vacant second homes than full-time residences, making it a fairly quiet area. The few extra cars she'd been seeing several times a day were definitely unfamiliar, and she knew it wasn't coincidence. As much as she disliked giving any weight to obvious scare tactics by someone, she couldn't help it. She had not felt safe for a moment since finding the body and, for the first time in her life, found herself afraid to go anywhere she might be alone and vulnerable. Possible bear encounters were one thing; encounters with gun-toting humans were a completely different story. When it had become clear that the same unknown vehicles were driving by her home repeatedly, it had occurred to Rachel that whoever was responsible for the murder, and her current predicament, might think the tactics would shut her up—clearly they didn't know very much about her.

Captain Taylor sighed. "Sometimes people see innocent things but make more of them when they are stressed or perhaps looking for irregularities. We get a lot of tourists up here driving around to check out the views. I understand you had a rough experience a few years ago, and perhaps that's clouding your, uh, judgment?" At least he had the decency to show some shame as he wrote her off.

Struggling to maintain her composure, Rachel calmly responded. "What happened then is completely unrelated, and I'm appalled that you would suggest otherwise. As for the present, Captain Taylor, I'm trying very hard to be understanding of your limitations, given the lack of a body. However, I refuse to sit around while someone is harassing me, whether *you* believe it or not. I have a job that puts me in remote areas, and I—"

"Maybe, Miss Winters, you need to reconsider your job then," he said, cutting her off. "I mean, if it's going to . . . scare you to be alone." That was it; he had touched a nerve, and Rachel couldn't stop herself.

"And maybe, Mr. Taylor, if you are going to treat the people you are paid to serve and protect like you're treating me, you should reconsider *your* job!" There was no help to be found here. Rachel turned around and swiftly walked toward the front door. But a few steps away, she noticed a bulletin board with pinned notices, business cards, flyers, and other local information. She saw a few cards for private investigators, but immediately dismissed the idea. She couldn't afford more bills than she already had. She was still paying off her student loan from getting her master's degree almost ten years ago. Footsteps approached on her left side, and a woman's soft voice emerged.

"Rachel, I'm not sure what's going on, but I have heard some talk. If you need help, that private investigator, Luke Reed, used to work here," she said, pointing at one of the business cards on the corkboard. "Word has it he was pretty good, just unlucky to be one of the new guys when budget cuts came."

Rachel looked at the woman. She appeared to be in her early twenties and was dressed in casual office attire. "Thank you. I just don't have much spare cash."

"Well, it can't hurt to ask, I suppose. Maybe he'll work out a payment plan or something. I think the first consults are usually free, so it might be worth a sit-down." Rachel nodded and grabbed one of his business cards.

"Thank you," she said, tucking the card in her purse. As the heavy sound of footsteps approached, the woman smiled and quickly walked back toward the front office to greet visitors coming in the front door. Rachel looked back around and noticed Captain Taylor eyeing her curiously.

"A bona fide private eye, huh? Well, it's your dime, Miss Winters," he said, nodding with what looked like sympathy but felt more like judgment.

"Well, Mr. Taylor, perhaps this PI can document the evidence you'll need to arrest someone when you find my lifeless body— make it nice and easy for you." Rachel gave him one of her thanks-but-no-thanks smiles and left the building. She climbed back into her pickup, leaning over to pet Bella who had waited patiently with windows open in the shaded parking spot.

"You're such a good girl, Bella," she pronounced in her typical "dog voice." As she started the ignition, she looked back at the building, which read "South Lake Tahoe Police Station" with "Serve and Protect" in smaller letters below it.

"Yeah, right!" Rachel muttered, slamming her foot on the pedal and whipping out of the parking lot intending to go straight home to figure out what to do next. Yes, she could call her parents and ask for a loan, but she knew they would ask why, and she had never been a good liar. If she told them the truth they'd be scared out of their wits. In fact, she hadn't even mentioned finding the body two weeks ago. They were on vacation having a good time and couldn't do anything other than worry for her anyway. But could she keep dealing with this every day? What about the work she needed to get started on in the backcountry next week? Rachel decided doing nothing wasn't an option, and she'd just figure out the money problem later. It was more important she and Bella remain alive.

After looking at the address on the business card, Rachel made the quick decision to head straight there. "Well, Bella, if you can handle another stop I know where this is, and it's not too far. What could it hurt, right?" She smiled as she rubbed the pup's soft ears. Bella tilted her head as if listening then turned back to the half-open window, her face in the wind.

~

"What was that about?" an officer asked the young woman behind the front desk, leaning over as if conspiring.

"Oh, that woman," she said as she worked, barely looking up from the file cabinet while responding. "That was Rachel Winters, I believe, although I might have her name wrong. It was the woman who reported seeing a dead body two weeks ago out on that hiking trail. She's been coming in or calling just about every day since, but I think the cap finally told her he couldn't do anything more. She was checking out some of the business cards on the board. Poor woman looked scared to death, but I think she was trying to cover it up with anger. Anyhow, I felt bad for her and suggested the private investigator that used to work here."

"Hmm, interesting." The officer paused then waved toward the stack of trays where various forms were kept. "Well, I did come here for a reason. I needed one of those blank request forms for some comp time. Do you mind?"

"Sure," she said, handing it over. "Got vacation plans?"

"Something like that," the officer said, smiling and walking away.

CHAPTER TWO

The investigator's office was a small dark-brown building with "Luke Reed" painted on the front door. As she parked in front, Rachel noticed there were no other cars in the lot. Not a good sign—maybe this was a mistake. Well, she was here, so she might as well at least go feel out the situation. The door was unlocked, and Rachel slowly opened it, knocking lightly at the same time to announce her arrival. She expected to see either a receptionist behind a small counter or the PI himself. She imagined him as a fifty-something overweight man, mussed-up thinning hair with a sweat-stained collar, although she knew it was likely a stereotype brought on by PI shows in her youth. Instead, she saw a small cluttered office with an expensive mountain bike leaning against the wall to her left and a thick glass-top desk covered with a laptop, small printer, and a coffee mug resting on a pile of papers to the right. Although she knew it was another TV-related stereotype, she smiled briefly, catching herself looking for a half-filled bottle of Jack Daniel's nearby. That was when she noticed someone behind the desk. Actually, she saw the top of a ball cap just a few inches above the back of a large old leather chair facing away from her. Was he sleeping?

"Hello? Mr. Reed?" she called out, ready to quietly turn and leave but feeling she should at least say something first. The figure in the chair, obviously startled by her presence, seemed to jolt upright, and the chair swiftly turned around as a man's voice began an apology. The first thing she noticed was the dark-blue ball cap inscribed with "Bike or Die." Second, this was no heavyset man twice her age as she'd been expecting. Instead, he was young, probably just a few years older than her, and handsome. Not the typical structured jaw and pretty-boy features often portrayed in *GQ* magazines, an image she had never been attracted to. Rather, he had the look of a seasoned cowboy combined with an obvious intelligence and touch of Harvard-school graduate. As she studied him, a rough image of him wearing a George Strait plain-black Stetson cowboy hat on his slightly scruffy dark-brown hair came to mind, and she felt an immediate, unwanted physical attraction. "Luke Reed?"

"Yes I am," he said with what sounded like a hint of "Who else would I be?" He looked her up and down, then to her pickup outside where Bella was likely hanging her head out of the window, mesmerized by unsuspecting birds nearby. "And, Miss, what can I do you for . . . I mean, what can I do for you?" He laughed. She didn't know what irritated her more, being called Miss by this man or his ridiculous line. Wonderful, another arrogant rich boy, she thought. His office screamed "money" with its cold, straight-edged furniture that probably cost more than she made in a year and looked completely uncomfortable. But the anomaly was the mountain bike. It looked well used— nice and dirty.

Rachel made no moves to sit in the rigid chair facing the front of his desk. "Well, Mr. Reed, I seem to have someone watching me because I witnessed a murder, sort of. But the police claim they can't help because the body disappeared. Apparently I'm imagining the harassment I've been experiencing since." She knew a mixture of fear and anger was obvious in her tone of voice. His expression didn't change from the curious look he'd been wearing since she began telling her story. "However . . . I can see this may be a bad time." As she turned to leave, she quipped, "Sorry to have bothered you." Rachel couldn't get out of there fast enough; this had been a complete mistake.

"Wait, please. If I seem disengaged, it's that you caught me off guard. I don't get many walk-ins, and you happened to catch me lost in thought. If you'd like, you can tell me what's going on, no charge, and I'll let you know if I can help." She had turned back around and noticed his gesture for her to sit in the rigid chair. Hesitating, she finally sat down.

"OK, thank you. Would you mind if I brought my dog in? It's getting a bit warm outside," she said, motioning out to her truck while eyeing the room for decorations or piles of paperwork that could be threatened by Bella's tail. It looked safe enough, so long as she led her straight from the door to the chair.

"Um, well, OK," he responded, and she saw him look around as well, probably worrying about the same thing.

"She's friendly, albeit a bit enthusiastic at times. I'll just bring her in and have her sit next to me." A few moments later, after attempting to greet Luke who seemed to hide from the dog behind his desk, Bella had finally resigned to sitting next to her owner's legs. "By the way, I'm Rachel Winters." After a brief handshake, she launched into her story, beginning with the body she'd found thanks to Bella's discovery of the glove, and the subsequent drive-bys, phone calls, and conversations with several officers, including her last one that morning with Captain Taylor.

"I realize everyone thinks I'm making it up for some reason, and maybe you do, too. But I know what we saw. Making matters worse, I believe the guy who did it was still out there and saw *us*, and for some reason is keeping tabs on me and wants me to know it. I feel like every corner I look around, some stranger is going to be there, waiting. And if he, or they, can make it look like nothing happened out there, even with today's forensics, then they can probably make me disappear without raising any red flags. I'm not sure what to do, but I can't keep living with this ongoing dread either." Rachel knew she'd been talking for quite a while, perhaps running on a bit as she did when she was upset. Luke had been quickly writing notes down, only occasionally interrupting with a brief question or clarification. She sipped the water she'd brought in with her and waited for his response, half expecting a repeat of her disappointing conversation with Captain Taylor.

"OK, give me just another minute," Luke muttered as he finished writing some notes on his pad. "And, what is your job, exactly?"

"I'm an environmental scientist, although I do a lot of advocacy, too. Not sure you've noticed, but Tahoe's politics are a nightmare." Again, her nerves were making her talk too much. Just shut up and see what he says, she told herself. His expression was still unreadable, and she was just about to stand up, thank him for listening, and rush out the door when he finally responded.

"OK, I do find it a bit strange that the police investigators wouldn't find any clues when they went looking out there with you. They are pretty good officers, at least those I worked with when I was employed there." At his response, Rachel's stomach clenched for the second time that day. Not interested in hearing yet another person disappoint her, she cut him off.

"How nice for you. Sorry to have wasted your time." She began to stand up when he spoke again.

"Calm down. I'm not done." She saw Luke smile as if amused by the situation and fought the urge to leave. Then again, she was acting quite hastily. He continued. "People have figured out how to get away with all sorts of criminal activities, so I try to keep an open mind. I know the station relies mostly on part-time regional crime scene investigators only brought into cases under certain circumstances, and I'm going to guess they were not tagging along when you took the officers out there."

"No, there were just two officers," she replied.

"OK, I figured that given their tight budget. Now, my other question is about the man you saw—did you describe him to a sketch artist, get some kind of image down?"

"The officers didn't think calling in a specialist was a 'valuable use of resources' since there was no evidence of a crime. I did try to make my own sketch, although it's not pretty. I'm good with nature scenes but pretty bad with people." Embarrassed, she pulled a folded sheet of paper from her purse and handed it to him. Rachel had gone home the night after her first visit to the police station and had done her best to recall his image, sketching it as well as she could. The officers had made a copy the next day, but she could tell they were basically going through the motions at that point.

He studied it before looking up at her. "It's actually not too bad. I don't think we could ID someone straight from it, but maybe if we had possible matches it could help for comparison purposes." He leaned back in his chair, set the paper down, and then looked up at her. "So, this is my proposal. I'll do some fishing around in MP—I mean missing persons—databases and see if anything pops up. Chances are the officers looked at the local list, but perhaps they didn't search any further out. Second, I'd like you to take me to the place where you found the body."

It took her a moment to realize he was actually taking her seriously. "OK, I can do that. When would you like to go?"

"I've got a conference call until about noon. Would around one o'clock work?"

"Today?" It surprised her that he could respond so quickly.

"Yes, I'm sensing time is of the essence for you. So, will that work?"

"Sure, but what's this going to run me?"

"We'll figure that out later. If I can't help, I'll consider it a nice afternoon hike with a beautiful woman. Today, I just want to get a fresh look at the scene, and we can go from there."

Grinning, he added, "Maybe you can cook me dinner instead." *Was he coming on to her? Really?*

"Mr. Reed, I do hope your investigative skills are far superior to your social skills." It was hard to keep a straight face and not laugh, though, since his suggestion seemed so out of place and yet so typical.

"OK, OK, guess I deserve that one," he laughed. "Maybe we can order a pizza instead." She glared at him, trying not to smile, but failed. The bantering had helped break the tense mood she'd been in earlier. Feeling like some of the weight had been lifted from her shoulders, she got up, Bella following at her heels.

Returning her smile, he asked, "So, how far up the trail will we be going?"

"Oh, about four or five miles. See you at one." She opened the door and stepped out, Bella in tow. Although she wasn't too keen on Mr. Reed's cocky attitude, she had to admit she felt better that someone was doing something. Whether it would help or not remained to be seen, but it was better than sitting around, waiting. And, well, he wasn't too hard on the eyes either. Might as well enjoy the scenery this afternoon.

~

Spencer had been shaken by the ordeal. He felt . . . guilty. He'd known he was involved in something serious and that tough decisions were going to come up, but he hadn't expected this one or how he'd feel about it afterward. Rather than sit and dwell on his anxiety, he decided to distract himself with some female companionship. He thought of Lori. She was ten years younger than he was, but he rarely noticed. They'd met in Gardnerville about six months ago, and he'd been happy to learn she did not work or associate with anyone in the business he worked in. There was no deep emotional connection, but they had fun together and were both content to keep it on a friends-with-benefits basis.

"Hey, it's me. Mind some company?" he asked into the cell

phone Mike had provided for side jobs.

"Sure, I can be at my place in forty minutes if that works for you."

"Perfect, see you there." He left, anxious to change out of the business-style khakis and designer shoes he'd been wearing for a meeting earlier.

~

Mike knew where Spencer had gone, having discovered his employee's new female companion a few months ago. In an unlikely irony, Mike had been keeping tabs on that particular woman for years. It wasn't the first time he'd seen her with a man. That bothered him, but nothing like the night when, to his utter shock, Spencer had emerged into his view as he peered into her apartment's window. Mike's surprise was quickly replaced with outrage, and after watching the couple undress each other, he'd put his binoculars away and driven home, filled with so much anger he'd almost driven off the road twice. He vowed that night—Spencer would pay.

CHAPTER THREE

Luke sat back in his chair, watching Rachel and Bella walk toward the dirty blue Tacoma pickup truck parked in front of his small building. When Rachel had first arrived, he'd been lost in thought; after learning his afternoon meeting was canceled, he was deciding whether to just take off on his mountain bike for the rest of the day. He didn't hear her drive up or open the door, so he was surprised when a woman's voice suddenly filled the room. It was a nice youthful voice, and when he turned around he expected to see a much younger woman dressed like a bank teller, although most people dressed fairly casual here in South Lake Tahoe. But, oh, had his first impression been wrong. She looked just a few years younger than him, with long dark-brown hair pulled back in a braid. A few loose strands had fallen out and were held back by the sunglasses resting on her head. She wore no makeup, although her lips were tinged with a light-colored glossy lip balm. She was dressed in light-blue jean shorts and black leather flip-flops and, in contrast to her otherwise tomboyish accoutrement, had painted her toenails a dark-pink color. She wore a basic T-shirt that hung slightly loose on her, but he could still make out her form well enough to see an athletic build. About five and a half feet or so in stature, the woman was pretty but a bit rugged looking. Far from the overly thin model types he'd grown up around near Hollywood. However, once he'd broken away from his family years ago and moved to the mountains, he'd come to prefer active women who played outdoors and ate real meals rather than a pile of lettuce. But, on the other hand, he'd encountered enough "mountain women" to know they were often too independent for their own good.

Or, like his ex-girlfriend Savannah, they pretended to be someone they weren't, all the while hoping to score what they thought would be a rich husband. Although almost two years had passed, the image of her betrayal still burned in his mind. After discovering her in bed with a coworker, matters grew worse when she seemed to feel no remorse at all, yelling at *him* for "leading her along, pretending to be rich." He'd never mentioned his family roots to her or discussed their financial situation. After breaking his family ties over ten years beforehand, Luke had long ago stopped associating with his family at the time he'd met Savannah. But she had apparently looked them up on her own and assumed he still had a large inheritance. After that, he made a point to stick with casual dates, period.

Yet Luke felt confident that Rachel Winters was not pretending to be someone she wasn't. She may have been wearing a rather casual outfit, but behind that mix of emotions on her face, he saw intelligence. In fact, the way she told her story sounded like something he might read in a technical brief. He had to stop her to ask what she meant when she mentioned words like "disturbed duff," which she explained as "decaying pine needles," or "downed Jeffrey;" she could have just said a fallen pine tree and he would have understood. She was clearly well educated but had apparently adopted the typical "laid-back" look of the people who lived here full time—let alone the attitude about the outdoors, based on her no-big-deal response to his last question—*oh, about four or five miles*—as if it was just a quick jaunt around the neighborhood. Although it did start to rub off on a person after being in the Basin a while. Luke laughed, realizing he, too, now thought of it as "the Basin"—how the locals referred to the entire Lake Tahoe Basin, even though it was well over thirty miles long from roughly north to south and divided in the middle with a deep blue lake.

As for the upcoming excursion he'd just agreed to, Luke knew the trail. It had been a while since he'd ridden there, but he remembered that after a couple of miles from Luther Pass, the trail grew relatively steep, and stayed that way until it crested and descended to the southern trailhead about a mile down, which was extremely difficult to access, the reason why he'd never ridden up from that side. The trail was located just outside of the Basin on the northwest edge of Hope Valley and, along with its steep terrain and lack of major views, was not very popular. Luke figured that would make it a great place to commit murder, if one was hoping to avoid witnesses. He looked over at his bike again, debating, but decided it was best to just trek along. He was in pretty good shape and could easily keep up with the smaller woman.

Three hours later, they were hiking up the latter half of the trail, Luke struggling to keep up and pretending his muscles weren't burning. They had started out matching paces the first mile or two, and talking was easy enough, but when the slope had grown steeper, Rachel's pace hadn't faltered. His had. She'd stopped, saying she needed to grab a snack, but he had a feeling she was just showing him some mercy.

"So, what did you bring along?" she asked, taking a bite from a protein bar.

"Basic supplies for collecting evidence and taking pictures."

"Hmm, so you haven't completely written me off yet?"

"That or it's part of a horrible, or perhaps kinky, seduction strategy."

"Do men ever think about anything other than sex?"

"Sometimes I think about my bike," he smiled, brushing his hand against her shoulder far too intimately before really thinking about it. "But seriously, no, I have not written you off. And I appreciate the pretend snack break, but I think I'm ready to get going again." Luke watched her grin, blush, take the last bite of her bar, and nod. Bella had spent the time focused on a nearby branch and now picked it up to carry along with her as Rachel continued on.

"So, Rachel, where are you from?"

"I grew up on a ranch a couple of hours south west of here in the Sacramento Valley, a pretty nice area back then, but from the first memory I have of our family coming to Tahoe, I always loved being up here. And you? Hmm, let me guess. Probably big city, wealthy, but I don't get the East Coast vibe. SoCal? Hollywood?"

She was right, and that annoyed him. "What gives you that impression?"

"Just a feeling I get. Your, uh, décor choices, among other things. More pretty than practical? I was afraid if I made one wrong move the edge of that glass table would slice right through my leg. Although, the bike in the office adds a nice effect, and that's a good start."

"What's wrong with my décor? I've got a good collection of Ansel Adams hanging around the office . . ." Luke trailed off, taking a deep breath.

"Yes, I saw those. Nice. But the rest is far too . . . clean edged and straight angled for the mountains. You need to have some local nature pictures thrown in and maybe a few corny woodsy decorations, along with a wall covered with crazy pictures of you with friends. Oh, and hang some of your mountain bike gear on the walls. Then it will start to look a bit more cozy," she laughed.

He frowned then said, "First, I'm afraid to see what your place looks like. And second, not everyone who lives here has to be, eh, rustic." At least she knew enough to look embarrassed,

Luke thought. "OK, yes, I did grow up in *Southern California*. And yes, we were quite wealthy, and my parents socialized with politicians and the like. Being the good son, I played on every sports team imaginable, giving them great bragging rights with their friends," he recited in a rushed yet monotonous tone, knowing it was a combination of annoyance with her obvious bias and the memories of how much he had disliked the dishonest people he'd grown up around. But that didn't mean everyone was that way. "Some things happened during my senior year that changed the course I was on, and I decided to do my own thing." He stopped, hoping to convey that he didn't want to keep talking about his childhood much either.

"Sorry, I suppose it's obvious I have some strong . . . *opinions*," she said apologetically. Then, after a brief pause, she tilted her head. "However, I must say that the rustic style of interior design can have a lot of character." Laughing softly, she picked up her pace and quickly increased the distance between them with every step. "Now don't burn out those hiking muscles too fast," Rachel called out behind her.

"Just wait until we bike together. Then we'll see whose muscles are on fire," he called out. Frustrating as she could be, Luke realized he was enjoying the banter. It was almost a requirement, given the circumstances. Much like the infamous skiers-versus-snowboarders "battle," the historic rivalry among hikers versus bikers was a long-drawn-out one in the mountain community. Arguments and cheap shots were expected between the two groups.

This time she didn't stop, and eventually he couldn't see her anymore—a bit surprising given she'd come to him in fear of a murderer finding her alone. Then again, Rachel had not let what she'd witnessed stop her these past two weeks, and the only changes she made to her routine were apparently to select more popular trails and check for familiar cars at the trailheads when they came back. Well, who knows what goes on in the mind of any female? He finally came around a corner about a half mile beyond the crest of the trail and saw her ahead, about ten feet off to the side of the path. She was sitting on a large granite boulder a bit less typical of this area, where rocks were smaller and more scattered. The dog was at her feet sipping water from a small dish. Luke stood for a moment, noticing how when Rachel smiled at Bella her whole face lit up. Gone was the slightly fearful and annoyed look he'd first seen in his office. With the sun's angle just right, it brought out the freckles that covered her nose and showed the glint of the small hairs that had fallen free of her braid. Luke shook his head as if it would stop his train of thought. Get yourself together, man; she's a client. Plain and simple. And clearly independent and stubborn as hell. You don't need this trouble.

"About time, cowboy," she said as she glanced up and chuckled at him.

Cowboy? Whatever gave her that idea? "Uh-huh. We'll deal with that cowboy bit another time, *miss*." He'd emphasized this last word, aware of how much it had angered her when he'd inadvertently said it in his office. "Lead on."

CHAPTER FOUR

Spencer had been drifting in and out of sleep after a frenzied rip-your-clothes-off interlude of sex when his cell phone rang, disturbing the quiet aftermath. Much to the frustration of the woman next to him, he answered it. Lori knew he would never refuse his boss, although she had told Spencer once that she couldn't understand why. As expected, it was Mike.

"I heard from the department. The woman has hired a PI to do some snooping, and they are heading out there this afternoon. You'll get a call soon with more specifics. Go take care of it."

He'd quickly disconnected, leaving no chance for Spencer to respond. Spencer hesitated for a moment, having hoped Rachel Winters would have chosen to move on. He'd been frustrated by the growing distance Mike seemed to be putting between them, at times acting like he was upset with Spencer yet trying not to show it. For now, unfortunately, he had his orders, and those orders had to be followed, although he wasn't sure he could go through with it. He got dressed and while Lori was in the shower, the phone rang again. The caller, a man he knew only as "the Frog"—a nickname clearly linked to the man's throaty voice—provided the specifics Mike had referred to earlier.

Once again, Spencer found himself slowly walking back up

the path, coming in from the opposite direction the woman and her PI would have taken, after a bumpy ride to access the trail's southern end. Hiking in from this side, it was less than a mile from where he parked to the place he had killed David that fateful day.

He still hoped he wouldn't have to do this. Maybe they had changed their minds or Mike's contact was wrong. Killing David had continued to bother him far more than he'd expected, and it had taken every bit of mental energy he could muster not to show any tension around Lori. Mike had asked him to do some nasty things over the years, and those he'd easily kept from others, but killing David was the worst—until now. He knew what was at stake, and he had a lot to lose—and a lot to gain as well. But he hadn't expected the payoff to come from "blood money." As he sat there, still struggling with what other options he could propose to Mike, his body froze the moment he heard the wind-chime sound of dog tags once again. *Damn.* He had just enough time to hide behind a thicket of trees before the woman and her dog came around the corner.

Spencer's heart sank. He didn't think he had a choice now. Although he trusted Mike, he was surprised to learn how far his boss was willing to go after the situation with David. Maybe he didn't know Mike as well as he thought. But this entire plan had been in the works for years, and if it got out he could be implicated himself for more than just David's murder. Worse yet, if Mike were linked to this in any way, Spencer knew his own stay in prison would likely be short, ending with a slit throat courtesy of some random inmate. Mike had some expansive connections.

"You have no other option, Spencer," he whispered to himself, exhaling and trying to get the nerve up to act. He did his best to wait patiently and quietly while watching her as she sat on a small boulder playing with her dog. Knowing what he was about to do as he glimpsed this happy, innocent moment made him sick to his stomach. She appeared to be waiting for the PI.

He thought about whether to just shoot her while she was still alone. He figured that would probably be about the time the guy showed up, and then Spencer could become someone else's target. Private investigators likely carry guns, too.

You are just stalling, he thought to himself. Sure enough, after only a few minutes, a dark-haired man in a ball cap slowly came around the corner and looked over at Rachel and the dog. *OK, they are here now.* He debated how to best handle this; with a brief shift in the direction of the breeze, the dog could pick up his scent and come checking, so he decided to use the distraction of the man's arrival to begin distancing himself while he considered how to best handle the three of them. Deep down, he knew what he was doing—or rather, what he wasn't going to do. Spencer couldn't go through with this, and he began backing up to a point where he could quietly withdraw down the trail, all the while keeping his eyes on the couple and hoping they didn't notice him. Then, for a split second, the unexpected shadow of someone behind him caught his eye, and before he could register it and turn around to look, the shadow moved and he felt an intense pain on the back of his skull. Everything went dark.

~

Rachel slowly made her way to the place where she had come across the body two weeks before. The memories played through her mind again, and as strong as she'd been trying to be, inside she was a tangle of nerves. Bella stepped cautiously beside her as if sensing Rachel's fear.

"I didn't bring Bella when I came out with the investigators," she said to Luke over her shoulder, half whispering although not sure why.

"Why not?"

"Well, I was expecting to find a decaying body and didn't want to subject her to it. Plus the investigators didn't seem to be, uh, dog people." She paused then called out while maneuvering across several feet of forest floor layered with pine needles. "He was just over here." To distract Bella, Rachel picked up a pinecone and threw it, but when Bella jumped up, ran after it, and brought it back, she realized she was more likely distracting herself. "That's the spot." She nodded in the direction of the large fallen tree. She watched Luke study the area intently, making no attempt to move closer.

"I can see some disturbance, but it doesn't jump out as anything strange to me. But . . . something about it . . . ," Luke murmured as he slowly walked around the side, pausing for a moment to stare at something. "There's some wear here on this tree that seems too clean. What do you think?"

She looked at where he was pointing and saw what he meant. The tree had several ragged indentations that, at first glance, looked like natural variations in the tree. But he was right—some of the pockets were many shades brighter than the wood around them, as if recently exposed. "I didn't notice that before. I suppose I was too intent on the dead man. But yes, that doesn't look like anything nature would do."

He nodded then seemed to be thinking out loud more than talking to her. "It seems a bit staged."

At Luke's comment, Rachel's spirits lifted. Finally some positive news. And if he could find something more, well, Rachel was afraid to get her hopes up. She was about to ask him what else looked staged when she realized a while had had passed since her last toss of the pinecone, so she whistled and called out Bella's name. The pup returned, but without the pinecone. Rachel watched, confused, as Bella stopped in front of her then turned back around again, signaling for her to follow. Her tail wasn't wagging.

"Bella, what did you find, girl?" Her voice was a bit shaky. This was starting to feel like déjà vu. "I think she wants to show us something."

"OK, but let me go first," Luke stated.

"What's it matter?"

"I've got the gun," he said, giving her a serious look. She had mixed feelings about that. She'd never liked guns or had any interest in using one. She used to shoot old cans off her fence with a BB gun growing up. But BBs usually didn't kill people.

"You'd better know how to aim it. Don't risk Bella for anything, got it?" Luke nodded and began walking behind the canine, Rachel falling in step in back. They came around a thick stand of young pine trees and saw the dog staring motionless at something still hidden from their angle. Two more steps and they both saw the subject of Bella's stare.

"Luke!" she blurted out with a mix of surprise and horror. There was another body. The man appeared fairly young, with scruffy brown hair, a day or two's growth of facial hair, and a pair of Ray-Ban sunglasses that had been knocked off to the side of his nose. His outfit, comprised of khaki pants, a white dress shirt, and tennis shoes, suggested that he was not simply a hiker enjoying the day. He looked like an executive who'd changed shoes for a lunchtime walk. Well, except for the thick drops of blood on the side of his head. As she stood there frozen, Bella at her side, Luke knelt down beside the man, reaching down to feel his neck.

"No pulse." After a moment of looking around, Luke spoke, glancing back at the man's body. "My first guess is he was slammed in the head with that." He pointed to a rock about the size of a baseball lying nearby. "Someone had to hit him damn hard to do *this*."

Rachel stuttered. "I . . . just can't believe this is happening again." She paused to refocus herself. She had to be strong. "Has he been dead long?"

Luke stood back up, wiped away the dust on his knee, and began looking around. "It looks fresh, but it's hard to say because the blood quickly mixed with the dirt. Although his body is warm. I see two different types of shoe prints. The smaller ones match our guy here, so the other set must be our killer's." He was talking very seriously, without any inflection in his voice, like an experienced officer who has learned to put off his emotions until another time, she thought. Although she knew it was better for him to look at this objectively, Rachel wished he'd show at least some fear, so she'd feel better about how nervous she was.

"So . . . should we get going so we can call someone?" Her wobbly voice revealed the anxiety she was hiding, but she didn't care at this point. She just wanted an excuse to leave, immediately.

Luke paused and nodded affirmatively. "But first, I'd like to check a few things out and take some pictures, since disappearing bodies seems to be a thing out here." He reached into his pack and put on a pair of disposable gloves much like the glove Bella found two weeks ago. "Can you handle one more minute? Are you okay?" He looked at her intently, waiting for a response.

Rachel nodded. "Yes, I'm fine. In fact . . . I'm angry. I don't like to be scared. It took me years to get over this kind of fear after . . ." She paused, catching herself. "Well, after something else happened. I'd finally reached the point where the only thing I worried about seeing was a mountain lion. But whoever is responsible for these two murders, it's like they are taking away what I worked so hard to get back." Rachel knew she probably revealing too much, but she was mad, and the memories of what she'd felt like so many years ago were flooding through her again. "I know that sounds selfish—two men are dead, and I'm complaining about my ruined hiking experience. But, I guess I'd rather feel the anger right now than to think about these men."

Luke paused, emotion flashing across his rigid features before once again retreating to the objective law-enforcement-officer mask. "No, I agree. Anger is good. It motivates." He turned back toward the body. "This time we'll have the police department investigators to help. But I'd still like to check a few things out here first," he said, leaning back over the body. Rachel could see he was trying to keep his footing and knee in the impressions he'd already made. After taking a few pictures with his cell phone, Luke tucked the phone in his back pocket then retrieved an unused evidence bag from his pack. He searched the man's pockets, and Rachel watched nervously as he removed some coins, wrapped gum, and a set of keys.

"No wallet. No phone. And obviously he didn't plan to go hiking today," Luke said, gesturing at the man's outfit. His gaze then went beyond the body toward a nearby sage bush. "Over there. I see a gym bag or something."

"I'll go get it," Rachel offered, needing to feel useful. But he cut her off.

"No, let me. I've got the gloves on, and we should try to leave it there for the investigators." Rachel stopped, although it was difficult to stand aside, doing nothing.

Luke rummaged through the bag. "There's a folded camping shovel, some clothes. And . . . oh, not good. A gun fitted with a silencer." He paused.

Rachel realized this could be the killer. But then, who killed him? She started to say "What the . . . ?" when she heard an electronic beeping sound coming from somewhere beneath one of the young pine trees. Luke heard it, too. He stood up, following Rachel as she tracked the source to a nearby collection of small trees. She heard the beep again and slowly reached out, pulling back the overhanging branches to peer underneath. Just a few inches from the base of one of the small trees was a black cell phone. It was turned on, and the phone appeared to be bouncing in between cell signal towers. The display was dim, but the words "now roaming" were perceptible across the front. Rachel started to reach for it.

"Hold on, Rachel." She felt the light touch of his hand on her arm and looked up at him. He held up his gloved hands and the evidence bag. She nodded. Luke picked it up and set it inside the evidence bag, and they read the display through the plastic. It beeped again, and the text on the screen changed to say "in network."

"Looks like it's doing what mine does out here. Not enough to make a call but enough to grab a signal here and there." At this point, Rachel was just inches away from Luke's neck, and she caught a quick scent of a masculine Western-like cologne. It wasn't the kind of thing she'd expect someone like him to wear, and she liked it. *What was she thinking?* Here she was a potential gunshot victim in the making, and she's thinking about how this guy smells? She stepped back, trying to make her voice sound even as she spoke. "Probably an unnecessary question, but can you tell if it's his phone?" Luke had been using the touchpad to run through the phone's menu.

"I'm trying to see if I can pull up any owner information. But it's empty—as if it were purposely removed. Yet a picture of the kid popped up when I hit this screen button." He held the phone over to the side, spreading the bag's plastic evenly across the surface so the display could be seen easier. Sure enough, there was a picture of the man, half smiling in front of what appeared to be a modular office building.

"So, he's got his picture here but no name or address?"

"Yes, doesn't make much sense. But . . . it's like someone purposely erased it to make it undetectable. At least the owner's information. I have a feeling this guy added the picture of himself on his own, maybe after it was cleared out by someone else first." He kept scrolling. "Well, here's a list of the most recent incoming calls. Let's see what pops up." Luke's voice sounded excited. "Only two. Not surprising—the history was probably cleared out, too. OK, the most recent call was from . . . unknown number. Just perfect," he said sarcastically. Then she saw him pause, look closer, and whisper, "I think things just got a lot worse."

"What's wrong?"

He looked straight at her with a strained expression. "I know the second number that called him just a couple of hours ago. In fact, it used to be my main number. When I worked at the South Lake Tahoe police station."

"OK, but what's the problem?" she asked, not immediately comprehending why he was so upset.

"He got a call from someone not long before we met up at the trailhead. I can't tell who exactly, but the call came from the main dispatch number of the station." He stood up, dusted his knee off with his free hand, and looked at her. "Right around the time you and Bella probably left your place to meet up with me." Another moment passed, and she understood.

"You mean there's someone at the police station alerting this guy of our plans?" she said, feeling like she was suddenly living through an episode of a clichéd TV drama. "I just can't believe all of this." She sighed then noticed Bella shift her position from relaxed to rigid, ears standing tall. Her front right paw was bent back at the midjoint and lifted slightly off the ground, an often comical position Rachel joked about to friends. Usually it meant another person or dog was nearby. She whispered, "There's someone else here."

They both looked up, following the direction of Bella's nose. Rachel didn't see anyone or any strange movements, but there were plenty of places to hide. She saw Luke slip the bundled phone in his back pocket then reach into a small pouch attached to his belt and withdraw a pistol. She had to admit her mixed feelings about guns were temporarily dissipated—Rachel was certainly glad he had one now. Luke motioned for her to get lower to the ground just as he did the same. They heard the sharp echo of a gunshot, followed immediately by a high-pitched sound whirring through the air about a foot above their heads. Behind them, a piece of bark burst from a tall pine tree. Before she could truly register what had just happened, Rachel felt the weight of Luke's entire body on top of her, pushing them both flat against the ground. She barely noticed the uncomfortable pokes and scratches on her back.

"I'm sorry about catching you off guard," he said, slowly moving a bit to the side but keeping low. Rachel looked around, fear for Bella flashing through her mind, and saw that the pup had followed their quick fall and settled low to the ground a few inches away, waiting for a reward for laying down. Rachel breathed a sigh of relief that none of them had been hit. "I'm going to give you this to hold," he said, and she felt Luke shift his weight to the side, balancing his upper body on his elbow. With one hand still holding the gun, he reached around with his other hand, trying to get something from behind him. The cell phone, she realized. He had a worried look on his face, but a moment later they both heard the now familiar beeping sound coming from a pile of rocks about a foot away. It was a good thing they hadn't landed there, she thought; otherwise she might have her own fatal head injury. Luke reached over and moved some rocks around to retrieve the phone. Rachel saw the empty plastic evidence bag nearby, half-sealed but apparently open just enough that the phone had fallen out. "Rachel, here, take this." She nodded, grabbing it with the tips of her fingers in the same manner as she would a coin found on the ground, hoping to avoid smearing possible fingerprints. But it was pointless, and she knew it. She wrapped her hand around it fully and slipped it into one of the Velcro-sealed pockets of her hiking shorts. At the same time, she felt him slowly move off of her.

"What about the bag . . . and the gun?"

"I'll try to go grab it. You and Bella get down that hill as fast as you can. I'll catch up with you later." He motioned to his gun. "I'll get a few shots off while you get going."

"But . . . ," she started to ask, worried about leaving him behind.

"Go! Please!" Luke pleaded with her. "I've done this before, just get down that mountain and go straight home. Don't call anyone, got it?" His voice was harsh, but she needed that to jolt her into action.

"OK." She nodded, slowly getting on her feet, ready to jump up and run. "OK, Bella, let's go. Time to run!" After she took off, the sound of gun shots echoed behind them. Soon she and Bella were over the crest of the trail, running back down, just as they'd done two weeks ago.

~

As Luke watched Rachel and Bella take off running, he strategically timed the three shots he fired in the general direction the bullet had come from, hoping to give her time to reach the crest and get on the other side. Then he waited, listening and debating about what to do. He could try to locate the shooter, and possibly take a bullet in return, or follow Rachel and Bella, making sure they were safe and giving himself some time to think this all through. On the other hand, what if this was his only chance to discover who the shooter was? The guy would probably keep trying to harm Rachel, and if he had someone on the force helping him out, he'd probably succeed eventually. The implication that someone on the force had alerted a killer surprised Luke. He hoped it was an odd coincidence, having worked with most of them—some longer than others—and never noticing anything out of sorts. In fact, he had admired most of the men and women he'd worked with. However, the evidence suggested someone from the station may have tipped the man off, and it was best to be cautious until they knew more. But more confusing was how it appeared that the two suspects— although one now a victim—were not working together, yet both were after him and Rachel. The gym bag indicated the dead man had come here with one purpose. So how did he end up dead, and who is the new killer?

He wanted just to grab the bag and run, but Luke was worried the shooter might sneak around the side and follow Rachel while he took the time to get it. It wouldn't be hard for someone to move out here unnoticed, given the thickets of pine trees and intermittent large boulders. Then he saw it: the slightest movement about a hundred feet away, just to the right from where the bullets had first come.

He slowly moved behind some trees, still low to the ground. The guy had stayed behind—good. Yet before Luke had another moment to decide his next move, a barely perceptible sound came from the tree stand, and a bullet ricocheted off the pile of rocks near where he'd toppled Rachel over. The memory of her body under his was something he wanted to think about more . . . later. Then clack, another bullet. He was forced to back up further into the dense trees. A third bullet, without a sound, just a dust cloud where it hit. A silencer had been added to the gun. Luke drew in a deep breath as a tall, slightly lanky shape wearing a dark-brown hoodie emerged. The figure moved stealthily, reaching around and snatching up the gym bag. *Damn.* Luke counted the bullets he had left in his gun. Just enough. He slowly advanced forward, aiming just in front of where he expected the man to move and pulled the trigger. He heard a slight curse, but the man kept moving. It looked like his bullet had, at best, brushed the guy's arm. The stranger returned fire, still holding the bag in one hand as he made his way over to a taller thicket of trees. Luke slowly moved from tree to tree, advancing in the man's direction. As soon as the figure came into view, he aimed and fired. The guy was too fast and the bullet missed him. He was now running farther away, toward a tall rock outcrop. Luke followed, adrenaline propelling him forward. The guy shot again, but the poor aim made it clear he was just trying to slow Luke's advance. The man's swift departure around the outcrop was followed by several loud shuffling sounds, then cursing, and, finally, silence.

Luke waited but heard nothing. Aware it could be a trap, he continued to hide behind various trees and scattered boulders while making his way toward where he'd last seen the shooter. He carefully came around the last rock, gun out and ready to fire, and saw open air. One more cautious step forward and he was standing on the edge of a steep cliff. The idiot had apparently gone over. Luke peered down the side and saw the drop wasn't as far as he initially thought. Too bad, he mused. The fall was not likely to be fatal. It looked like a huge gully had recently formed from heavy rain, and the sides appeared too straight and eroded to climb up or down. As he was examining options to continue the chase, movement farther downhill caught his attention. The shooter was dragging himself down the washout, but with the steep terrain and wind funneling up from below, Luke couldn't get a good shot. The man still had the bag, and Luke debated about whether he should find a way to get down and follow him. But the only way down appeared to be a good fall, and he couldn't risk it. Luke was stuck. He did note some blood where the guy had apparently landed, and his first thought was to tell the crime scene techs to get some samples. But then he realized until he knew who had called the first man, that wasn't an option. He backed up carefully, stopped, and took a few more pictures of the other man's body and surrounding area, then took off running in the direction Rachel and Bella had gone—what now seemed like hours ago.

~

Mike was not going to like this, the man thought as he slowly climbed around the snagged roots and loose dirt that comprised the sides of the gully he'd fallen into. His arm was throbbing thanks to the bullet from the PI. At least he still had the bag. Now he had to deal with Spencer's body. This had been in Mike's plans for a few weeks, although his boss's change of heart about Spencer had come as a surprise. When he asked why, Mike had just stated that "Spencer had messed with the wrong woman." Chances were little Spencer had done some frolicking of his own with one of Mike's female friends; yet, the idea was a bit hard to believe given the timid nature of the kid. Well, Mike's reasons didn't matter. He had his orders. Then things were expedited by the girl's meddling.

He'd received a call from Mike earlier, explaining what was going on and instructing him to get out here and resolve some "issues," including Spencer. At least that was taken care of, but now he had to get back and figure out how to get rid of the couple at another location. Then again, maybe there was another way. He knew he wasn't the smartest bull in the pen, but he'd learned quite a bit about manipulation from his father and could figure a few things out. He'd seen their little tangle in the brush, watching as the man reached over for something in the rocks. He couldn't see what he had been reaching for, but what mattered now was the recollection of him picking up the rocks.

As a new idea formed, the shooter knew that, if needed, they could get help from law enforcement. Mike knew someone in that station, although who it was and why they helped was a secret known only to Mike. Yes, he felt this new idea might work much better than trying to clean up three bodies. It took some time, but he made his way back to the trail and ascended to where he'd left Spencer's body. A few things strategically moved around here and there, his own shoe prints brushed out with some pine branches, and he was good to go.

CHAPTER FIVE

Rachel was playing Frisbee with Bella to dispel some of her nervous energy. She kept glancing up at the clock over her door and looking out the window, hoping to see Luke's Subaru pull up. They'd been home for about twenty minutes now, and she was too keyed up to sit. That bullet had scared her to death. She did not like guns and always figured if she tried to shoot a "real gun" someone would easily grab it from her and turn it back on her. So, she kept other things around, like bear pepper spray, which she expected she was more likely to use on a human than a bear.

She heard the sound of a vehicle out front. Bella clearly had as well, letting go of the disc and rushing inside to greet the visitor. Rachel was so relieved that she ran over and opened the door just as Luke reached the top step on her porch. She hadn't intended to do any more than invite him in but found herself reaching for him and pulling him into a tight hug. It was obvious by his surprised reaction that she'd caught him off guard as much as herself, but then she felt his body relax and he wrapped his arms around her in return. And there was that wonderful musky scent she'd noticed earlier. Her face was tucked close into the crook of his neck, her lips so close to his skin he could probably feel her breath. She noticed how warm his body felt so close to hers, and a small rush of desire spread throughout her body. What was going on with her? Sure, Luke was nice to look at, but he was arrogant, stubborn, and from a completely different world, one she often fought against. She pulled back, apologizing and stepping aside so he could come in. His look of initial surprise was soon replaced with a grin.

"Miss me?"

"You wish," she rebounded and then made the mistake of moving her eyes up toward his, pausing first on his soft, inviting lips. What would it feel like to taste the sweet scent of the cinnamon she'd noticed on his breath? Feeling the flush in her cheeks and hoping Luke would blame it on the sunny afternoon, she quickly stepped back and distracted herself by petting Bella, now patiently sitting next to the door, waiting for the signal that it was okay to greet him. Luke stepped inside, a barely perceptible smile flashing across his features before he glanced around her home.

"Nice place. You were right—mountain rustic. It's . . . inviting, I suppose." It was unclear if he meant it as a compliment or if he was just trying to be nice. She didn't care, mostly thankful for the distraction from thinking about how his body felt against hers. "What's with the empty tables?" Her decorations were at least four feet up, set on top of a tall hutch.

"Bella Bomb," she laughed then threw a ball to the other side of the bare coffee table. Bella excitedly chased it, her tail swishing back and forth, sweeping across the top of the table.

"Got it," Luke chuckled.

"How did you get away?"

"Long story, but unfortunately he's still out there, and I wasn't able to get the kid's bag. He has it, and, on that note, I suspect he's going to continue to go after you, or rather both of us. Although I think thanks to a timely fall he's going to spend tonight on ice packs and pills."

"So what do we do?"

"Well, I think for tonight we stay at my place so you're not alone. I can start looking up some information on this, see what we can find."

"Your place?"

"Of course," Luke responded. Rachel waited for him to elaborate. When he didn't, her irritation crept up a notch.

"Do you have a state-of-the-art security system or something?"

"No. My place is bigger, and my stuff is there. Plus, I'm the ma—" Rachel's eyes must have burst wide open, because Luke stopped before he could finish his statement. They stared at each other, the only sound in the room the swishing of Bella's tail, which was getting slower. The dog must have felt the tension in the room. Luke finally broke the silence. "Look, it just makes sense," he said calmly. Perhaps he thought his comment would diffuse the situation, but his statement only upset her more.

"Fine. I'll pack up my less important woman things from my tiny little cabin and be ready in a jiffy!" She turned toward her hallway, intending to go pack a bag in her room while cursing him out in her head, but she felt like taking one more dig. "Oh, and I'll ask Bella not to move at your place. Wouldn't want to mess up those fancy decorations of yours or get dirt on your precious leather furniture." Rachel paused. She suspected she had just made a bad situation worse.

"First," retorted Luke, "what's with the attitude? I'm just trying to help. Second, yes, I like some finer decorations in my home, but I earned every penny I've spent. And third . . . have you ever felt what it's like to sit down on a soft, cool leather-covered sofa? To fully sink down into it and prop your legs up while your head just melts into the side cushion? It's heaven."

She didn't know what to say. He'd gone from being a complete chauvinist to making her think about what it would feel like to be on that sofa—with him next to her. Rachel wasn't quite sure how she felt, so she opted to wave a white flag, so to speak, and just let it go. "OK . . . sorry. We can leave Bella in the truck while we head in and get your house ready. Let me pack my things." She saw him look around some more, then sigh, and speak with a resigned voice.

"Wait a minute. OK, Rachel, I'm not sure what I said that ticked you off so much, but I'm sorry. Regardless of *how* you did it, you have made your point. It would take too much time to make my place safe for, or from, Bella, so how about I go and get my supplies and come back here for tonight?" Rachel nodded in agreement, surprised by his compromise. Luke continued, "Although I know this valley is a bit out of town, based on what you mentioned about working from home, I'm assuming you have high-speed Internet access?"

"DSL." She paused, adding, "And Luke . . . thanks." Rachel was still confused and upset about the housing debate but decided it was best to lighten the mood. They did, after all, have to spend the night in the same house. "How about we order some pizza when you get back? Sounds pretty good at the moment, and we can get delivery."

She saw a strange look pass over his face before he smiled and said, "Yeah, sounds good. I should be back within an hour. Keep your guard up, and, by the way, do you have a gun?" he asked tentatively, although his voice gave away his suspicion she didn't.

"No, but I've got a fountain of pepper-hot burn-your-eyes-out spray." He paused a moment then nodded.

"Bear spray. Got it. Well, keep it handy. And don't use it on me when I come back." She heard him quietly laughing as he closed the door.

"I'll think about it," she called out, although he probably didn't hear her remark through the closed door.

As Rachel began packing a few things herself, preparing in case a quick departure was in order, she started thinking about where they could go. No way could she afford a hotel room, and she wouldn't put any nearby friends in danger. She thought about her parents' home just a couple hours away, currently sitting vacant for a month while they traveled. However, when they left for long periods of time like that, the house was completely shut down—no water, no power, no air conditioning. Let alone, if someone could find *her* address that easily, they could no doubt find her parents' address with one or two additional keystrokes. Her older brother was too far away to help, even if he did have time, but he could barely call her once a month he was so busy right now. Her younger brother only lived a couple of hours away, but he had his own problems at the moment, and Rachel knew she couldn't add to them. As far as places to go, she'd just have to cross that bridge if, and when, she came to it.

~

Luke had driven home quickly. As he walked into his house and viewed it from the perspective of the Bella Bomb, he agreed it could be a very messy and possibly expensive undertaking to have her there for a few hours, let alone days, as he expected it could come to. As he began stuffing clothes and toiletry items into his bag, his mind recalled that hug. He had been surprised, but once he felt Rachel's sweet warm body against his and the tickle of her breath on his neck he had started imagining what it would feel like to have her lips touching his skin. Then she had to go and stare at him the way she had, and he was certain she was thinking the same thing. It made him want to forget all reason and move in to taste her sweet mouth. Thankfully he hadn't, and now that he was removed from the intense situation he wondered how he could be reacting so strongly to a woman as stubborn as Rachel Winters. He liked independence. He also liked athletic women. He'd grown up surrounded by young, starving model types or women his mother's age who underwent plastic surgery and attempted to fit into tight clothing that was far too young for them by about three decades. Then there was his poor sister who nearly killed herself because of the too common preoccupation with being thin. He also liked a woman who relied on him, at least on some level; a woman he could take care of, who would appreciate a few of the finer things in life that he worked so hard for. A woman that would be *thankful* to have him watch out for her.

"Why am I even thinking any of this?" he said out loud. Luke had plenty of women to date—women he could go have fun with and not have to worry about any long-term commitments, something he'd made a point to avoid since the engagement fiasco with Savannah. He needed to get it together and focus on the job at hand.

He was still struggling with the knowledge that someone he might have worked with in the past had apparently tipped off the killer, although it was also curious why whoever was behind this didn't just let things go after Rachel's initial report led to nothing. Legally, nothing could have been done about her sighting of the first victim; therefore, she posed no threat as a witness in any murder trial. The officers followed up on a citizen's report, found nothing, end of story. Which begged the question—what harm could come from her going back to revisit the area if there was nothing to find? Which meant there was something to find. Maybe not there, not physically, but someone threatened by what she'd seen had apparently been keeping an eye on her, going so far as to—what? Scare her into silence? Ironically, he figured she probably would have eventually been forced to let it go, if not for the obvious signs that someone was watching her every move.

Luke returned to Rachel's place almost an hour later. Based on the echoes he heard from the backyard as he pulled up he concluded Rachel was playing ball with Bella. When she unlocked and opened the front door, he noticed she'd packed a couple of bags for Bella and herself, stowing them nearby. That was good thinking. He unloaded a bag of clothes, a shaving kit, a laptop, a small portable printer, and a leather bag full of a few other electronic devices that could come in handy. Luke was thankful the atmosphere in her home was much lighter than an hour ago.

"All right, let's get that pizza ordered. Not sure what you like on yours, but I need to have at least three layers of meat. Beyond that, I'm pretty flexible. Well, except pineapple. Or anchovies," she smiled.

"I'm guessing you ramble a bit when you're anxious?" he asked.

"Maybe," she said, quickly changing the subject. "Now, the pizza?"

"Speaking of pizza, I thought you worked in the environmental realm. Aren't you all vegetarians or vegans, something like that?" Luke said haughtily.

"Are you kidding? Hmm, now who's projecting stereotypes?" Rachel laughed, admitting sheepishly, "OK, I did try the vegetarian thing once, but it didn't work out."

"Hmm, all right, let's get the works then," Luke chuckled.

After phoning in the order, he set up his laptop and spread out some other electronic gadgets. "Got the cell phone?"

"Yes, here." She handed it to him. He spent more time going through it, but didn't find anything more informative than what they'd found earlier.

"Well, the phone hadn't been used that long. It was probably recently purchased at a convenience store. There are no outgoing calls, or at least if there had been, they've been erased."

"I suppose I'm not surprised."

"How about we see what we can find online? Can you get me your wireless code?"

"Sure." As she headed into her office to write the password down, there was a knock on the door.

"Great, I'm starving!" Luke said, getting up. A few minutes later, he sat in complete fascination as he watched Rachel douse her pizza with red pepper flakes then dip the slices in ranch dressing. "Want some pizza with your pepper flakes? I mean, my God, woman, doesn't that burn your taste buds?"

"Hasn't yet. I like things spicy," Rachel said, averting her gaze.

"Oh, so do I." He liked hot things, too, but it wasn't food he was thinking about at that moment.

CHAPTER SIX

"Captain, we've received a call from someone saying they were out hiking the Yova-Pioneer Trail this morning and found a body." Captain Taylor looked at the young officer, a tall, lanky rookie named Nolan who tended to keep to himself but seemed good enough at his job.

"Are you kidding me?" Ron said, frustration in his tone. The kid nodded.

"The one off Luther Pass."

"Oh, I know which one, damn it," he snapped then calmed himself down. "Did the caller leave a name? Phone number?"

"No, dispatch just handed me the information. They said the caller refused to leave a name, but he wanted to let us know." Unfortunately, it wasn't uncommon for people to call in a report and hang up when questioned for their name.

Ron sighed, brushing his mustache in nervous habit. "Just what we need. OK, go find Ted. And have him take whoever went out there with him last time."

~

Wearing a fresh pair of disposable gloves, Officer Ted Benson searched the man's pockets for any identifying belongings while the other officer slowly walked around nearby, attempting to locate a cell phone signal strong enough to call in what they'd found. Ted broke the temporary silence. "No wallet. Looks like the poor fellow was slammed pretty hard with this rock, maybe once or twice. I found a couple of different shoe impressions, although it's so dusty I'm not sure how much they can tell us." At forty-three, Ted looked ten years younger, thanks to a healthy lifestyle and the good heredity that blessed his family with thick heads of blond hair until the day they died. Ted searched the area around the body and noticed a blood-smeared rock just a few feet away.

"I'm surprised a little rock could do this. Then again, suppose if someone were strong enough and motivated enough. Poor guy." He took multiple pictures of the scene, including close-ups of the shoe impressions lined with a small ruler to help them determine shoe size later. He placed the rock in an evidence bag.

"Don't you want to leave that for the crime scene techs?" the other officer asked.

"Normally, yes. But I'm sensing from your obvious frustration that we don't have the ability to call this in from here. Someone needs to head back down the trail until the signal is strong enough. Add to that I see some possible thunderstorms forming over to the southwest that could easily come this way."

"You're right. No signal. What about heading down the shorter side here?"

"Then we'd have to walk out to the highway from the trailhead, several more miles. Then you might get a signal, might not. Probably about the same distance either way. We should just stick with the way we came in." He tried not to show his mild annoyance with the officer's gripes.

"OK. Who stays?" the officer asked, clearly hoping to be the one leaving.

"You. And do not leave this area for any reason. As I mentioned earlier, a woman reported another body that had disappeared from around here just two weeks ago."

"I thought she was some New Age hippie looking for attention."

"I admit I had doubts at first, but I have to say this makes me reconsider her story," Ted waved at the body. The other officer nodded.

"All right, I'll hang out here."

Ted left instructions to secure the scene and collect any additional evidence if it appeared thunderstorms might develop. Then he began his descent, hoping he didn't have to go too far before he could connect enough to send a text. Two miles back down the trail he was able to get a text message through to Captain Taylor. Several minutes passed before he was rewarded with a short response. "OK. WILL SEND CSI TEAM. GET BACK HERE ONCE THEY ARRIVE."

It had taken a few hours for the technicians to show up. They didn't look happy about having to carry their bags of equipment up the trail. Ted could have suggested the shorter route, but from what he'd heard, the old dirt road was torn up and hadn't been maintained in years. Crawling their van across the streams and other obstacles would shake up their $500,000 worth of equipment.

After setting their bags down, one of the techs said the medical examiner—or rather, their half-time ME since her services weren't often needed in this area—was on the way with additional officers to help carry the body down. Realizing the late hour, they had brought along extra flashlights and headlamps, handing one to Ted for the rest of his descent. He left the other officer there again, this time keeping watch until relieved by the officers that would arrive with the ME. Just what the department needed—more overtime charges.

"I'm going to run this rock back to the lab tonight, see what we can find," Ted said, holding up the bagged evidence to the other officer who'd stayed behind at the scene. "Sorry you have to stick around a while longer. I'm sure these guys can entertain you, though." He waved at the forensic technicians who were fully focused on the scene, oblivious to any conversation around them. He received an annoyed look in response. "They may ignore you at first, but I've learned a lot from them. Might be a good opportunity for you." Ted waved then took off for yet another trek back down the trail.

The clock on the laboratory wall read 9:03 p.m. Ted's stomach growled, reminding him he'd skipped dinner. Thanks to an inquisitive mind, and extra hours spent working directly with techs labeled "squints" or "lab rats" by various television shows, he'd learned a few things about retrieving fingerprints from almost any surface. The rock was rough, but because of the type of dirt in the area, when the rock landed, just enough dirt stuck to the oil left behind by someone's fingers that Ted was able to decipher the ridges of a thumbprint. Through the wonders of technology, an image was scanned into the computer, and a search for matches in the national fingerprint database began immediately. Expecting it to take a while, if it worked at all, he began to skim through a sports magazine someone had left behind. Before he could even finish looking through the "Letters to the Editor" page, the computer beeped. Ted looked up, surprised and excited at the same time.

But the name and face displayed on his screen couldn't be the perpetrator. He knew the guy, had even worked with him at one point, although he hadn't spoken with him since he was laid off a few years back. There was Luke Reed's face with the words "MATCH FOUND" on the screen.

CHAPTER SEVEN

Rachel woke up in her normal fashion, with a slight shift on the other side of the bed, the whiff of dog breath, and then . . . the stare.

"Good morning, sweet girl." She rubbed Bella's ears, going through their usual morning routine. She had just a moment of peace before the previous day's events came back to her. The realization that Luke was sleeping in the next room ran through her mind before being distracted again by Bella's instant nudging.

"OK, OK, I'll let you out." She threw on her robe and quietly led Bella to the back door, hoping that Luke didn't wake up until after she'd showered. Luck was on her side this morning as the house remained silent.

Emerging from the bathroom with wet hair and almost awake enough to communicate, she found him in the kitchen, searching through her cabinets.

"Hey." She struggled to sound cheerful, but there was no disguising it. She was not a morning person.

"Oh, hey." He sounded half asleep, too, and his dark-brown hair was mussed in every direction. It was kind of . . . sexy, she mused. "Got coffee?" he croaked.

"You okay with one of those instant packets?" She saw the

look of disappointment on his face and added, "It's strong."
Speaking of strength, groggy as she still was, his bare chest and
toned arms had not gone unnoticed either. The man was
definitely athletic.

"So long as it's leaded." He reached for a coffee mug after
she'd pointed toward one of the cabinets and turned to look at
her. "You seriously don't drink coffee? My God, girl, you can
barely speak, and yet you've already showered."

"The mere fact it's morning has always overpowered any
potential boost I'd get from coffee." Trying to smile, again half
failing in the early hour, she reached for the instant packets she
kept around for such emergencies. "So, find anything last night?"
Rachel had felt a bit guilty when, by eleven p.m., she could barely
keep her eyes open.

"Yes, a few things that I think you may understand better
than I can. But let me get some caffeine in my bloodstream first,
if you don't mind." Luke filled the mug with water and placed it
in the small microwave nearby.

"Sure, and I'll fix some breakfast, too. Eggs, sausage good?"

"Hell yeah."

By the time they'd finished breakfast Luke had downed two
cups of coffee, and they sat in the living room reviewing what
he'd found.

"It took some digging, a bit strange since usually everything is
mentioned hundreds of times online. After you'd gone to bed, I
found a legal notice for an RFP from about seven years ago that
mentioned the Yova-Pioneer Trail." He handed her a printout
and she looked it over. Rachel knew what RFPs were—requests
for proposals. Typically, at least in her line of work, government
agencies often seek estimates from private consulting firms to
perform the environmental review for projects or to do the actual
on-the-ground work. Companies hoping for the contract write
and submit proposals describing how they would complete the
work and what it will cost; then the agency selects which one to

hire. She scanned over the printout.

"It looks like the county planning department was seeking RFPs for erosion control work in the vicinity of the southern portion of the trail. I guess I'm not surprised I haven't heard about it. That end of the trail is so hard to get to, and I think last year's floods took out parts of the dirt road people use to access it. Things don't tend to get much attention out there."

"I'd believe it," Luke said. "Unfortunately, after another hour looking for more information, I came up with a long list of trail maps, motor-vehicle use maps, forest maps, and a whole bunch of hiking books I can 'buy now for 20 percent off' from the local forest service office. But I have a feeling you'll have a better idea of where to look for this sort of information." He stood up. "And on that note, how about you take over the research while I shower?"

She nodded, already typing away on the keyboard as ideas ran through her mind about what to look for and where. "Fresh towels are under the sink," she thought to call out at the last minute. The last thing she needed was to think about that man's amazing body—in her shower, all wet. Rachel silently chastised herself. Girl, get your mind out of the gutter. She'd simply been working too hard for the last couple of years. That must be it.

Ten minutes later Luke reappeared, wearing a clean pair of jean shorts and a black T-shirt. "Got another packet of coffee?"

"Are you serious?"

"Yes, three's my limit. Also my minimum requirement."

She waved at the kitchen. "Feel free. Ever tried just inserting an IV into your vein?" she laughed.

"Once. Too difficult to ride my bike and keep the needle attached." As he walked into her kitchen for the third packet, Rachel thought about that. She honestly wasn't sure if he was joking or not.

"Find anything?" he called out.

"Not yet, but I just got an idea. I keep typing things, and the search engine wants to autocorrect or fill in my phrase. I'm thinking about how often I've run across typing errors in government documents or newspapers, let alone how much I rely on spell-check, so I'm trying some different ways someone might spell one of the trail names or phrases wrong." About the time Luke was stirring the coffee grains in his last mug of coffee, Rachel yelled out, "Got something!"

He came over and sat next to her, looking at the laptop screen. "What did you find?"

"It came down to three spelling errors that together the auto-searches couldn't figure out. I started including the old forest road number in the search terms, and that's what did it. Looks like just a few months after the RFP was published the newspaper included a small follow-up article. There's a picture here with a quick description." She moved the screen so he could read it, meanwhile smelling the aroma of his coffee and thinking about the nature of the first two typos, *Java* instead of Yova; another coffee addict had probably written it either pre-drug or post-drug. As for leaving the *r* out of Trail, she could grant that it was probably an easier mistake to make:

> One of our well-established and locally-owned businesses, Row Environmental, has just received a big boost after winning the bid to construct and operate the West Hills Erosion Control and Forest Recycling Project, which will be located just northwest of Forest Road 41298 (mostly known for providing jeep access to the Java Recreational Tail).

There were five people in the accompanying photo, posing in a forested area with hard hats and shovels—including a younger version of the man they'd found murdered yesterday.

"Yep, that's our guy," Luke said, staring at the image.

"Well, now I have a starting point," Rachel said, sending the image to the printer and opening more tabs on the computer. She went straight to the forest service website covering the location of the project and, after a few more clicks, found it. After sending a few more files to the printer, Rachel explained her find to Luke. "I've found the project's RFP and the EA that followed it. The forest service did eventually approve the project." At his questioning look, she quickly explained. "Sorry, I'm a bit too used to acronyms. As part of the National Environmental Policy Act, or what you may hear referred to as NEPA, federal agencies have to look at the various ways a project could be completed, including what the environmental impacts and benefits of each way would be. Often you'll hear reference to an EIS, or environmental impact statement, which is the most detailed analysis they can do. An EIS can sometimes end up being thousands of pages." She sighed, remembering some of the lengthy EISs she'd had to review over the years. "Anyhow, when smaller projects meet certain criteria, a less detailed review, called an environmental analysis, or EA, is often sufficient. That's what they did here."

"OK, I think I get it. But will this EA thing list names or anything?"

"Yes, but not everyone who, say, just went to the meetings will be listed. However, attendees should be listed in the minutes—those are the typed-out notes of what happened at the public meetings. Hopefully, they took good notes. Some agencies are really thorough while others are so ridiculously thin it's almost a waste of time."

"The environmental firm in that notice," Luke pointed to a line of text on the screen, "have you ever heard of them?"

"You know, now that I think of it, I *have* heard of them. But I don't know much about them. I think they are usually more involved in mining projects over in Nevada. Although they've picked up a few forest restoration projects in the Basin over the years, just not in the areas I usually work in." Rachel looked at the picture a bit closer. "So what is the connection between this forest project and two murders?"

"We're going to find out," he announced confidently. She could see the excitement on his face and got the feeling he lived for this sort of thing.

"OK, how about this? I have a few other cases I'm working on, but being shot at moves this one to the top of my list. Let me make some calls and put off the other cases for a bit."

"Good idea. I should probably shift my workload as well."

Eventually, Rachel sat down with Bella lying at her side, preparing to read through the EA document. Luke was leaning back on her sofa, laptop balanced on his knees, when he shifted, and she saw him grab his phone. He mumbled, "I'd better check my messages at home." In the Basin, cell service was not guaranteed, so many residents kept landlines in place, attaching answering machines as backup. She didn't pay much attention to his call at first, more interested in what she was reading on the computer. But when she heard him whisper, "Son of a . . . ," she looked up. He had the phone next to his ear, still listening to what was apparently a long message.

She set the papers down and leaned forward. "What's wrong?"

He ended the call and slowly set his phone down, and she saw a look of worry mixed with anger on his face. "Well, the good news is the cops won't doubt there was a body this time. The bad news is he's been found, and I'm being asked to come in for questioning."

"Which is bad news because . . . the murderer wanted this guy found and somehow you've been connected to him," Rachel surmised.

He nodded. "Which, as you can imagine, is rather quick given that you and I are probably the only people who have been on that trail in the last two weeks. Well, except for the dead kid and whoever was shooting at us." She could see his mind was already turning with possibilities.

"You think the person at the station somehow alerted them? Why would they do that? Why would they want this guy found so quickly?"

"Good question."

A moment later, Rachel's home phone rang. They both looked at the caller ID display. The same seven digits that they'd seen on the dead man's cell phone glared ominously in her display. She heard Luke say, "Let it go to voicemail."

"No problem," she said, sensing more bad news. A minute later, they listened to the message on her speaker phone. It was Officer Benson, whom she remembered from their excursion to the site of the first body. He'd been friendly and worked to keep the mood lighthearted as they'd hiked up. His voice had a similar tone on the message now. She suspected he was trying to make his request to speak with her sound like a nothing-to-worry-about routine-questioning kind of thing.

"Isn't there anyone you can trust on the force?" she asked, feeling a bit helpless.

"I thought I could trust them all," Luke responded, disappointment evident in his tone. "Maybe I misjudged someone or it's a new hire. Or maybe the perp just used the station's phone. Until I know who that is, or who *they* are, we have to stay away. Once they catch us, we might lose our chance to figure out what's really going on here."

She looked down at Bella, reaching down to rub her neck. "So what do we do?"

"We go somewhere no one would look for us, and then we focus on finding out what this is about." He moved to turn off his computer. "Know any places we could get Internet service, a roof over our heads, and where no one would expect you to go?" Grabbing his laptop case, he slipped his machine inside, grabbed the portable printer he'd brought, and placed it in its own bag.

Although she'd given it some thought the day before, she'd never quite settled on one specific place, hoping she wouldn't have a reason to need one. Rachel ran through some of the places again in her mind and settled on one that might work, if just for a night or so.

"I know a place about two hours away we can bunk in for at least a night. Even my friends wouldn't expect me to go there."

"All right, works for me. I say we take your Tacoma—more room for Bella, I expect—and you drive."

Soon they were heading east out of the Basin, through Hope Valley, and after leaving the canyon and passing through the small settlement of Woodfords they continued east toward the Nevada desert. Luke hadn't realized Bella always rode in the cab. The pup had no problems sitting on the backseat when there was another human passenger, with one exception. It hadn't taken long for Luke to give up trying to keep Bella from resting her chin on his left shoulder.

Rachel took the opportunity to explain where they were going.

"Several years ago, my parents retired from teaching and wanted to find a place in Nevada with more acreage, but unfortunately, they were looking during a time when the housing market was extremely overpriced. They ended up several miles north of Yerington, a small desert community. Ten acres and not one tree. My mother couldn't stand it. Anyway, they fixed it up quite a bit but soon put it up for sale, hoping to move farther north where they could still be in the mountains with the pine trees my mother longed for, but away from the tourist traffic and snow we deal with in the Basin. Lucky for them, an older couple from Maine or Vermont—pardon my poor East Coast geography skills—wanted to get away from the busy life and actually bought the place. The couple managed a good six months or so in the new place then headed back. It was too quiet for them. They kept it though, and periodically come for a week here and there. But they avoid the summers—too hot and too dry. Lucky for us, though, they leave the utilities on year-round; please don't tell my coworkers I just said that," she laughed.

"Guess you'd better be nice to me then," he said. Rachel fake punched his arm, and after an overly dramatic "ow," Luke continued. "Sounds like a good spot. Do you have a key? Not that we couldn't get in . . ."

"No, but I know how to lift the sliding glass door to get around the lock. They don't leave much of value lying around, so apparently security wasn't a big issue. Let's just hope they haven't changed anything since they last e-mailed my parents."

"Sounds like you are close with your parents? That's great."

"Yes, I'm pretty lucky. Although when I was a kid, like everyone, I thought they were unfair and didn't understand me at all. I believed they loved my brothers more." She laughed a bit at this last thought. "I take it you aren't?" Rachel probed, hesitantly, but he'd broached the subject and she could use a good mental distraction as she drove down the sage-lined highway, trying not to think about why they'd left.

Luke sighed. "Well, my parents weren't good at . . . being parents. I was caught up in their world but, at the same time, alone. My younger sister was playing her role perfectly, just like I'd been doing. But, the event that changed my life, I guess you could say, was a car accident. A good friend of mine, Trenton, was driving a bit too fast and lost control going around a corner. He broke his leg, and I almost lost my eye. In the meantime, I wasn't allowed to play football, but I still needed to do something. I found myself taking my road bike out on the dirt trails nearby, which is when I learned why dirt bikes have wider tires," he laughed. "After that, I got into hiking. The next thing I knew, I was organizing camping trips for the summer with a huge group of friends. Trenton even started going along, once his leg healed. He'd been doing his parent's bidding on the sports circuit, too, although he seemed to like it for himself—which was good. I was never quite into it as much as he was. But then several months after the accident my father did something I could never forgive, and my mother meekly stood by letting him run the show." She heard the anger creep into his voice.

"What happened?"

"My dad was a big-time attorney. He never said a word to me before he suddenly slapped my friend's family with a huge lawsuit. My buddy was only sixteen, so his parents were legally responsible." He paused as if trying to remain calm while telling a story that was clearly difficult to talk about. "My jerk of a father sued them for everything they had. When I begged him to change his mind, he told me to shut up and deal with it, that it was for 'my future.'"

"How did the lawsuit end?" Rachel asked after a brief pause.

"My dad won, of course. Trenton's family lost their home. He had two younger sisters, and they all lost their college funds and had to move into a small apartment. Unlike us, they had earned their money the hard way, saving every penny and being careful to invest it for the kids to be able to afford college. We got ours the old-fashioned way—we inherited it."

"That's horrible. What happened to Trenton?"

"He refused to talk to me. I called him every few days for over a year, but he never answered. I eventually gave up. He ended up working full time and going to a community college. Kind of lost track after that. I tried a few times over the years to get in touch with him, his parents, even his sisters, but they wouldn't return any messages."

"Sorry." She didn't know what else to say. To her surprise, he continued.

"And worse yet, know what my parents did with all that money? Aside from putting some into a college fund that already held more than I'd ever need, they bought themselves a new vacation home along the coast. And a new car. While my friend's family struggled to put food on the table! When it came time to go to college, I wanted to get into criminology, become an officer, and *help* people. My parents wanted me to go to Harvard or Yale and then take over my dad's law firm. I refused, so they cut me off, focusing everything on my sister. I didn't care about the money at that point, except that I'd planned to give it back to my friend's family once I turned eighteen and could access my inheritance—if they were willing to accept it. So instead I worked, got through school, the police academy, and then saw the opening at the station here in the Basin a few months out of college."

"That had to take guts, what you did. I really respect that." Her voice had grown serious. After a few moments of silence, she tried to cut through the ominous mood with another lame joke, but she couldn't think of what to say. "I guess that explains the Harvard-boy vibe. So you just need to work on some of that pretentious behavior, and you'll be good to go."

"Pretentious?" He shifted in his seat. "Says the woman who decides the entirety of who someone is by how they decorate?"

"Touché," she said, seeing him smile. Well, it had worked.

~

"I understand the body of a young man was found beaten to death on that trail," Mike said without pretense when his phone call was answered.

"Yes, they don't know who he is yet, but word around the station is they've tied the body to a local PI involved with the woman who reported another body on the same trail recently," the informant relayed.

"Oh, well now, that's quite an interesting turn of events." Mike paused, taking in this new information and starting to see the significance of the situation. "Have there been any arrests?"

"Not yet. Apparently they can't find either of them. There's no official be-on-the-lookout alert yet—they are just wanted for questioning at this point."

"I see. I appreciate the update. I'll talk to you later." He carefully placed the phone down and smiled at how things were turning out. He no longer had to worry about Spencer and Lori.

Unfortunately, his excited mood would be dampened after the next call he made. Mike was supposed to be keeping Jerome in the loop on this deal. The problem was Jerome worried too much. He liked structured plans that followed nice clean steps. When adjustments had to be made, Jerome got nervous.

~

Standing across their expansive living room, decorated with expensive items that meant nothing to her other than a means to show off their wealth, Diane looked over at her husband of almost twenty-five years. Jerome was not aging well. Stress and a life of overindulgence had left him with an extra forty pounds, high blood pressure, and thinning grey hair. His stomach hung over his belted pants. He attempted to cover this up by buttoning his suit jacket. She'd married him young, caught up in the romance of the times, surrounded by friends who were all getting engaged and married. Having grown up primarily in boarding schools only the wealthy could afford, most of the friends she'd made in school had simply found rich men to marry—attorneys, politicians, and businessmen—content to become accessory wives. Jerome had seemed to be different. Yes, he had started a career in politics, was slowly but surely moving up the ranks, and did come from a rich and powerful family. However, unlike other men in the same situation, he also seemed to cherish her, wanting a partner rather than a trophy wife. He'd courted her for over a year, sharing sweet romantic gestures that often made her friends jealous. They had both become well known and liked in their circles. Both friends and those pretending to be friends for political favors attended their enormously lavish wedding.

However, just six months after returning from their honeymoon, Jerome started growing distant and keeping things from her. She thought it was one of those typical lulls in a marriage that people just had to work through. It continued, and six months later, she missed her period. Seven months after that, her son arrived, and she spent less time worrying about her husband's distance and more time focused on her little baby boy. Three more years went by before Marie was born. Now almost two decades had passed, the kids had moved away, and they were living their own lives with children of their own that Diane hadn't even met.

She was once again alone with a man she barely knew. He had been elected to one of the most influential positions in their town, and while that came with many perks and political connections, the salary alone wasn't very high. About ten years ago, Diane noticed they seemed to be spending far more than they could afford. Curious, she'd started to pay more attention to his schedule, noticing a surge in their investments or other extravagant purchases that tended to follow the approval of the larger development projects in the area. But those projects were few and far between, not enough that she figured anyone other than she might take notice of, and so, resigned to the life she'd chosen, she had let it go.

"You look stressed, Jerome" she said, disinterested but sensing the phone call he'd just received had troubled him.

"That obvious, huh? Yes, I've been working on a project, and there's been a slight hitch. My people tell me not to worry about it, but I don't like it."

Diane sat down and took a sip of her Chardonnay. "Want to talk about it?" She couldn't recall the number of times she'd said those words over the years and never once had he taken her up on her offer. Unlike her, he seemed perfectly content with the pretend marriage they now had.

"Thanks, but I'll work it out." He stood up, grabbed his glass of whiskey, another one of his increasing indulgences, went into his office, and quietly shut the door behind him. She sat for a moment, dreaming about a different life but feeling forever stuck in this one. The phone rang and the caller ID said it was her older brother. Well, at least she would have a momentary distraction. Her brother wasn't the most personable guy, and she never saw him much, but she didn't have many friends calling her anymore and hadn't heard from her kids in ages.

CHAPTER EIGHT

Rachel silently apologized to the couple who'd purchased her parents' home years ago as she worked the sliding glass door open and entered the dining room. She never did this kind of thing and reminded herself it was a life-or-death situation. She promised, though, that she'd clean up after Bella before they left—if there were supplies—more to ease her conscious than over fears of their stay being discovered. For now, it was a good place to hide for the night. The nearest neighbors were miles away, and empty sage-covered desert managed by the Bureau of Land Management surrounded the lot on three sides. Thankfully the house was furnished with an old sofa, a chair, decent beds in the rooms, and some basic appliances. She noticed Luke glance into the kitchen and smile.

"Would that huge grin be related to that coffeemaker over there?" she asked, laughing.

"What else?" Luke set up his computer and attached it to the satellite modem he'd found in the living room while Rachel put out food and water for Bella. She soon heard him typing on his keyboard.

"While you do that, I'll keep looking through the EA."

"Uh-huh," he said, not paying full attention.

About ten minutes later, she heard Luke shift in his chair and say, "I think I found him." Anxious and excited, she marked her spot, dropped what she was reading, and came to his side. He sat in the large worn leather chair where, according to the sports magazines tucked in the side pocket, the husband probably spent a lot of his time. Not thinking, Rachel moved to sit on the arm of the chair to lean in and see his screen, but overestimating the width, she lost her balance and fell into him. To stop her fall, she'd instinctively put her hand out, catching his shoulder. She could feel the muscles under his shirt that she'd admired earlier that morning and paused, realizing where her thoughts had again drifted. Not again—what was wrong with her? She awkwardly mumbled an apology and readjusted herself, immediately trying to steer her focus, and his, back to his laptop screen. But she had a feeling he'd known exactly what was on her mind, and she was thankful he was going to pretend he didn't.

"How about we move over on the sofa and put the laptop on the coffee table?" Luke asked. Rachel agreed, stood up, and stepped over to the sofa, careful not to disturb her sleeping dog. Carrying the laptop in his right hand, Luke traced the same path around Bella and sunk down into the deep sofa next to Rachel, placing the laptop on the short table in front of them. "I think his name is Spencer Wells."

"Think?" In this day and age, that any one couldn't be easily found online was surprising to her. He nodded.

"Curious thing. There's a list of employees for Row Environmental dated a few years ago where his name is included among various subcontractors and consultants. It looks like an old link that hasn't been updated in some time, plus the current employee and subcontractor directory on their main website includes pictures next to their names and bios. None of the pictures match our guy. According to the computer here, this website was last updated today. What do you make of that?"

Something tickled the back of her mind. "Wait a minute. Let

me check something." She reached for the stack of papers she'd been reading earlier and looked through the last few pages. She paused on a page titled "List of Authors/Contributors." Toward the bottom there was a note thanking "Mr. Spencer Wells, grandson of Lloyd Wells, for his ongoing participation and assistance in the development of this project."

With shared enthusiasm they both stared at the screen as Luke typed in Spencer's name on a generic people-finder website.

"Usually I hate these websites that let you locate anyone, but at this moment I'm temporarily over it," she smiled.

"Yes, great for stalkers, bad for their victims," he said nonchalantly. She thought of Matt and tensed. He had no idea how close to the mark his statement was. He must have felt her stiffen a bit; thankfully he quickly continued. "Sorry, bad reference. I do know what you mean, though I admit I do use them sometimes in my line of work." A new page opened and they read two similar names: a Spencer Wells Jr. born in 1979 in Denver, Colorado, and a Spencer Wells born in 1960 in a small town in North Carolina. "I'm going to say our guy is the one from Denver. What do you think?" he laughed.

"Yes, unless he discovered the fountain of youth."

Luke typed a few more times, and eventually they started to hit on a few searches. "There's a graduation picture here. Looks like the kid and maybe his grandfather?"

Rachel leaned in closer, looking at the details in the picture. It was the dead man in the forest, although probably over ten years ago, wearing a blue graduation gown. He was standing next to an older man who could be the young man's grandfather. The older man appeared to be in his sixties, hair mostly grey, wearing a very pristine suit and tie.

"I'm going to take an obvious guess here and say that must be Lloyd. But Spencer doesn't look like he's very fond of his grandpa," she observed. In the picture, Spencer's smile looked strained, his hand around the other man's broad shoulders appearing not fully committed to the familial gesture. "Where did you find this picture?"

"It wasn't easy, but it was one of a few archived pictures from the *Denver Post* website. Unfortunately, it's a stand-alone. No story to go with it."

"Well, at least now we know his name," she said.

"Yes, let's just hope we can find out more."

Rachel settled back a bit. "How about I fix us some dinner while you keep looking? I'm starving."

"Good thinking. I hadn't even thought to pack food. What did you bring?"

"Aside from Bella's food, I threw in some leftover barbequed pork ribs and green-bean casserole. There's a microwave here. Sound good?" Rachel heard a moan of pleasure originate from the vicinity of the sofa and took that to mean Luke agreed.

~

As they sat on stools eating the leftovers, plates resting on the stone countertop, Luke couldn't help but notice how close she was. Earlier, when she'd lost her balance on the side of the chair, he'd reacted immediately to the feel of her hip and arm on his body. He hadn't wanted her to move. He imagined her falling on his lap, where he would push her thick hair aside and run his lips along her soft neck.

Luke reminded himself to get it together. Besides the fact she was stubborn, too independent, and some kind of environmental-feminist or something, they were also from two different worlds. My God, she lived in a small forty-year-old cabin *by preference* and decorated it with ski and bear knickknacks intermixed with who knows how many scented candles. Add to that, the dog was allowed on the sofa—and on the bed. In fact, he'd found a few dog hairs in his pizza the night before and tried to carefully pull them out without being noticed. None of that seemed to bother Rachel one bit.

Then again, Bella's pretty sweet and fun to have around. He'd also learned the mountain lifestyle was very accommodating to dogs. Often places advertised outdoor patios that were "dog friendly," and a lot of people he knew brought their dogs to work with them. Growing up in the circles he did, the only dogs he really knew were carried around in purses and dressed up in frilly little clothes. He had always felt bad for the poor pups, thinking no animal should ever be treated like a fashion accessory, regardless of size. In the Basin, most dogs were treated like dogs and never put through the embarrassment of wearing a pink tutu. As his thoughts continued, the unfortunate childhood image of his parent's Chihuahua always dressed in a pink ballet dress flashed through his mind. When Rachel broke through his little visit down memory lane and asked, "So, find anything else while I was getting this stuff ready?" he silently thanked her again with a little smile.

"Some, but not enough. On that note, ever been to Denver?" he asked, licking sauce off his fingers before thinking about manners. He was not eating alone. Luke tried to shed a lot of what he had deemed excessive manners growing up, like eating a leg of barbequed chicken with a fork—he had always wanted to yell out, "It's finger food, people!"—but licking his fingers . . . may be a bit much. Then again, she didn't seem to notice. In fact, a moment later, she did the same thing. Luke laughed.

"What's so funny?"

"Nothing, just remembered something. So, back to my question: Denver?"

"I lived there for a year. Always thought a road trip back through the Rockies would be fun. But I have a feeling we're talking good old-fashioned Denver metro, right?" He sensed she was trying to be indifferent, but there was some level of tension in her voice with the mention of Denver. Clearly she didn't want to talk about whatever it was, and he wouldn't push it.

"Unless I can get into some electronic copies of records, which have likely been buried very deep and strategically, I'm not sure what else we can do from here. Looks like his grandfather was rich but spread a good portion of the wealth to charities and nonprofit groups, mostly conservation-based. However, he passed away after his second heart attack a few months ago and left most of his fortune, minus the estate and a minor portion of his assets, to his grandson, Spencer Wells." He took another sip of water then added, "It almost seems like he made a point to keep the media coverage minimal for both of them, at least after the kid graduated from high school. I found a brief reference indicating his parents had died in a car accident during his freshman year and that his grandfather had taken him in."

As Luke helped her clean up the few dishes they'd used and carefully placed them back in the cabinets, he couldn't help but make a comment. "You have a, uh, pretty good appetite." Then realizing how that might sound, and knowing women were often sensitive to weight issues, he quickly added, "For someone your size."

"Thanks, I think. You do seem very surprised by my eating habits. What's that about? Date some anorexic models back in the day?" She'd clearly thrown it out as a joke, but she couldn't have known how much of a nerve it hit.

He paused. "Well, my younger sister—who stuck around and got caught up in the life—began starving herself when she was maybe seventeen or so. I think from the pressures of being surrounded by models and having to meet my parents' expectations about who to be friends with. I don't understand it all, but I've heard it can stem from self-esteem issues and a need to control something for yourself, which my family certainly had never let her do. She had never been overweight, just not the size-two model type, and there was a lot of pressure to be excessively skinny. She ended up in the hospital, in part because it was affecting her heart. That's all I know, since she refuses to see me. So I guess it makes me appreciate a woman who's healthy and doesn't starve herself. That's all."

She had paused to give him her full attention as soon as he had mentioned his sister. "Sorry about your sister. That's hard. Do you know if she overcame her eating disorder?"

He nodded. "Last time I heard from some old friends down there she was out of the hospital. But beyond that, I have no idea."

After a few more moments of silence, Rachel broke it, and Luke knew she was trying to steer them out of a depressing conversation. "So, yes, my strategy is the more miles I hike or snowshoe, the more pepperoni slices I add to the pizza or the larger the bowl of ice cream for dessert." She smiled, and he found relief in the laughter that followed, having broken the strain of memories of his sister's situation.

"Good strategy. It works well for you," he said, smiling. He looked down at her hips and bare legs and then back up to her face. She was staring at him, struggling to hold back a laugh. He'd been caught gawking—best to move on. "I'll dive back into the Internet and see what else I can find."

"Sounds like a good plan."

During the time it took Rachel to walk Bella, shower, and unload their sleeping bags from her pickup, he'd found . . . nothing. "Unfortunately, I think we are looking at a trip across good ol' Nevada and Utah tomorrow," he sighed, leaning back, arms raised over his head.

"I kind of had a feeling that was going to happen," she replied. "Well, road trip it is then!" she added cheerfully. "It's probably a good idea to put more distance between us and home now anyway."

Although he could tell from their first meeting she seemed to be a strong woman, her features had been dominated by a more fearful and stressed look, with the exception of when she was involved with Bella. But tonight her expression had relaxed, and she was smiling a lot more, telling jokes, laughing at herself. He liked it. She had a beautiful smile when it came right down to it.

She reached down and rubbed Bella, who was once again resting at her feet, caught up in the wonders of pulling the stuffing out of what had once been a toy monkey with squeakers in its limbs. "Well, girl, you'll get to see some new territory."

"How do you want to handle . . . sleeping?" Luke asked awkwardly. He meant it platonically but was sure she'd see it otherwise.

"As much as I'd love to abandon all inhibitions and just have sex with you for the next few days, there are three bedrooms and they all have beds." He froze, staring at her. He had *not* expected that. He was speechless. "Calm down, just giving you a dose of your own medicine, Mr. Reed," she laughed. "I'll take my sleeping bag and spread out on the bed in my room. I mean, the room I always slept in when I visited my parents," she corrected, looking a bit sheepish.

"Dose of . . . er . . . right. Beds . . . oh, OK, I'll grab one of the other ones then."

The next morning, after a night of tossing and turning, Luke felt half awake, eyes closed and frustrated because the shower nozzle barely dripped any water on his face. Come to think of it, everything but his face felt bone dry. That was odd. Struggling to crawl further out of the sleep haze, he realized he was still bundled up in his sleeping bag on the king-sized bed. But he wasn't alone. He opened his eyes and saw two dark-brown eyes cradled by floppy ears staring straight at him. Bella, her tail wagging so ferociously her whole body moved, reached out and licked his face again.

"My God, your tongue," he mumbled. Funny thing, he'd thought something like that would disgust him, but he laughed and found it endearing. He reached out to rub her while also gently pushing her back so he wouldn't get attacked by her tongue again. Twice was good enough for now. "Good morning, Bella. Fancy seeing you here."

"I figured it was about time for you to get up," he heard

Rachel say from another room, laughing. "Thought we'd give you the full treatment this time."

Two hours later, they were heading east on the "Loneliest Road in America," as Highway 50 was termed. Luke was driving, pushing the speed limit to the imaginary boundary he thought highway patrol wouldn't waste time enforcing. Before leaving the house, Rachel had located the couple's cleaning supplies, and after taking Bella outside she vacuumed, mopped, and dusted. Luke went around wiping surfaces, more to prevent detection of fingerprints if it came down to it. They both hoped the brief stay might not be noticed when the couple made their next trip west, likely months from now when the desert temperatures had cooled. For a while, discussion centered around where to begin their search in Denver, but eventually the lulls in conversation grew.

"I know you moved here because of the job opening at the station, but when you were laid off, what made you stay and not look elsewhere?"

"I did consider it at first. Sure, I'd bought a house, but I could probably rent it to cover the mortgage payment. But I'd become attached to the lifestyle, the community, the types of people here. It's an active, outdoorsy, fun place, and people tend to support each other. I like that. So I struggled with options—waiting to see if they'd eventually rehire more officers or do something else. I started looking into the private investigator option and thought that would be a good thing to try in the meantime. I ended up really enjoying it. Being your own boss has its perks."

"That it does." She smiled.

"What about you? How did you end up doing the independent enviro-consulting thing as opposed to a government job or something like that?"

"First, I do like what I do now, but getting into my current career involves a long story. Sure you want to hear it?"

"We've got the miles, baby."

"Excuse me? Ba—"

"Sorry, the line came from an old movie that apparently you haven't seen." He smirked. "Yes, I'd like to hear it."

"Cute," Rachel said, looking at the road in front of them as she spoke. "I was in a situation where I needed to leave Denver quickly. The bright side was I did miss Tahoe and my family out here, but when I came back, I didn't have a job. I started talking to people I used to work with and volunteering with conservation groups, and eventually they hired me to do various consulting jobs. I loved it—still do—because I get to put my work toward where my passion is."

"Good deal," Luke said, waiting for her to continue.

"Indeed," she responded, taking a sip of water. "They didn't have offices in town, so I began working from home and found I really enjoyed it. Some times are more strapped than others, but at the end of the year, it usually balances out. And it's also what I wanted to do with my career—use science to help guide policy and try to protect these beautiful areas. It's pretty difficult sometimes, but I enjoy it."

"Mind if I ask why you had to leave Denver?" Luke inquired but then thought maybe he should have just left it alone. Something bad obviously happened.

"How about the short version. Couple of dates with someone who turned out to be the son of one of the owners of a very profitable company. That's not why I turned down a third date—I just wasn't feeling 'it.' When I tried to explain this, he turned violent, apparently having imagined us to be in a deep committed relationship. I got away, and he began stalking me and eventually attacked me again, so I had him arrested. Then his wealthy and connected father stepped in and made sure he was protected from legal action. All I could do was run."

He could sense the tension in her voice as she told this story. "Did he leave you alone then after you moved back?"

"No, he followed me and . . . some things went down. It

wasn't easy to go into that station and report the body I'd seen given the experience I'd had there years ago. I shouldn't have been too surprised that some of them would write me off like that. Politics and money protect a lot of people who don't deserve it."

"That's true," he said, feeling he understood better her slight aversion to wealth—and him. Not everyone with money or power had bad intentions or broke the law, but she had a tough experience in not one but two places and was continuously exposed to the consequences of greed through her job. Who wouldn't have developed some feelings of bias after that?

"So, how about some tunes?" Rachel clearly didn't want to elaborate any more on what happened.

"Sure." He leaned over and hit the power button and was surprised when a Garth Brooks song blared out. Luke was not a country music fan, but everyone knows Garth Brooks. "You like . . . country music?" he asked, the last two words said with some inflection of surprise.

"Yeah. And . . . ?" she challenged.

"Just didn't expect that, I guess. But really—cowboys, bull riding, chew . . . you like that sort of thing?"

"Not all of it. Chew is disgusting and I don't watch bull riding. I do listen to other types of music, too," she chuckled.

"I don't get that country stuff."

"That's too bad. Cowboys are sexy." And in the moment it took for him to gather his wits at that, she turned on a different mixed CD and turned the volume up as she rolled her window down. For an hour Luke patiently waited through her music, wondering what each new track would bring. Her odd CD mix began with Brad Paisley and ended with Lady Gaga.

"Got any Zeppelin?" Luke asked when it ended, and an awkward silence filled the cab.

"I can take over driving if you'd like." She dodged the question. He let her, and they switched positions at the next off-ramp. Another mixed CD began, and when a popular Carrie Underwood song came on, Luke prayed for something, anything, to knock him out until the torture ended.

"Finally, Grand Junction. Time to get out of this box and move," Rachel exclaimed as they drove down the main street, looking for a hotel that would allow pets. Luke had thankfully nodded off, although he recalled hearing intermittent parts from her unique blend of music every so often. "And, I'm curious, Mr. PI. How should we pay for this? I mean, could someone be tracking our accounts?"

"I've got a few special, uh, identities I keep around for extreme circumstances. I'll use one of them." He noticed her accusatory expression and cut her off before she could say anything. "And don't worry, the name may be different, but it's all me. I'm not ripping someone else off. I pay the bills on them."

She relaxed. "Sounds like a good idea then," she said, exhaustion clear in her tone. They located a room, walked Bella around outside, and barely managed to unload their things before sleep overtook all three of them.

~

Ted was walking alongside Captain Ron Taylor, taking the opportunity to talk to him about the case as Ted followed him to his car.

"I'm as surprised as you are, Captain. I remember Luke as an upstanding cop, never breaking rules and rarely pushing the lines. It just doesn't make sense, but those are his prints I found, and they've clearly gone on the run, which in my experience innocent people don't typically do," Ted sighed. "I keep hoping there's another explanation here. I'd like to have the techs go back to the area, look where we found the body again, and where Ms. Winters reported seeing one before."

Ron, who years ago instructed his officers to refer to him as "Captain" when on the job for appearances sake, looked frustrated and in a hurry to get somewhere. "If they are innocent, they should turn themselves in and help us figure out what's going on." He reached his car and paused, continuing his directions to Ted. "We don't have the budget to keep sending people out to scour the area. If you want them to take a second look at the rock you found, OK. But I can't approve any more than that." Ron opened the door of a shiny new Lexus SUV and sat inside. "And let me know if they find anything else. I'm out for the rest of the day, so let's touch base tomorrow morning." He was about to shut the door when he focused on something behind where Ted stood. Turning around to follow Ron's gaze, Ted heard him call out, "Hey, you two, did you have a good lunch at that new barbeque place?"

The chief of police, Timothy Parker—known as "TIP" to his friends due to an unconscionable middle name from hippie parents, Incense—was walking nearby with one of the current younger officers on the force. The chief appeared a bit distracted at first and then responded. "Yes, it was pretty good, Ron. You should give it a try sometime." Without breaking stride the two continued walking into the precinct as Ron closed his door.

Ted nodded and watched the captain drive away. Odd, he hadn't noticed that car before. Ron usually drove a brown Subaru Legacy. The Lexus was not only, well, a Lexus, but it appeared fresh off the lot.

He headed back inside and over to his desk, ready to call one of the CSIs about the rock. The desks were set up in typical cop TV show fashion, forcing partners to not only work together all day or all night long, as happened frequently enough, but also to uncomfortably face each other at their desks. His partner, Leona, a beautiful, slightly overweight Hispanic woman in her early forties, was excitedly talking to one of the other female officers— easily identifiable as Officer Shelby Coats due to her long red hair, who was flashing what looked like a large shiny engagement ring. "Congrats again, Shelby," Leona said as they shared one of those women-only conspiratorial smiles Ted easily recognized.

He thought about the ring. Ted considered himself a bachelor by choice. He didn't need any relationship woes right now, and he'd seen far too many divorces lately. Yet women seemed so intent on getting married and settling down, and maybe in their haste they kept picking the wrong partners. Who knew? He'd also noticed women were so excited about getting engaged that they'd tell anyone and everyone they saw, even strangers on the street, unceremoniously flashing the ring in people's faces. He'd often joked about the "crazy fiancée syndrome" with other unmarried friends. Now, before he could say something to Shelby that would probably be akin to putting his foot in his mouth, Leona noticed his concentrated look and interrupted his thoughts.

"Whatcha working on?"

Happy to be spared the subject of Shelby's impending nuptials, he responded, "It's this Reed case. Something's bugging me, so Ron approved another quick review of the evidence." He sat, hearing the annoying squeak his old chair always made. "Leona, have you noticed Ron's new Lexus? A bit flashy for him."

"No, I hadn't. Although I don't come through that part of the lot when I ride my bike." In recent attempts to improve her health and stamina, Leona had taken to riding her bike to work most days. She lived about five miles away, and after a month on her new wheels she'd dropped a few pounds and said she had more energy than before. Her new arrangement didn't cause any who-drives-today vehicle problems for them, since Ted preferred to drive his Explorer when they were on duty. He was glad to see her enjoying the new commuting lifestyle. Although she didn't say much about money, she had once referred to saving on gas money, confessing things were a bit tight lately. Her husband had been laid off from his engineering job at the county, and they had three young kids to support.

"That's right—the bike rack is in back. Glad that's still working out for you." As he reached for his desk phone, it rang.

He answered it and ended up discussing another case with the local prosecutor. While they were speaking, he happened to notice Leona write down some lengthy notes—a bit strange because she usually typed everything. She glanced at her computer for a minute, quietly scooted her chair back, and headed in the direction of the women's restroom.

CHAPTER NINE

Just as Rachel remembered from her summer there, June in Denver could be hot, and sure enough, it was roughly ninety degrees and barely noon when they drove east toward the tall buildings that comprised the downtown area.

"I still can't believe I used to work in one of those. I was miserable here. Don't know what I was thinking when I took that job, except that I needed to try something new," she sighed, looking over at downtown and the surrounding cloud of smog.

"I definitely can't picture you there. I imagine you were like a fish out of water, huh?"

"Pretty much. Not only did I dislike being in a big city, but I definitely didn't fit in with anyone. I missed my family and friends back home, let alone the Sierras. The Rockies are nice, but it takes a while to get to so many places up there when you're living in Denver. And there's just something special about the Sierra Nevada." Then she laughed. "One of the worst things about it—I couldn't wear jeans to work every day. I had to wear ridiculously uncomfortable dress suits and, don't laugh, *dresses*."

"Oh my God! Call the guards out!" She heard him chuckle and speak up again softly. "Then again, you *would* look sexy in the right dress. Only for a special occasion, of course. Otherwise, I'd never take your jean shorts away from you. Actually, let me rephrase . . ."

Rachel opted to quickly change the subject before turning red. "Thanks, I think. So, first we hit Fourteenth Street and get to the Denver Public Library, right?"

"Yes, then maybe we can manage a meet with Lloyd's attorney. I couldn't locate a name anywhere online but figured we'd have better luck with it here."

She found a spot in a parking garage, and the three of them walked a few blocks to the library. As they strolled along the downtown streets, she was tense but trying her best to hide it. Memories of her previous days here, especially when Matt began to torment her, flooded into her mind. She tried to push them back and focus on the situation at hand. He would never bother her again, that she knew. "Somehow I doubt anyone would believe Bella's a trained assistant dog, so I'll stay outside with her and hop on a Wi-Fi signal, see what I can find."

"That works. If you need something, send a text. I'll let you know if I'm making any progress." As he turned to walk up the steps into the building, Rachel watched him go. The more time she spent with him, the more attractive she found him. When Luke told her how he'd walked away from millions to do his own thing, she'd been impressed. But, she reminded herself, he was still a bit cocky at times. Why did it matter, anyway? She wasn't looking for a relationship and certainly not with this guy.

An hour later she saw Luke emerge on the front steps of the old building and flinch. She figured he'd been caught off guard by the wave of heat after being in the air-conditioned library. She had stretched out on a nearby patch of grass below several trees and was casually tossing around loose leaves for Bella to retrieve with one hand and typing on her laptop with the other. She looked at him anxiously. "Well?"

"OK, first, we can forget about our second stop."

She stood up and brushed herself off. "What do you mean?"

"Lloyd's attorney was killed in a hit-and-run not long after the old man died."

Rachel didn't like the sound of that. "Not good . . ."

Luke handed Rachel some documents he had copied inside. "Thankfully, they had recently been converting older archived documents into a searchable PDF format. That's where I was able to find a few things out. There's someone we should visit nearby—how about I tell you as we walk? And I need to get out of this horrible heat!" Luke wiped the sweat already forming on his forehead.

"I'm with you on that," she concurred, thinking about how once someone gets acclimated to the cooler temperatures in the mountains it is a lot harder to take anything over seventy degrees. A lot of Tahoe locals traveled in fall and spring, otherwise avoiding trips to anywhere "off the hill," where temperatures were often twenty degrees warmer during the summer.

He signaled for them to begin walking north. "Lloyd had several medical issues the last few years of his life, so he hired a personal nurse, a Ms. Melanie Kline, to help him out, although people speculated she was more than that. I found her because a reporter from a local paper stopped her as she was leaving the wake and asked about her feelings regarding Lloyd's will. She was quoted saying that it didn't make any sense. Lloyd had seen the 'little shit' going down a bad road and was trying to teach his grandson some responsibility. Lloyd was paying him a good salary but making him earn it for a change. Lucky for us, she was quoted verbatim. The reporter also asked a few other attendees their opinions, trying to get their reactions to her outburst. Some suggested that she was just jealous because she expected to get a big inheritance when he died. It never went anywhere after that. The good news is she's still here and happens to live in a loft a few blocks over."

"That sounds encouraging."

"Yes. In fact, I called her before I came out, and she's

expecting us. I told her we were volunteers for a small land conservation group and were looking for more information on Lloyd. She seemed hesitant until I asked if she would mind if a dog came along as well. She perked right up and asked us to come right over. Hmm, you dog people are tight, aren't you?" He laughed.

Rachel watched the excitement in his features as he relayed what he'd found, anxious to see where the next lead went. She admitted she had a few butterflies in her stomach as well but wasn't sure if they were from fear, worry, excitement, or the attractive boyish look lighting up his face right now. Perhaps it was a combination of all of the above.

Rachel knocked on the door of the woman's third floor loft. "Hello, Ms. Kline?"

"Yes?" responded a pleasant voice from inside the doorway. Rachel suspected she had been waiting for them.

"It's Luke, Rachel, and Bella. You spoke with Luke earlier. About Lloyd Wells." The peephole cover went dark for a moment and then the door slowly crept open the few inches allowed by the chain. The woman inside looked down at Bella, who had keenly slid her nose into the gap, wagging her tail. That's all it took. "Oh, sweetie, move back a bit so I can get this door open all the way," she said to Bella, rubbing the dog's nose through the opening. Rachel called Bella back and the door closed then reopened all the way. Bella immediately walked up to Ms. Kline, tail wagging, rubbing against her legs.

"Hello, and please y'all, call me Melanie." The woman, appearing in her seventies, had grey hair, a slim and athletic build, and wrinkles that revealed a lifetime of being outdoors. She was already rubbing Bella when she bent down, saying, "And this must be Bella, right?"

"Yep, and be careful. She'll tumble you over trying to get you to rub her belly if you let her." Rachel laughed, cheered by the obvious happiness on the woman's face. She had an idea why having the canine visitor meant so much to this woman. There were several pictures on the wall showing a younger version of Melanie hugging a grey-nosed chocolate lab. But no signs of the dog remained—no loose fur lined the floors, and no food dishes, toys, or dog beds could be seen. Chances were the dog had recently passed away or had to be put down.

"Please, come on in." Melanie waved. They followed behind her as she made her way through a short hall to a small living area. Melanie sat in a plush recliner but remained perched on the edge so she could continue to rub Bella. Rachel sat down next to Luke on a large sofa a few feet away.

"Oh, she's a sweetheart. I can just see it. Kind of reminds me of my Bo. I do miss him." She was massaging Bella's ears, and the dog happily stood in place, soaking up the attention. "He got cancer last year, and I had just two weeks with him after that. Sure leaves a gaping hole in your life when they pass."

"Yes, they do. Is Bo the lab with you in those pictures over there?"

"Yes. He was up there in years, but we still walked the foothill trails quite a bit." She smiled, appearing lost in memory, then refocused on the couple. "So, what can I do for you two kids? You said you have some questions about Lloyd?"

"Yes, and thanks again for letting us impose on your day like this," Luke said.

Melanie nodded. "It's nice to have visitors, especially Bella here. No offense."

"None taken," Luke laughed. "We are here because we are volunteers with the Sierra Nevada Land Conservation Group, and we're trying to find out more about Mr. Wells. We understand he made some charitable donations out our way as well, and we are working with a consortium of groups to honor private donors." As Luke relayed the story they'd come up with, Rachel thought again about how awkward if felt to blatantly lie to this woman, but as they'd discussed on their walk over, it was probably the best way to find out what they needed without getting her caught up in what was really going on—or having her drop everything and call the police.

"It's twofold," Luke continued. "We want to honor those who have helped preserve lands for public use, but the attention often generates a few more donations from other parties. We couldn't find much information online, but we came by an article about you and thought you might be able to help us."

She nodded. "Let me guess, the article where that no-good chicken-shit reporter caught me off guard mourning the loss of my best friend?" A disgusted look flashed across her face. "Yes, you're right. Lloyd made an effort to keep the media coverage down for them both. After the kid's parents were killed—car accident—Lloyd became Spence's guardian. He'd seen younger kids growing up in wealthy political families, sucking up attention from the paparazzi because they weren't old enough to know better. He worried Spence would go down the same road and thought maybe he could protect the boy by shielding his exposure." She then leaned in as if about to reveal a secret. "Frankly, his parents—may they rest in peace—didn't do a very good job with Spence. He was getting into trouble all the time . . . even had a few arrests under his belt by the time he was but thirteen. His folks had been too busy attending parties to raise their boy right. When I met him, he'd lived with Lloyd for several years, but in my opinion he was a lost cause. Lloyd, however, had a good heart and just kept on trying." She sat back. "Sorry, that's not what you're here for."

"Don't worry about it at all—it's nice to hear more about Lloyd's background," Rachel said, knowing the information could prove valuable.

Melanie smiled and continued. "As for the land . . . yes, he did buy up a lot of land both throughout our Rockies and a few patches over your way. I think it's a bit ironic—his love of nature grew in the first place *because* of Spence. Lloyd researched outdoor programs for troubled youth, thinking he could help shape the boy up. Mind you this was before Spence's parents had passed; Lloyd suggested a whole bunch of places but could never convince his no-good son and daughter-in-law to send their son to one. Lloyd said he'd been pretty dang impressed with what he saw—experiences with nature helping kids turn their lives around and all. *He* also loved being in nature and began hiking and getting out of doors on his own—heck, helped me get back in shape, too." She stopped, sipped from a nearby coffee mug, and continued.

"Then one of his favorite hiking areas was set to be rezoned to condos after a land sale. Well, he looked into it and learned that part of the land had been privately owned, although most people didn't know because it was surrounded by public land. The owners weren't able to keep paying the taxes on the land—had no choice but to sell it off. Lloyd, good man that he was, offered to buy it for more than the condo developer; then he donated it to the state with the agreement they kept it open for the public." She paused, appearing to once again be lost in a memory. "I tell you, he made some enemies on the local planning board with that one, but there was nothing they could do. Those owners had every right to choose who they go selling their land to, and the damn government can't tell them otherwise. Plus, the state was happy to draw up the agreement to keep it open like that . . . on someone else's dime, of course."

Bella rolled over with the classic rub-my-belly request, and Melanie leaned down to comply. "After that, Lloyd started looking for similar places—private land crossing public land. It was hard for him to choose what to buy. He'd go visit the place, hike around, talk to people he saw, find out histories about the place. Then he'd come back and lock himself in his room for a day or two and figure out which ones he thought would benefit the public most. He had plenty of money from his family's estate, and he'd made some darn good investments. Wanted to do something good with it rather than just leave it to his grandson—who'd no doubt party it away or put it up his nose. I sure do wonder what changed Lloyd's mind, though," she sighed. "Doesn't make any sense, I tell you."

"Where did he look for potential land to buy? Did he have any employees or partners helping him do research?" Rachel asked, filling the silence after Melanie's pause.

"Most of his purchases were out this way, I suppose because he lived here and it's where he spent most his time. But a few years back, he made a trip out to your Sierras to meet up with some buddies and go hiking in 'new territory,' as he called it. Lloyd came back and couldn't stop talking about some private land he called 'out of place.' Said he was going to look into buying it and consider branching out beyond Colorado. By that point, he'd also built a reputation for his donations and was getting a lot of good attention, and other well-off folks began to join in. Whether they really cared, wanted a tax write-off, or just liked the publicity, he didn't know—didn't care, really. The more of them people interested in doing what he'd started, the more land they could preserve."

"Do you know if he ever followed through on those lands in our neck of the woods?" Luke asked.

"I know he bought some land up near Mount Lassen and I think down by Yellowst—wait, Yosemite. That's it, Yosemite." She paused. "Probably more places I didn't know about. Or he could have set it up to have someone else purchase and donate them."

Thinking of her own tendency to document everything, Rachel asked, "Did he keep a list of his purchases?"

"You know, I told that man he needed a list for himself—partly to keep track of it, partly to see the amount of good he'd done, but I'll tell you what. Lloyd was not a man into organizing his own affairs. Drove me nuts, in fact! However, his attorney and, I believe, his accountant both kept good records for him.

Unfortunately, Joseph—bless his soul—was killed not long after Lloyd passed, and there has been no one to take over his clients. But now Janet—his accountant—she's still around. Let me see if I can find her number for y'all." She stood up, promising Bella that she'd be right back. She returned with an old well-used address book, sat back down, and began flipping through the pages. "Oh yes, here y'all go—Ms. Janet Fields. The last address I have for her is down in Castle Rock. Got a phone number here, too. Just not sure if it's up to date, but I'll write them both down for you. And if you do speak to her, please send my best." She leaned over to the side table and grabbed a notepad and pen.

"Oh, that would be great. Thank you!" Rachel beamed. "Lloyd sounds like a wonderful man. I'm sorry we didn't get the chance to meet him."

"Yes, good old Lloyd. Miss him. And, oh, he sure would have loved your little pup here, too. He doted on my Bo as if he were his own." She handed them the paper. "Sorry, now I'm keeping you here with my ramblings."

"Please, don't worry about it," Rachel smiled, noticing Luke glance her way with a smirk.

After sticking around a few minutes more sharing pet stories, they thanked Melanie for her time and stood to leave.

As they headed out the door, Luke turned around. "Thanks again. And if you don't mind, would you happen to know where Spencer is these days? I doubt we'll want to talk to him, but it can't hurt to know in case something comes up." They both knew exactly where "Spence" was, but Rachel understood how it might help to find out what the woman had heard.

Melanie tilted her head a bit. "It's been a while, but I do recall that boy getting involved in some project out in Nevada or thereabouts. Kinda funny because it'd been Lloyd's idea, and Spence was sure ticked off because it meant he had to actually earn himself a living. I think something about mining, but I'm not sure. Sorry I can't be of more help. But I do hope I never see that little nitwit again, frankly, after the way he treated his dear grandfather."

After Melanie squeezed Bella one more time, they said their goodbyes and headed out. Back inside the truck with Luke behind the wheel, they drove south on I-25 toward Castle Rock. Rachel stole a glance over toward the northern end of Littleton, a suburb of the larger Denver metro area where she'd once lived, remembering the good parts of her time there. One positive that had always stood out about her time there—her neighbors were extremely friendly.

"Do you want to try calling Janet's number and see if we can get through?" he asked.

"Sure." She picked up her cell phone and reached into her pocket for Melanie's note. The call went to a woman's voicemail system. Rachel's message was short, providing a similar story about searching for information on lands Mr. Wells had donated and having been referred by Melanie. She asked Janet to call them back on Rachel's cell number and mentioned they'd be in the area that evening. "Well, guess we'll see if she checks her messages today."

"Let's hope."

Just a few miles outside of Castle Rock, Janet returned the call. She had spoken with Melanie about their message and offered to meet them at her office at eight p.m. that night. After getting directions, Rachel thanked her and hung up.

"Well, we've got a whole hour to kill. Whatever should we do?" Luke laughed then glanced sideways toward her, a sexy look telling her what his suggestion was.

"Keep dreamin'," she remarked, although she had to admit the thought was slightly appealing.

~

Mike was tearing David's home apart. When the hydrologist had entered Mike's office a couple of weeks ago, he had complained results weren't matching the samples he'd run "on the side" for quality assurance. David then asked how much experience Mike had with the lab they'd been using to test their water samples. Feigning surprise and confusion, Mike responded he'd used them for years and felt confident in their results. But, if David had some concerns, they definitely should to look into it.

Mike later reacted in haste, getting rid of David before learning where and how the man had found these conflicting results. Who had run them on the side? Mike envisioned David as a bit of a loner. He had never mentioned family or friends or anything other than work.

That morning, under the guise of billing questions, Mike had made several calls to various laboratories that ran the type of water samples they'd been collecting, asking if they'd logged any business with his company or under David's name. No one had any official record of recent jobs. He continued going through David's files, hoping for some hint of who it could have been. He didn't like loose ends—this had to work out. Lori was too important for it not to.

~

Where in God's name is the rock? Ted stood staring at an empty evidence locker. He'd logged it in there himself after running it for prints, securing it where only a few other officers could gain access. In fact, no one had signed in the log book since his last trip to place it inside. Ted closed the solid metal door and walked back out to the young man sitting at the security desk. His lack of attention to Ted's exit, combined with the books and notepaper spread in front of him, suggested a young college recruit studying for classes. Finally, the young man looked up when Ted stood directly in front of him.

"Get what you needed, Officer Benson?" he asked politely.

"Not quite. Looks like someone got there before me, but I don't see anyone logged into the book. Did you let someone else in who maybe *forgot* to sign in?"

"No, sir, rules are rules," the kid said, a brief flash of

nervousness registering across his face.

Ted nodded then leaned down to rest his elbow on the counter, moving in closer to the boy's face although not enough to seem threatening. "Any chance you maybe slipped out for a bathroom break without locking the main door? I know sometimes it comes on pretty fast . . ."

The security guard paused, his expression giving Ted all the answer he needed. "I suppose it's possible I forgot—but I was only gone for a few minutes, I swear." He held his stomach as he stuttered, "I . . . uh . . . really had to go." He stared down at his books, unable to look Ted in the eye.

"OK, for now we'll leave it at that. If I understand correctly, there should be video footage aiming at your desk?"

The rookie's facial expression paled even more. Ted almost laughed; the kid hadn't known there was a camera there, recording his every move. Good, it serves him right. "I'll check with the tech guys then." Ted turned to go, figuring he could follow up with disciplinary action later. "And kid, lock that door if you aren't at your desk, period. I don't care if you need to wear diapers."

Ted went straight to their station's sole computer expert to locate and view the videotape. Carlos, the most skilled technician Ted had ever worked with, was a shy older man who didn't leave his office much due to an overwhelming phobia of germs. Ted watched from a foot away while the video played in reverse. His recent visit and conversation with the kid flew by backward and in double time on the screen. About ten minutes before Ted had discovered the missing evidence and approached the counter, the kid ran to the bathroom as if his life depended on it.

"Let it play forward from there," Ted interrupted. Although the image came close, the camera's angle didn't quite capture the front door that was supposed to be locked before leaving the desk. Ted and Carlos watched, mesmerized, as the movement of a straight shadow indicated the room's front door opening, after which someone walked in so quickly, the person had to have been waiting outside for the young recruit to sneak away. A moment later, something wet was sprayed onto the video lens, dripping just enough to distort the image.

"Damn!" Ted said. A blurry figure in dark clothes and a large hat walked into the evidence locker, brushed right past the desk, opened the locker with the code, and then strolled back out. At about the time the person would have been back by the front door, what appeared to be a cloth covered the lens and wiped the substance off so the images once again appeared clear, barring the few minor smudges along the sides.

"I can't even tell if that was a man or a woman. Anything jump out to you, Carlos?"

"Nope. Can't even guess at a possible height. I can work with the numbers guys and see if we can get more from the footage. Too bad that other camera was turned off during that last round of budget cuts."

"Agreed. If you can work anything up with the numbers that would be helpful. Hey, one more thing. Can we watch what happened *before* the kid dashed off to the restroom?" Carlos nodded and hit a few keys, and the image once again scrolled backward. "It looks like he's eating something. There. I can see it's a Tupperware container." He pointed, narrating out loud mostly to himself. They watched as the kid entered the room with the container, holding the bottom with some thick paper towels.

"Go figure. I can tell he had to unlock the door when he came back with his food," Carlos sighed.

"Yeah, but I'm thinking we need to cut him a bit of slack. I think there was more in that container than what he packed before work." Ted's theory was confirmed as they watched the kid take a few bites of his food before suddenly hunching over in obvious pain. He dropped the fork he was eating with and ran straight to the bathroom. Poor kid might not have made it had he locked the door, although that wasn't an excuse.

~

As he rebandaged the bullet wound on his arm, the man thought that although he expected his little setup to fool the cops on the first go-around, when Mike warned him that one of them was taking a second look he was concerned it might not hold up to further scrutiny. It's a good thing to have friends in the right places. Even better—when they found an empty locker, they would have to wonder how someone could get in there and steal the evidence. And who better to know how to get around the station's security than someone who used to work there—and their prime suspect?

With that potential problem avoided he could focus once again on finding the couple, who had managed to disappear. He'd done some research on their backgrounds, and both of them were avid outdoor enthusiasts and experienced at backcountry camping. Chances were good they were hiding in the forest somewhere. Maybe they'd stay there until fall comes around, and by then it would be too late anyway. Regardless, he needed to find them both and take care of them for good. He had spent the last couple of hours accessing phone company records and putting a few other feelers in places he suspected they might go or contact. Eventually something would pop up. This was no longer just a job he was doing for Mike. Now—it was personal.

CHAPTER TEN

Janet Fields was definitely prompt, Rachel thought, as they watched a woman pull up and park in front of the small office and climb out of her compact SUV. They'd arrived just a few minutes early and had stayed in the pickup, air conditioning on high. Janet unlocked the door and went inside, and a moment later several lights came on in the building.

"Well, here we go," Rachel said, opening her door. After she got out, she opened the back cab door and let Bella out, grabbing her water dish to bring along. It was too warm to leave her in the truck without the air conditioning, but she didn't want to leave the truck running with the keys in the ignition either.

"So, what are you going to do with Bella? Not sure they are as . . . accommodating around here as back home," Luke asked.

"I figured I could tie her on that rail there. Looks like Janet's office is mostly glass, so I can keep an eye on Bella easy enough. And there's shade there, too."

"You know, you might very well have the mind of a detective, the way you observe and process things so quickly," he chuckled.

"I suppose I do investigate things. Like making sure the science referenced in an EIS actually supports the conclusion in the EIS. It's amazing what they'll—"

The front door opened and Janet Fields smiled, waving them in. Rachel knew she'd probably been a few seconds shy of completely boring Luke. Janet's timing had been perfect.

"Luke, Rachel, please, come on in." The woman had a pleasant voice, and there was a warm, inviting feel to her office. "Oh, and please feel free to bring in Bella. Melanie told me all about her," Janet said enthusiastically as she stepped aside so they could enter.

Janet opened a small refrigerator and reached in for a can, at the same time asking, "Would either of you like a drink? I've got soda, milk, and some juice boxes." She laughed. "In case it's not obvious, I have two young kids." She waved to a large eight-by-ten picture hanging on the wall showing a smiling Janet next to a handsome man in his forties, two young boys with freckle-specked noses standing in front of them, and a light-colored Labrador retriever sitting next to the boys. Rachel recognized that it had been taken from the top of Pike's Peak.

"You have a beautiful family."

"Yes, some nice looking boys there," Luke said, looking at the picture then back at Janet. "Oh, and thank you. Yes, a soda would be great."

"I'll take a juice box, thank you," said Rachel.

After Rachel led Bella in and they settled in various chairs, Luke once again spun the tale they'd told Melanie, shyly saying he understood if she could not share that type of information but since they were out here they thought they'd ask.

"So, all you're looking for is a list of properties that Lloyd purchased in—what—California and Nevada? Nothing more?" Janet, with her dark-blonde hair pulled into a loose ponytail, appeared to Rachel to be just shy of fifty. The sign of her time spent outdoors had begun to show, and a few mild wrinkles appeared as she raised a brow, smiling like someone who knows more than they are saying.

"That's it," Rachel said. "If more information is readily

available, like who he sold the property or properties to, or what agreements were made to ensure public use of the lands, that would certainly save us some additional legwork, but just having that list would be a helpful start." She couldn't help but shift a bit in her chair, probably a physical manifestation of her discomfort with the lie, because the chair itself was quite comfortable.

"If they were still in his ownership we could get what we need from databases in various assessors' offices. But, unfortunately, we haven't pulled up much information, and a lot of the smaller counties don't have all of the records online. It would take a long time to go to each office and look through boxes just to see if his name pops up." At that point, Rachel feared she may be over explaining.

Janet paused, leaning forward ever so slightly. "I can give you a list of his known properties until right before he passed away, including which ones he donated or sold." She began typing while continuing to speak. "In fact, he talked to me about continuing to deal with his finances after he'd passed, although unfortunately I kept shutting those conversations down, telling him not to talk that way because he was still fairly young and so active. Maybe I should have let him talk about it more, I don't know. But, oh, I do miss him," she sighed. "After a couple of times he did eventually stop bringing it up. I was quite surprised when he donated a lot of his land to his worthless grandson," she said with a slightly guilty look, pressing her fingers to her mouth. "Oops, did I just say that out loud?" She laughed.

"Not a problem." Luke smiled. "We've heard about Spencer from Melanie. Sounds like a real piece of work. We just hope he doesn't mess up any plans that his grandfather may have had in the works."

"I agree," Janet said. "I guess the second part of that is that if the kid botched any deals that weren't final or sold off some properties after Lloyd passed away, I won't have that information since I don't work for the family anymore." She typed a few more items on her keyboard as she continued.

"I know the will prohibited access to the money until his twenty-fifth birthday, which had already passed when Lloyd died, but I never knew what it said about the properties Lloyd owned. Then after Joe was killed in a hit-and-run, the kid found a new attorney to administer the estate and a new accountant to take over the financial matters. He wanted nothing to do with me, which is his choice to make, except it was difficult for me to see him having any control over what Lloyd had managed to build up." The sound of the printer turning its first page came from a desktop just behind Janet. She leaned back a bit, smiling as one does when reliving good memories. "Lloyd was such a good man. When I first met him about fifteen years ago, he came off as a bit caught up with himself, and too focused on money, but still seemed to have a good heart. Then when his son and daughter-in-law died a couple of years later, he changed, and he really tried to help Spencer. Although I don't think he succeeded much; at least it served as the catalyst that led him on the path of improving his own life, and he was a much happier man for it."

"Melanie pretty much said the same thing. I could tell she was very fond of him," Rachel said. "I wish we could have met him."

"Yes, that would have been nice," she sighed. "People thought there was something going on between Lloyd and Melanie those last few years, but I just think they became really good friends. She helped him with some medical issues, but I think she also gave him the companionship he needed, too." Three sheets later the printer grew quiet again, and Janet reached around for the list.

She set it in front of her then looked up at them and paused, the pleasant, reminiscent look replaced with a slightly serious, if not accusatory, stare. "You seem like a really sweet couple and that dog clearly loves you more than herself, which tells me something about the kind of person you are." She directed this last comment at Rachel. "But I have a feeling you're holding something back. Now, I won't ask what it is. This list is basically a compilation of information you could find on your own; it just might take you a lot of time, like you said." Rachel noticed Luke move a bit in the chair next to her, as if preparing to respond, but Janet charged on. "I would love to see Lloyd honored for what he did. That said, whatever your intentions are, all I ask is if you can make that happen somehow, please do. And better yet, if you can prevent that loser grandson of his from messing up any more agreements he made to preserve land, even better." She handed the sheets across her desk to Luke.

"Oh, we will certainly do our best. On both counts."

"Good." She smiled and stood up. "Now, if you don't mind, I'd like to get back to my family."

"Of course," Rachel responded and exited her chair as Luke did the same. "Thank you again for your help." They all proceeded toward the front door.

"It was nice to meet all three of you," Janet spoke, opening the door.

As they walked through, Rachel turned back around. "Janet, thank you again so much. I do want you to know we will do our best to honor Lloyd's memory."

"I have a feeling you will, Ms. Rachel Winters and Mr. Luke Reed," she said, looking at each of them intently, her eyes showing more understanding than her big smile would otherwise suggest. She shook their hands again, reached over for one last rub on Bella's ears, and turned and headed toward the only other vehicle in the parking lot. Rachel looked at Luke, who was in turn looking back at her, sharing the same surprised expression she had on her face.

"We never gave her our last names, did we?" Rachel asked.

"No, I'm pretty sure we did not."

"I think Janet did a bit of homework before our meeting tonight." She started walking toward her pickup. "I can't help but admire that."

"Yes, in fact, I'm at this moment reconsidering hiring a nonlocal accountant." As they all got back into the truck, Rachel mentioned the time.

"So, should we drive back to Denver for a hotel then?"

"Yeah, probably the best, and least expensive, idea," Luke said and Rachel saw him looking around the new, large buildings in the area. Then he paused and looked at her with a concerned expression. "I only know what you've told me about your experience in Denver, so are you okay with staying there overnight?"

His question had caught her off guard. He *had* been paying attention. "Oh, uh, yes, I'm fine. It's been quite a few years, and I've been able to think back on the good times. I even came through the area again on a summer road trip so I could meet up with some old friends. It helped put more of a positive spin back on most of my time here. But . . . thanks for asking." She started the ignition, and they both reached to turn up the AC knob. They laughed, and it was enough to break the serious mood that had settled over them. "I know a few hotels around where I used to live, at least the names. How about you grab that cell of yours and look up the numbers, see if we can find a dog-friendly place?"

"No problem. But I think after this we should find some disposable cells phones, and take the batteries and memory cards out of ours, just to be on the safe side . . ."

"Do you think the cops are already tracking our phones?" The thought worried her. Although they'd been using cash for everything, this seemed to really bring home the seriousness of the situation they were in.

"I don't think they'd be that far along yet. At least until they officially release arrest warrants. But it's not the cops I'm necessarily worried about. They have to follow the rules and procedures."

"Well, apparently not all of them," Rachel responded.

CHAPTER ELEVEN

Although it was a bit early in the morning, Jack Stine picked up the phone to try to get in touch with David again. He had expected to hear back from him a couple of weeks ago after sending him the water sample results. It was just over a month ago now that his old friend had called him, out of the blue, concerned the lab they were using for a project he was working on had contamination that could be affecting results. Jack had agreed, and the samples had arrived on ice the next day. After some evenings spent processing them off the clock, Jack e-mailed David the data—although the exact same methods were used to test them, the results from the two batches did not match. But he hadn't heard back from David, and his calls and e-mails had gone unanswered.

"Where the heck did you go, buddy?" he said out loud as he once again heard David's voice message greeting come on. He knew that David, a single workaholic who lived alone and didn't socialize much, was often out collecting water samples or writing the follow-up reports in his office. David lived for his work, plain and simple, and he had been that way since Jack met him back in college. In fact, he had always wondered if he was David's only friend. After Jack married and moved to Oregon, conversations with David had grown shorter and less frequent. As the Internet boomed and e-mail became common, they had reconnected through a thread of occasional e-mails. But until recently, Jack didn't think he'd actually spoken with David for a year or two. So when David called him asking for an important favor, Jack knew it had to be serious.

Maybe Claire will know something. She was David's sister, older by barely a year. She had moved somewhere back on the East Coast years ago. David had said she'd married at eighteen and pretty much written off their parents after that, although David never offered up any reasons why, and Jack never felt comfortable enough to ask. But he did meet her a few times during their college years and talked once or twice since. He didn't have her recent phone number, so he looked her name up online, plugging in any details he could recall to narrow it down. It didn't take long to search, and he found the number for a Claire Gooding in North Carolina. Well, it's worth a shot, he thought, dialing the number.

A woman's voice picked up in two rings. "Hello?" She sounded a bit confused, probably curious to whom the strange number on her caller ID belonged.

"Claire, is that you?"

He could hear the hesitancy in her voice when she paused. Then she responded, "Uh, yes, and who is this?" The sound of kids laughing echoed in the background. He'd known she had at least two and suspected probably more.

"This is Jack Stine, David's old friend," he said with question in his voice, wondering if she'd remember. She let out what sounded like a relieved sigh.

"Jack. Wow, it's been years. Yes, I remember you . . . but . . . how did you get my number?" Before he could respond, she spoke again, this time fear in her voice. "Wait a minute . . . is David okay?"

"I don't know. That's what I was hoping you might be able to help me with. Have you spoken with him recently?"

"Well, we talked about a month ago. I admit I was only half paying attention. The twins were screaming in the backseat, and I was trying to focus on the road. I didn't want to answer the phone with all of that going on in the background, but he calls so rarely I didn't want to miss him."

"Did he say anything . . . *odd?*"

"Let me think. Actually, can you hold on a second?" Without waiting for his response, he heard a strange noise and then the muffled sound of a mother scolding her kids to quiet down. Apparently it worked and she returned, again fully attentive to the call. "Sorry about that. These kids haven't yet figured out that if Mom's talking to someone on the phone they need to wait their turn." She chuckled but in that slightly frustrated way parents often do when they are fed up with something and trying not to show it. "Well, let me think. He asked about the kids . . . asked if I'd talked to Mom recently, which of course I haven't. That was an odd question, I suppose." Jack worried she was getting distracted again, but then she continued. "I asked him about work, and he said he was doing part-time contract work for a small environmental firm out in California. Or Nevada. Something like that. He was monitoring the water runoff from a new project. He was always so excited about his work, which I could never understand. I mean, it's water. And dirt." She laughed. "Now that you mention it, he did seem worried. I remember something about how he sounded made me wonder if he thought the company might sever the contract. He'd mentioned it was his only income and finding work had been tough. I guess I'd just assumed he was worried about money. But that's about it. I cut it short so I could pull off the road and get the twins to calm down before we got to their soccer practice." He heard her shift the phone in her ear; then she spoke again, no longer reminiscing. Instead, she must have picked up on his worried tone and matched it. "Jack, why are *you* calling about

David? I didn't think you two talked much."

"It's probably nothing. He asked me for a favor, and I was just trying to follow up. But I know he sometimes goes out for days at a time in the woods or desert and doesn't always have good cell coverage. I'm sure that's all it is," he said, although he knew he wasn't convincing either of them.

"Well, if I hear from him, I'll call you, and please let me know when you talk to him, okay?" she said. He agreed and just before she hung up, he heard a child's shriek in the background.

He sat back in his chair, breathing deep. Now what? He lived two states away with two kids and a wife. He couldn't go running off on some spontaneous road trip. If he knew which firm David was working for, he could try calling them. But he had no idea. David did mention it was a mining-turned-forestry outfit once but didn't elaborate. Well, they might brush him off, but it was worth a shot. He'd go ahead and call the local police station to file a missing persons report or at least see if they could check up on David. After his mapping program revealed David's mailing address was part of Douglas County, Nevada, he located a number online for the Douglas County Sheriff's Department and dialed.

~

"Rest assured men, this deal will go through," Jerome said, feeling beads of sweat running down his neck under his collar. He faced two other men, dressed in suits and ties, and an older woman wearing overly extravagant jewelry, all of them sitting at a small white nondescript table.

One of the men, the only one wearing glasses, leaned forward. "It better. We have been very patient, and we have a lot riding on this. *You* have a lot riding on this." The man was glaring at him.

"Yes, I know. And remember, I'm the one who brought this plan to you. I warned you it would take some time, but trust me, it will be worth it in the end." Jerome knew that by now they had likely heard about the recent events in the area. "Things are moving along as planned. In fact, we are at a point where we can finally pick the pace up a bit. That said, Mike will have more information for us in a few days. After that, let's meet here again in say, two weeks?" He hoped, prayed, that they'd leave it at that and agree. With some obvious sighs of frustration, they did.

Minutes later, after everyone left the building and drove away, Jerome sat inside his car for a moment, keys still in his hand. The irony of the recent development had certainly not escaped him. He knew Ms. Rachel Winters. In fact, that bitch had been a thorn in his side for years, raising questions about technical reviews they'd done a bit of estimating or skimping on. Big deal. So they didn't look at the exact boundaries of special wildlife habitat, or, God forbid, they'd failed to consider a few extra cars or that a little dirt might run into a stream for a year or two. She'd been working for local environmental groups, helping them find ways to hold up good projects. How did those people think the town was going to survive without some new building? The extra kickbacks he got on the side were just a nice bonus. After all, he wasn't serving on the Board of Supervisors for the pay, so when he found out that *she* was the one who had caused this hitch in their plans, he couldn't believe it. Then again, if she happened to disappear as a result of this ordeal, it might just be a double blessing for him.

~

The sun was out and temperatures hovered around seventy degrees. "This was a good idea. I needed the exercise," Luke said from behind her as they walked along the narrow foothill path a few miles east of where they were staying. Rachel had told him about the open-space trails up and down the foothills as he drained his second mug of coffee that morning, and although he seemed a bit hesitant, he had agreed to come along. Not that she gave him much choice—she needed to walk Bella, and she wasn't going to wait around. Stubborn, yes, she knew it. But she couldn't help herself. She was a bundle of nerves, and Bella was pacing the floor, not to mention being fairly harsh on her toys.

"Thanks again for coming. I know you weren't too keen on the idea."

"Well, I was one cup of coffee short of consciousness."

"You really need to get off that stuff," she laughed. When he grew a bit quiet she turned around and noticed he was messing with the new disposable cell they had purchased the previous night. How to connect it to the Internet was quite the mystery that morning, but finally they'd figured it out. "Find those parcels on your phone app yet?" The new smartphone apps, and frankly smartphones in general, were still a bit foreign to Rachel—she still had an older flip phone with a good old-fashioned qwerty keyboard. It was part preference, part hesitancy to spend a lot on a newer model when she rarely used her cell phone.

"I've been able to get a general idea of where the California parcels on Janet's list are located. I guess I'd have to download another app if I wanted more info. But let me try something . . ." He kept walking as he continued struggling to see the screen on the small phone, and Rachel wondered to herself how many steps he would take until he tripped. It took three.

"You okay?"

"Yes, fine, thanks." He hadn't completely fallen, but the blush on his face revealed his embarrassment. "So, one of the properties is up by Mount Lassen, another down by Sonora Pass. But third time's a charm. Our last parcel is located near the southern end of the Yova-Pioneer Trail. Quite the coincidence, don't ya think?"

"Very . . . oh, *great*." Her tone changed from curiosity to annoyance as she turned back around and looked in front of them.

"What?"

"There are three loose dogs ahead, and they don't look all that friendly." She guessed the dogs each probably weighed a good seventy-five pounds, and although they weren't growling, they had that challenging, dominating look that worried her. They appeared to be purposely advancing toward them, hackles raised. She moved between the dogs and Bella, taking an assertive stance.

"What are *you* going to do, fight them off?" Luke asked, sounding perplexed.

"No, I've just learned if I exert more of a calm, alpha-type vibe, it rubs off on Bella. Helps prevent her submissive behavior that's invited attacks before." She tried to sound calm, eyeing the dogs and carefully standing her ground. But they continued to approach and Rachel was worried. Luke must have sensed her concern.

"That really works?"

"So far, but I also have pepper spray in my pack . . ." Her words trailed off as the distance between them and the dogs grew shorter.

"Hey, call your dogs!" Luke yelled to the owners, a younger couple that appeared deep in conversation and oblivious to what their dogs were doing. Then it all happened fast. Rachel heard Bella cry out as the dogs launched forward at them. A snarl to her right, a howl to her left—then she felt a tooth sink into her leg, and in her attempt to step back she tripped, lost her balance, and fell backward. After a quick flash of pain, Rachel spun back to see Bella, now bleeding from a wound on her upper front leg, cowering to show submissiveness to the other dogs. The three canines had retreated yet appeared ready to lunge forward again. But before they could, Luke reached down and carefully grabbed Bella, who curled up like an oversized puppy in his arms. Relieved, Rachel now had the opportunity to grab her pepper spray and aim as she stood and regained her balance. For a brief moment, she tried yelling and stomping against the ground, hoping that would scare them off. Apparently unfazed, they advanced on Rachel, so she released a quick squirt of the pepper spray in their general direction. Whimpering, they ran back toward their owners, and she noticed the distant couple was still unaware of the entire ordeal. She wished she could spray the dogs' owners with the pepper spray.

"Oh, Bella." She walked over to where Luke had her.

"I wasn't sure how far away to keep her from that spray," Luke said as he gently set Bella down.

"Good call. Thank you so much for getting her out of that," she said, almost in tears while she checked the wound she'd noticed on Bella just moments ago and then searched for more.

"Did they get you too, Rachel?" She'd almost forgotten. She looked at where she felt a tooth sink in and noted it was just a surface scratch.

"I'm fine," she said dismissively and continued inspecting Bella. A second later she heard Luke mumble.

"I can't believe they are trying to get away." He took off running, trailing the three dogs back to their owners.

An hour later, they were at a small vet office in Littleton. The other dogs' owners were out in the waiting room, unhappily stuck there until the final bill was ready. The vet finished examining Bella's wound. "She's going to be fine, Ms. Winters. Looks like she'll need some stitches and a good cleaning, but other than that, just some daily care and maybe limit the hikes a bit. I sent my assistant out to get information on the three dogs out there, and we checked. They are up to date on their shots; they just weren't registered with the county. And since Bella's up to date on hers, we're fine in that respect." Rachel breathed a sigh of relief, rubbing Bella as she calmly lay on the floor in front of the vet, belly up, obviously hoping for more rubs.

Then she remembered. "Oh wait, sutures. When I first adopted her, she had a reaction to the sutures that were used for her spay. My vet said they'd eventually dissolve, but he was going to call the vet who performed the spay and document the type of sutures used to avoid them in the future."

"Oh, yes, we've had that happen a few times here too. Do you know what type she reacted to?" The vet was older, probably close to seventy, with greying hair and a wide, concerned smile.

"I can't recall at the moment," she said, still shaken by the attack.

"No problem. We can call your vet and find out." He stood up, rubbed Bella once more, and said he'd go make the call and then get her stitched up. About ten minutes later, Bella had three short sutures across the bite wound and was in the lobby of the vet's office, once again wagging her tail, looking around for other dogs to greet. Rachel watched as the reluctant couple paid the bill, sat back down, and waited while their dogs were treated for the spray. Apparently they weren't talking to each other. Luke walked up to the counter next to where Rachel was waiting for the antibiotics the vet had prescribed. A young vet technician covering the phones looked up.

"By the way, you wouldn't happen to have the number for the local animal control, by any chance?" Luke whispered. The woman smiled back.

"Why, yes sirree, I have it right here. And I believe they are open all day until four thirty," she said, handing him a paper with a number scrawled across it in feminine handwriting. Rachel smiled, and a few minutes later they left to drive back to the hotel. Luke was driving this time. Rachel held Bella on her lap, although, thankfully, the pup seemed to be over her scare.

"So, how did you get them to follow us back there?"

"I pulled out my old badge—I've been carrying it since we left. I figured it might come in handy. Anyway, they had been taking illegal drugs back there, so I threatened them with arrest if they didn't come and pay the bill. They believed me."

"How . . . convenient," she laughed. "But seriously, thanks for doing that."

"No problem. I'm growing a bit fond of Bella myself, you know," he said, reaching over to rub Bella's ears.

~

"Hey, it's me," the man's throaty voice said the moment Mike answered his phone.

"What's up?" Mike asked, sitting in the chair in David's office, having given up his search.

"They are in Denver. The idea to tap a few recurring phone numbers on Miss Winter's phone bills paid off. My God, that woman is obsessed with that mutt, paying vet bills left and r—"

"What did you find?" Mike cut him off.

"Sorry . . . we traced the caller to a vet in Littleton." Mike had intently begun listening after he heard the word Denver.

"What in hell are they doing out there?" Mike spout. Plus, how could they possibly have already figured out who Spencer was, let alone his ties to Denver?

"Interesting question. I'm thinking maybe it's a good time to get out of town for a few days, check out that Rocky Mountain high people always talk about."

"Yes, good idea. You deserve a vacation. Good job with our young ex-colleague, by the way. Keep me informed." Mike hung up the phone without waiting for a response. He thought about whether to get the Denver police involved. After all, as of this morning, Luke Reed and Rachel Winters were officially suspects on the run. But then again, if the problem could be resolved quietly and permanently, getting cops involved might just get in the way. He'd wait for now.

~

Ted had relayed his findings from the previous afternoon to his partner, waiting to inform Captain Taylor when he arrived.

"Well, I guess it means you were probably right to take a second look at it," Leona said, listening while half caught up in something she was reading. "But who could get in there? Even with the kid gone, there are still a few bells and whistles he or she would have to get through."

"Yeah, that's what worries me. Only someone close to, or *in*, the department could do that," he sighed.

Leona looked up at him pointedly. "You know, I hate to say it, but Luke used to work here, too. He could probably figure all of that out." Earlier Ted had confessed to her that he doubted Luke and Rachel's guilt, and now he suspected she was concerned about his objectivity.

"Yes, that certainly occurred to me. But we've already matched his prints to the rock we found, and he knows it by now. So if he were innocent, wouldn't he *want* us to take a second look at it?" He tapped his pencil on the desk, a habit he failed to notice anymore but one that Leona frequently reminded him drove her crazy.

"True. But, just to play devil's advocate here, maybe he figures if the evidence against him is gone, or chain of evidence is broken, legally there might be no case." She reached over and gently placed her hand on the tapping pencil. He looked at her, laughed, and set the pencil down.

"I was doing it again, wasn't I?"

"Yep. Good thing you have me to stop you," she chuckled. Leona leaned back and looked down again at the paper in front of her, worry lines again forming.

"You OK? Looks like something has been bugging you lately." He nodded, looking down at the pile on her desk. Her eyes immediately began filling with tears, and he moved his chair over by her side, placing a hand on her shoulder. "Leona, what's wrong?"

"Oh God, I told myself I'd keep it out of the office. But, I'm a mess . . . don't suppose I can hide it well," she paused and took a deep breath. "A few months ago, we took Nick to the doctor because he seemed to have a flu virus that wouldn't go away." Nick was their middle child, about six years old. Ted had met him a year or so ago.

"They ran some tests and found out he has cancer." She began to cry, and Ted, although childless, imagined how scared and helpless he'd feel if one of his nephews were sick.

"Oh, Leona, I'm so sorry. Is there anything I can do?"

"Thanks, but I don't think so." She grabbed a tissue and wiped her eyes and nose. "The doctors are optimistic at this point, otherwise I'd probably completely lose it. But to make matters worse, the treatments are only half covered by insurance, and we've already run through our savings. With Marcus losing that county job, things were already a bit tight." She looked at the paper in front of her. Ted couldn't read the details, but it had the look of an invoice or bill. "I picked up the mail on my way in this morning, and the most recent bill from the hospital was in there. I guess it just hit me hard again." She was recovering a bit now, folding up the bill and stuffing it back into her purse. "Please don't say anything to anyone else, OK?"

"Of course . . . of course." He walked back to his chair and watched her slowly rise and head again toward the women's restroom. He couldn't even imagine the kind of heartbreak she had to be going through, let alone the financial stress. Although they didn't know everything about each other or socialize much outside of work, Ted felt like they'd become good friends over the years. Initially he'd been a bit upset to be stuck with a rookie cop, let alone a woman from somewhere in the Plains. But she had quickly proven to be smart, capable, and agile, and able to chase down a perpetrator with the best of them.

Knowing all he could do was be there for her when she needed it, Ted tried to focus back on the case. It was hard, though, thinking about what that sweet, innocent little boy and his family were going through. He supposed it also explained some of her additional sick leave lately.

Time to get back to work and figure out who broke into the evidence locker, Ted decided. He was pretty sure it wasn't Luke, although he had a feeling once word got out his opinion would be in the minority.

Just as he was finally able to refocus his mind on the case,

Shelby walked over with an unpleasant look on her face, twisting her new engagement ring around her finger. "Hey, everything okay with Leona?" she asked, disapproval in her tone. "Looked like a pretty serious conversation. One she should be having with *her husband.*" The implication was not lost on Ted, but he decided to let it go and play dumb. He knew some people thought of him as a bit of a player, but he'd never mess with a married woman, let alone his partner. It annoyed him to be accused of doing so.

"Oh, yes, she's fine. I think she went to the bathroom if you wanted to go check on her." He quickly glanced back down at his notepad, hoping the officer would get the hint. He knew Shelby and Leona had become office friends but didn't think they spent much time together outside of work and wasn't sure this was something Leona would have shared with her. But Shelby had a reputation for being a bit intrusive, and perhaps a bit too interested in office gossip.

"Thanks," she said then briskly walked in the direction of the women's restroom.

CHAPTER TWELVE

Jack called the number and after explaining the reason for his call was transferred to the officer who handles missing persons. Naturally it went straight to voicemail, where a young-sounding officer named Brian Choe asked the caller to leave a message with the reason for calling, phone number, and so on. Jack kept it short, repeated his phone number, then hung up, sat back, and hoped it was something as simple as a dead cell phone battery. But given David's recent call and how upset he sounded, Jack had a bad feeling. Thankfully Officer Choe called him back less than ten minutes later. He assured Jack he'd go check out David's place first and be in touch.

~

About an hour after speaking with the man in Oregon, Brian Choe was standing next to one of his station's newer officers, peering into the window of David Payton's home. He had to raise his hands to his forehead and block the sun's reflection on the glass to be able to see inside. The interior space bore the look of a long empty home, and his car was gone. Chances were the guy just wanted to get away for a while and was simply avoiding calls from family and friends. It happened more often than people realized. But as he scanned the room inside, paying more attention to the details, he saw a few red flags. First, an empty laptop case sat open on the counter. Second, an old-fashioned answering machine—not really uncommon in areas where cell reception was poor—was blinking the number twelve. That was a lot of calls to accumulate between checking messages. Perhaps the most troubling observation was when Brian moved to another window, looking inside at what was clearly a home office, and saw the tossed-about look of the room. He had heard jokes about how scientists weren't always the cleanest or most organized people, but, regardless, this room looked like it had been frantically searched. He went back to the front door and called out.

"Mr. David Payton, this is Officer Choe from the Douglas County Sheriff's Department. If you are in there, please come to the door now. Otherwise, we will enter by force." He waited another minute and repeated his statement, but after no response he kicked in the front door. He and the officer who accompanied him carefully searched the entire home. There was nobody there, living or dead. But there were several more hints that the man hadn't simply taken off on a trip somewhere. A shaving kit sat open on the sink. An electric toothbrush rested in its charging cradle on the side. The refrigerator contained rotting fruit and vegetables. Brian turned to his fellow officer. "I think we need to get some more people out here and get an official MP report going. Can you make the call?"

"Sure." The officer turned and headed toward their vehicle.

Brian removed the gloves he'd put on for the search, and retrieved the phone number he'd written down from Mr. Stine in Oregon to report what he found—and to get the information he needed in order to file the official missing persons report.

~

Resting on one of the beds with Bella asleep next to her, Rachel finished reviewing the printout of the environmental analysis and picked up her laptop to connect to the motel's wireless. She looked over at Luke, who had nodded off not long ago, his laptop sitting on the small round table in front of him, head slightly tilted back. She knew he'd tossed and turned a bit the night before, the noise of his shifting having awakened her a few times. He'd downed the foul-smelling generic hotel coffee that morning like it was the last fluid left on earth; then again, it seemed like he did that every morning. She spent a moment looking at his face, now relaxed and peaceful. He had what she'd call a bit of a baby face combined with the rugged look of a bull rider. She liked the combination, including the day's growth of stubble. There was a small scar just below his right eye that she hadn't noticed before. He'd been wearing his sunglasses quite a bit, but even without them it was barely visible. Just as she found herself imagining the feel of her fingers gently tracing the scar, he seemed to catch himself, head rising up straight again, eyes opening quickly. He looked right at her and was obviously surprised to find her gazing intently at him. Grinning, he inquired, "See anything you like there, *mountaingirl*?"

She knew her face must have turned bright red. Bella—she'd look at Bella. That would be a good, safe focal point. "Sorry, I was just about to tell you what I found when I noticed you were asleep."

"Uh-huh," he said, his tone indicating he didn't believe her one bit. Then he gave her a slight wink and as he got up and came to sit next to her. "OK, I'll go with it. What did you find out?"

She'd been caught. She paused before continuing, "There is a reference to a two-hundred-acre parcel of privately owned land in the EA, although it's quite vague. I think it's safe to say it's the Wells property. It appears when they wrote the EA, the preferred project—the one the government was pushing for—included treatment on that parcel." At that, she saw the questioning look on his face.

"What 'treatment,' and why would the private acreage matter

anyway?"

"Oh, sorry. This may shock you, but I have a tendency to get lost in my 'work speak,' as some of my friends fondly refer to it."

"Wow, I'd never have guessed," he said sarcastically.

"I'd like to think it's part of my charm. But seriously, how about I back up a bit. So first, the treatment. The water in that area essentially flows toward the valley, supplying water to people down in the Carson Valley. They still have to remove pollutants from the water before it's potable, but there's been a lot of attention, *finally*, on the need to repair unhealthy forests upstream. Not just for the sake of the forests, but also to improve the quality of water that's making its way down the mountain to urban areas. Because our forests are so unhealthy, things are all messed up environmentally. There is a lot of erosion. Basically too much dirt is getting into streams and rivers. That causes a whole set of other problems, but I'll spare you the details . . . unless you want to know." She laughed, but as often happened when she talked about her work, she was getting riled up about some of the issues. She tried not to sound preachy, as she'd learned everyone had their own opinions and challenging them wasn't a good way to work together. But she couldn't help it; she cared too much.

"No, I get the idea that it might take up the whole evening and possibly next week," Luke said. Yes, Rachel could sense he'd figured her out on that deal.

"No comment. So, anyhow, they've been working on ways to help reduce erosion and put the right nutrients, so to speak, back into the dirt. One of the more common treatments has been to mix wood chips into the soils on sloped hillsides. According to the EA, the project was about mixing wood chips into the dirt with a few variations to test which works better. Regardless, it should all improve the water quality in the area."

"Wood chips, like what people landscape with?"

"Yeah, kind of like that. The hope is to use the trees and

branches they cut out of forests to reduce fire danger to make wood chips and get some benefits out of them."

"OK, got it. I recall reading some articles about that now. So, what's the deal with including the private property?"

"The project's boundary appears to have been delineated in a way that captures the full area of the mountainside. Runoff from the area drains to the West Fork of the Carson River, and people and animals in the Carson Valley eventually use that water. If they had to exclude the two hundred private acres from the project it would really put a dent in what they could do, and a project like that may not get funded in the scheme of public agencies."

When he didn't respond right away, she looked up at him, worried she'd again gotten too preachy. But he was shaking his head with an odd smile on his face.

"Politics. How you can work in that world amazes me."

"Criminals. How *you* can live in *that* world amazes me," she retorted, smiling.

"OK, good point. Although I don't suppose the two are really all that separate, are they?"

"Oh, do not get me started. If people only knew some of the stuff these politicians are doing . . . ," she laughed. "But, yes, I'm aware that not all of them are evil criminals. OK, back to the case at hand." She focused once again on the laptop, calling out with false enthusiasm: "Time to dig back into the political muck."

"Don't get too dirty. I'd hoped to go out for dinner."

"Ha, now that's a knee-slapper," she said, slapping her knee. "And if you're paying, yes, dinner out sounds great."

"I'll add it to your bill," he responded. Before she could muster a witty response of her own, the computer screen caught her eye and she smiled.

"OK, I think we're getting somewhere." Rachel sat up in excitement. "There was a meeting in 2002. No consultants had been selected yet. The RFP we found was from 2005. So let's try a meeting later in that year." She clicked on a meeting held in October 2005 and began to scroll down the pages. "And there it is. The list of attendees includes several people who worked for Row Environmental, starting with Michael Row, owner, and then three other names. And below that, our Mr. Spencer Wells. According to this, he was, *quote*, 'representing Lloyd Wells, private land owner.'"

"What the heck kind of mess did you stumble on, girl?" Luke said, and Rachel thought he was talking to her until she looked up and saw his gaze fixed on Bella, one hand rubbing her neck. Then he stood up and went back over to his own laptop. "Let me see what I can find out about that property. How is it that the entire area isn't in public ownership already?" he asked as he began his own search.

"Well, have you ever seen a land map that has a sort of a checkerboard design in terms of colors?"

He nodded. "I've seen that on some of the maps I've looked at for bike trails."

"The checkerboards are basically one square of public land, then one square of private, then public again. It goes back to the construction of the transcontinental railroad in the 1860s. The government offered every other square mile of land to companies, hoping to incentivize construction of the railroad, at the time retaining the remaining intermittent parcels. Although for decades efforts have been underway to get more of the private land into public ownership in certain areas, there are still a lot of private squares out there. Based on what we've learned about Lloyd Wells, I'm guessing he bought it so he could get it into public ownership." She paused when they noticed Bella apparently having one of those running dog dreams. Her paws twitched and then all four legs began to paw at the air. Rachel looked to make sure she didn't move too much and pull her stitches.

"As expected it never got finalized, and the delinquent

grandson became the legal owner," Luke said, remaining focused on his computer screen.

The room fell silent, except for the slight whooshing sound of Bella's moving legs. After a minute or so, Rachel perked up. "So Lloyd buys the land, intending to deed it over to the US National Forest system. But then Lloyd has another heart attack, dies, and Spencer gets the land. Before that, Spencer was already representing the family at the project meetings and working directly with the environmental firm that won the bid. Nothing suggests Lloyd's heart attack wasn't natural, and he had a history of heart problems. Maybe someone figured out a way to capitalize on his death after the fact?"

Luke cut in. "Although his health history could have also been used to the benefit of someone wanting him dead," he speculated. "Why wouldn't Lloyd have already signed the property over right away? Years ago?"

"Hmm, maybe it was somehow his way of making sure the project happened as he'd intended. Or to make sure that the forest service wouldn't allow logging or something. At least, that would be my guess. Another headline for you, Luke—a lot of people don't trust the forest service."

"Yeah, I got that idea after that last big fire in the Basin."

Rachel knew what he meant. The Angora Fire was started in 2007 from an illegal campfire built by juveniles on forest service land and kicked into gear by winds. The fire eventually consumed hundreds of homes. But the forest service and a few other government agencies took the brunt of the public outrage, and things got pretty tense in town for a while.

"So then the question is, what could Spencer do . . . or have done *with* the two hundred acres, that would be a motive for murder? And how was the first murder victim, involved?" she asked, thinking out loud. Then Rachel thought of something else. She'd always heard greed or love were the primary motives for murder. And in her world, when it came to land use and development, it seemed the greed was endless. "I just pulled up the land-use maps, and it looks like, at first glance, the land could be approved for one big estate." She sat back and let her next comment slip out without thinking first. "Just what the world needs, another rich schmuck looking for a weekend getaway, not caring at all about the resources his new mansion uses up."

"Classism, anyone?" Luke retorted.

Rachel was going to apologize for her comment at first, but for some reason his response just aggravated her more. She knew she sounded unreasonably annoyed, but couldn't help herself.

"Oh, yes, sorry, how could I forget?" she said.

"And just when I thought we might be able to have a pleasant dinner later. By the way, yes, I wrote off my wealthy family, but not all people with money are bad, you know."

"I know, but I run into a lot of self-absorbed rich people in my line of work who seem to care nothing about the environment and have no problem stepping on the rest of us poor minions to get what they want." Now she was letting her attitude get the best of her.

"Well, I'm sure we all do," he snapped back.

Feeling a bit chastised, and knowing she probably deserved it, she tried to change the subject and looked back at her laptop. "OK, how about we end that conversation?" His silence and motion to look back down at the computer suggested he agreed, but she could still see the annoyance on his face. Perhaps they both needed a reminder that they'd come from two different worlds before she let those moments of physical attraction go anywhere. "OK, although building a big mansion and selling it could make some good money, I can't imagine it would be profitable enough to go to the trouble Spencer and who knows how many other people have gone through for this. Now condos or subdivided land—*those* could be a big money motive. But they'd have to change the zoning, and I don't see how they could meet the environmental and legal requirements."

He nodded. "Yeah, the timeline seems off, too. Lloyd bought it before this Row group or Spencer ever got involved. If getting ownership had been Spencer's goal from the start, why wait so many years?"

At that point, a large grumbling sound filled the room. Rachel flushed at the sounds of her stomach begging for food. "Well, on that note, still want to go out for dinner?" She really didn't want to go sit and stare at him at a restaurant but couldn't ignore the rumbling sound of her hunger and thought it would be worse to call off the idea altogether.

"I suppose a break wouldn't hurt." He got up and stretched, a hint of reluctance in his voice.

He's just as excited as I am about this, Rachel thought. Oh joy, isn't this going to be fun? After she'd asked, she'd been hoping he'd say no. Frankly, she'd rather stay here with Bella and eat a protein bar than make awkward conversation over dinner, but now she was stuck. She just hoped the food was good.

~

Having arrived at Denver International Airport an hour ago, he'd managed to rent a car and get going soon thereafter. Scott, also known as "the Frog" to some, presented identification in the name of James Smith for the airline ticket and car rental. He was not fond of airports—delays, security checks, taking your damn shoes off for God's sake. Plus enduring the pain from the gunshot wound, not to mention his subsequent fall, and he wanted to kill the couple simply for the misery he'd endured on the flight. Adding insult to injury, he ended up having a three-hour delay at the stop in San Francisco, due to a mechanical problem with the plane.

By the time Scott arrived at the vet's office in Littleton, it was closed. No problem, he thought, as he examined the pathetic deadbolt lock that was their primary security measure. He grabbed the small black case of tools he'd packed away in his checked luggage and had the deadbolt unlocked in under sixty seconds. Stepping inside, he stopped and briefly listened for the sounds of any people or beeps indicating additional security. Nothing. He walked farther in, entering what appeared to be the main file room. Perfect. He began looking under Winters, expecting to find the dog's file from that morning, but there were no files for Rachel Winters. Next, he checked under Luke Reed. Again, nothing. Frustrated, he kicked one of the nearby chairs, creating a loud whacking sound as it flipped over. In response, multiple dogs began barking in a nearby room. *Damn.* He should have expected they'd be boarding pets overnight. He hated dogs—had since the day his ex-wife had brought home some mutt that had systematically destroyed half their furniture. He'd let that dog know exactly how he felt about it, before letting his wife know, too.

Now he had to hurry it up. There was a good chance a staff member might be remotely monitoring for disturbances. The file had to be there somewhere. He walked into the front office where, as far as he was concerned, people would wait to spend half their month's earnings for a lousy dog or cat. On the shelves next to the computer monitors were a few wire baskets with handwritten labels attached. The first one on the left read "In-box—for doc's review." The next basket over had another label: "To be filed." That had to be it. He began looking through the files seeing many typical dog names: Spot, Fritz, Lady. Eventually he found a file with "Winters, Bella" written across the top with the day's date next to "intake form." The first half of the page included basic contact information, clearly written in female handwriting, with all of those ridiculous curves. Regardless, it was legible, and all he cared about was that she had written down the hotel they were staying in. She hadn't noted a room number. But that was easy enough to find out. He placed the files back in the pile and walked toward the back door he'd entered through. The ongoing barking and growling of the clinic's overnight patients hadn't stopped. Scott slipped through the door, originally intending to lock it back up with his tools but noticed two headlights had turned into the lot. Yes, someone had been monitoring after all. He stepped back into the shadow of the trees, hoping he was fully hidden. He didn't have any reservations about taking out a possible witness; he just preferred to avoid the mess and extra time involved.

Lucky for the young on-call technician, she didn't see him hiding in the trees. Scott quietly watched her as she reached for her key, put it in the deadbolt, turned it, and seemed to pause for the slightest moment. She shook her head, opened the door, and stepped inside. He heard the click of her relocking the deadbolt. After a moment, he quietly left his hiding place, sticking to the shadows provided by trees and poorly angled streetlights. He got back into his rental car, a small Camry. He'd been frustrated when they'd had no trucks or SUVs available, but what could he do? He started the ignition and drove away, heading toward the hotel that was listed in the dog's file.

In the lobby, he played the part of the traveling businessman in need of a room. There were three hundred rooms in this place, and the clerk claimed to have just a few left on the first floor. What a scam, he thought.

After entering his room for the night, Scott debated about his next move. Trying to find Rachel and Luke's room tonight would probably be a waste of time. They would likely leave in the morning, or they'd come down and go outside to let that dog do her mess. Either way, if he got up early enough, he was bound to see them leaving. He smiled, turned on the television in the room, and began pushing buttons on the remote to find the guide for the extra channels. There was a special porn flick on pay-per-view that might be entertaining. Pricey, but Mike wouldn't complain about cost so long as he did his job.

CHAPTER THIRTEEN

"Wow, this is really good chicken parmesan," Rachel remarked, twisting another fork of chicken with the penne pasta. They'd found a small Italian restaurant with outdoor dog-friendly seating just a few blocks away from the hotel. Now she was feeling a bit tipsy, Luke having generously poured them both wine, probably as a distraction from awkward conversation, or lack thereof. It looked to her as though he was far more composed than she was.

"I agree, my dinner was great," he said, dipping another piece of bread into the balsamic vinegar and olive oil blend.

Was? She looked over at his empty plate. He was wiping the sauce with another dinner roll. "I guess it was," she laughed, taking another sip of wine. She wasn't a huge Chianti fan, but it had tasted surprisingly good. Or maybe after the last few days, she just really needed the alcohol.

"OK, Rachel, you have to admit going out was a good idea, right?"

"All right, yes, I'm glad we came," she reluctantly agreed.

"So, I won't push you for a thank you, because after all, that might be *too much*," he said sarcastically. She was about to retort when he cut back in. "How about a temporary truce? Until we get all this figured out and then we can go back to disparaging each other's stereotypes."

She knew it was a good idea and probably not easy for him to extend this olive branch. "OK, truce."

"On that note, you can tell me to leave it alone, but . . . mind if I ask more about what happened in Denver? I get the idea it explains some of your . . . views." He appeared to be sincerely interested. Rachel sighed—she didn't like to talk about it, but he was right. It had a lot to do with her attitude about some things.

"OK. And I know I probably do have some issues with . . . 'classism,' as you called it. I'm working on it." She smiled coyly. "So the guy I went on a couple of dates with when I lived out here—Matt—turned out to be the son of one of the owners of the big electric company I was working for in Denver. But I didn't know it. We'd met at a coffee shop, and following some nice conversation he asked me out for dinner. After the second date, it was clear to me there was no attraction, at least on my part. Plus, we didn't really have much in common, as you can probably imagine. So when I thanked him for dinner and he asked about meeting up again, I was honest and told him I just didn't feel the connection. I couldn't see how he could feel one either."

"And how'd he take that?"

"He got really angry, throwing down the take-home container he'd carried out and grabbing me, trying to pull me along next to him as he walked. He called me some names, said I was just another woman trying to get a free ride, that sort of thing. I got loose from his grasp and left him there ranting while I ran to my pickup. I just wanted to get away as fast as possible and never see him again."

"Sounds pretty intense," Luke said, leaning toward her.

"Yes, it had completely caught me off guard. I'd hoped that was the end of it. He'd never been to my house, and, so far as I knew, he didn't know where I worked, only that it was for a private energy company. I then started getting repeated calls, with messages apologizing for getting upset, please, *honey,* take me back . . . very strange stuff. Then, he started showing up outside of the building I worked in and, eventually, my house. I had a two-year-old Akita mix then, Shila, who rarely barked, yet she began barking just about every night, and I soon realized that he was out front, parked or standing in my driveway. I called the police and filed a restraining order against him."

"And I'm guessing that didn't work?"

"Nope. I went into work the next day and was called into my boss's office. He asked me—and I quote—'What the fuck were you thinking filing a restraining order against one of the owner's sons?' I was shocked. I tried to explain I had no idea who he was, although it shouldn't matter given what Matt was doing, but my boss cut me off and said my womanly *antics* had no place in the company, that if I wanted to keep my job, I'd rescind the order and play nice. I was given the rest of the day to 'think it over.' I went back to my office, packed up my personal items, and went straight home. I had no idea what I'd do, but I couldn't stay there. I was inside my house, down in a basement room with my other dog, Koda, when I heard Shila barking ferociously out back. By the time I got upstairs, Shila was quiet again, and when I came out back, I saw Matt standing there, in my backyard with a syringe in his hand. Shila was lying on the ground, and I couldn't tell if she was breathing. He begged me to just hear him out, and I ran inside for the phone. He followed and grabbed me, knocking me to the floor and pinning me there with his weight. When I felt his hands reach for the buttons on my blouse, I screamed louder than I'd ever screamed in my life." Rachel stopped and looked over at Luke. He was looking at her, listening intently, but harboring what looked like anger—not aimed at her. He also looked tentative about responding.

"He didn't . . . get that far. After my scream, we both heard a strange howl from Koda downstairs. It distracted Matt enough that I managed to twist my arm free and slam my elbow into his groin. About then my neighbors burst through the back door. One ran over and kicked him off of me while the other helped me up. Then, at least, he'd only given Shila a sedative. I called the police again, and he was arrested. The next day one of the friendlier officers stopped by off the clock. Turns out he was there to warn me that Matt's father had hired a huge law firm, and they were going to claim I led *him* on in order to work my way up the ladder at work. When he refused, *I* attacked *him*. The officer alluded to the higher-ups in his department being bound to support Matt's story due to political connections and upcoming elections. He suggested if charges were dropped against Matt, and I moved out of town, it would most likely all go away. I realized I had no choice. I didn't have the money or power to fight something like that. My neighbors were witnesses, sure, but they were also married gay men and, according to the officer, were likely to be discriminated against by jurors."

"My God."

"So, I moved back to Lake Tahoe, which I'd been giving thought to anyway, just not under those . . . circumstances. I had no job but, as you may have noticed, a passion for the environment, so that's when I began volunteering with the environmental groups and eventually became an independent consultant. It seemed the officer had been right. The charges against Matt were dropped, and no legal action came my way. But about six months later, the calls started. Then Shila's evening barking sprees began to occur. Finally, I saw Matt outside, hiding behind a fence across the street, just . . . watching. I called the police. They sent out a patrol car, but he'd left by the time they arrived. I explained everything to them about what happened in Denver, and although I was hesitant they convinced me to file a new restraining order. So I did. The next time I saw him I called them, and he was escorted back to the station. Of course he called his daddy, and Daddy called some lawyers, and he was out the next day. I'd gone to a city council meeting, telling myself there was nothing to do but keep busy since he was locked up. Well, I'd left Shila outside because she loved to run around in the yard. Koda stayed inside when I was gone. When I got back that evening, it was so . . . quiet. Usually she'd hear me drive up and start making excited little yelping noises until I came and greeted her. I went into the yard to look for her and found her in the corner. She was dead." At this, her voice cracked, and her eyes watered. But she wanted to finish the story, so she went on. "That creep had laced a raw steak with rat poison. Half the steak was still in the yard." Now, the tears fell, and she saw Luke reach across to gently touch her hand.

"I'm so sorry."

"Thanks." She wiped her nose with a napkin and continued. "I called the police again, and that's when they told me they'd released Matt that morning. I was fuming with anger and full of grief. I didn't know what to do, so I took Koda with me and drove straight to the station. I demanded they arrest him immediately. They said without any proof connecting him to what happened to Shila their hands were tied. I couldn't believe it. I gave up, went home, and called my mom. She said they'd help me pay for an attorney to go after Matt if I wanted. I didn't know what to do, and I didn't want to see them drain their retirement to fight someone who obviously had unlimited resources. I sat there that evening and all night, holding Koda, afraid Matt would show up. The next morning, I got a call from one of the officers at the station, who informed me they'd received a call from a patrol unit in Salt Lake City asking about a man who's name popped up with an RO filed in South Lake Tahoe. Turns out he was speeding down I-80, hit some loose sand blowing across the interstate, and fishtailed off the side of the road. The gas tank exploded immediately. They'd figured out some way to get prints and matched them to Matt's."

"Good riddance," Luke whispered.

"Agreed. His father still blamed me, and for a while made it difficult for me to get work, even out here. He seemed to have connections in all the right places, reaching across thousands of miles. The environmental organizations, however, knew me and trusted me and didn't care what others thought, so they continued to hire me for work. It took years for the supposed scandal to calm down. But I never trusted the police after that, or rather the idea that they'd be able to help me. I still wonder what I was thinking to even go there when I found that body. I should have known better."

"That all sounds pretty rough. I'm sorry you had to go through that. I guess it was before I worked there. Well, normally I'd say there are still many good cops out there, but, then again, obviously someone in the department is against us on this."

"Yes . . . and I know not all wealthy people are that way—in fact, look at the good Lloyd was doing. Plus there are a lot of large donors to environmental causes around Tahoe, too. And I'm also aware not all politicians are that way, but I just get so upset that bad ones get away with so much and have plenty of help in doing it." She stopped, reached for her wine glass, and took two long sips. "OK, moving on. What should we do next?"

Luke paused, and Rachel wondered if he was debating whether to let her change the subject or to keep asking her about what happened. Apparently he decided to let it go. "Well, I'm thinking two things. But first, you said Row Environmental typically worked more in the mining arena, or at least they used to?" She nodded, chewing another bite. "OK, here's my proposal. First, we need a copy of Lloyd's will."

She started to question how they'd get it when he cut her off, guessing correctly at what she was going to ask. "Leave that to me. If no one has taken over for the attorney yet, maybe no one has cleared his office out either. Regardless, I have my ways." He grinned. "And my ways may work better in the dark . . ."

"OK . . . ," she stuttered. The double meaning certainly hadn't escaped her.

"While I do that, I think it would be helpful for you to find out more about this environmental firm. I could set you up with a few of my, um, special passwords, give you a few more places to look." He emphasized the word *special,* smiling guiltily. After two small bowls of spumoni ice cream and Rachel finishing another glass of wine that Luke had quietly poured as she told her story, they walked back to their hotel room. Rachel had been speaking incessantly about irrelevant things and going on about childhood experiences she'd never tell anyone if she were sober. Then she stopped walking, Luke also pausing at her side, and looked over at him. "How is it that I'm so tipsy and you seem fine?"

"Well, I could say it's a man/woman thing, but I'm sure that would offend you. Honestly I slipped a few extra sips into your glass. It was just really nice to see the sad, worried look disappear for a little while." He was looking straight at her. He brushed away a wisp of hair that had fallen across her cheek from the slight breeze. They froze, facing each other, close.

Rachel knew better. She was less inhibited from the wine and damn if he hadn't looked good walking along the cobblestone streets, the breeze catching his hair just right, but she couldn't help it. Once again, her gaze met his, and she remembered the scar she'd seen earlier. Reaching up to touch it, she asked, "Is this from the accident when you were a kid?"

The moment her finger touched his face a warmth ran up and down her entire body. "Yes. I forget it's there half the time, and not many people notice it, or at least ask about it." He stepped just an inch closer to her, leaned down, and his lips brushed against hers. She couldn't help but stiffen at first, caught off guard by the intimate moment, but then relaxed, falling into the outline of his body. His hands on the sides of her neck, he gently but passionately drew her mouth toward his.

When their lips touched this time, it was an instinctive need. Rachel didn't realize she'd pressed herself against him more. She didn't want to stop. This felt too good. His warm hands caressed her neck and she lost herself in the moment, with his body against hers and the taste of his gentle, sweet lips. And then, reality. Bella, who had been calmly standing next to them, unexpectedly tightened the leash looped through Rachel's arm. The slight tug pulled Rachel away from Luke's embrace, and, reluctantly, she stepped back. "Bella, what is it?" she asked, concerned, until she noticed Bella's attention focused on another dog across the street. Rachel felt disappointment at the interruption but at the same time thankful.

"I'd apologize for kissing you, but it would be a lie," he said, slipping his arm through hers, beginning to walk again.

She fell in step next to him. "Just remember, you did have to ply me with wine first."

"Fine. Next time, no wine, no excuses," he said seriously, which made her start thinking about the next time, and she felt herself warm up all over again. Rachel didn't know what to say to that. She certainly enjoyed the kiss and had not wanted to stop, but a relationship, of any kind, could only complicate their current situation. Plus, how could anything between them last? They were so different. So she said nothing, murmuring to Bella as they strolled back to their hotel room. While Rachel got Bella set up with her bed and checked her sutures, Luke booted up his laptop. He pulled up several bookmarked webpages and wrote down the various passwords associated with them.

She sat down in front of his computer, her buzz almost worn off. "I'm still not sure I want to know where you got these pages. Nothing legal, I'm sure."

"Relax," he said. "And frankly, it can't hurt you to live a little. Go ahead. Look up someone you've always been curious about. Snoop a little." He laughed, stood up, and pulled a light coat from its hanger. "I guess I'll get going and see what I can do to get a copy of that will. Joe's office is just a few miles north in Lakewood."

"Good luck," she said, and then, pausing, she looked up at him. "Please be careful," she said. He smiled and shrugged as if saying, "When am I not?" and started to head toward the door. Behind him, she had started typing again but paused and smiled, casually saying it just loud enough for him to hear: "I just don't want to have to bail you out of jail, that's all." She could almost hear him smile.

~

Luke had spent the ten-minute drive to the attorney's office mulling over what Rachel had told him about Matt. It certainly explained some of her opinions. Now that he knew the full story, he couldn't really blame her. In fact, as she'd talked about it, he'd felt the overwhelming need to find the guy and break some bones. He wasn't sorry to admit he was relieved to hear the guy had basically killed himself. But that he'd also taken the life of an innocent dog before doing so—poor Rachel.

Then there was the kiss. If not for Bella's interruption, they might still be standing there on that street, tangled in each other's arms. He wanted her more than he'd wanted any woman in a long time, but not just physically. He wanted to know more about her thoughts, her life, her childhood. What was happening to him?

Luke stood in front of the back door of a small office building, focusing on the task at hand. He'd driven by the front, which still read "Joseph Tilman, Attorney-at-Law." There had been an attempt to tape something over the door to cover his name, but the paper now hung below it, attached by an inch of tape.

Luke parked a block down the street and carefully made his way back up to the office building, approaching from behind. He had to admit, he was a bit excited about some hands-on investigating of something other than cheating spouses. After putting on a pair of disposable gloves, Luke carefully opened the locked door handle and entered the musty office of someone who probably worked too many hours and enjoyed very little before his life was cut short by a reckless driver. He drew out his flashlight, not wanting to turn on any lights that might be seen from the street.

He found Joe's desk, and while he sat in the chair, Luke looked around and saw evidence of what he'd suspected. A lonely, single man, with no one to pack up his belongings when he passed away. There was just one personal picture—a man, maybe around fifty-five, sat in a park with a short and pudgy basset hound at his side. He was smiling, holding the dog, who like his human companion, had a few extra pounds around the middle, and several areas of grey. No other pictures were displayed, nor were there were any outlines on dusty surfaces that might indicate photo frames having been removed by a friend or family member. He picked up the one picture that was there and turned it over. Sticking out of the backing just enough to be noticeable was the corner of a note that had been tucked into the frame. He pulled it out and found the words "Gus, RIP, 2007" written in the typical straight-edge scrawl of a man. So Joe had just one bright spot in his life, and he'd lost him years before. Sad. The attorney reminded him, somewhat, of people he'd known growing up—those who worked most waking hours, never taking time for themselves. They usually just ran themselves into the grave that much faster. Certainly not the life he'd wanted. He'd once heard the saying "No one on their deathbed ever says they wish they'd spent more time at work," and that phrase helped him remember that, although more money from extra jobs might be nice, he needed time to enjoy life every day. You only live once. And on that thought, once again, the image of Rachel floated into his mind—kissing her soft lips that sparkled with that lip balm she always wore.

"Oh man, get a handle on yourself," Luke whispered while looking around the office. He saw the file cabinet behind the desk—a good place to start. He carefully opened the poor locking mechanism on the front, thinking at first that it seemed to open too easily. He looked closer and noted what appeared to be a slight scuff mark on one of the small edges of the keyhole. *Curious*. He found it a bit difficult to rummage through vertical files stuffed in the drawers but eventually made his way to the "W" folder in the back of the lowest drawer.

Luke pulled it out to study the contents. Inside, about ten packets of stapled papers were neatly set together. Luke flipped through three before finding "Wells, Lloyd" printed on the top of the first full-size sheet. He looked around and noted a copier in the corner of the room. He couldn't tell if there was power, but he pushed the ON button anyway and was relieved when it came to life. He made a copy of the entire will and went to place it back in the folder. But as he was carefully setting it back in place, he saw the edge of another piece or two of paper sticking out from the very back, stuck in the metal rod intended to help contain overstuffed folders. He carefully tugged on it a few times before it came loose. It was just two sheets, with *Wells, Lloyd* noted at the top next to the page numbers. He compared the papers to the matching pages in the copy he'd just made, and, at first glance, they appeared to be the same. But then he noticed small variations in the lengths of each line of text displayed on the right side of the page. As if someone had printed a page out and then added a few words, and the processing program had automatically adjusted the lines to fit in the margins. He added the other pages to his stack and then spent some time checking the drawer for other loose papers. He also went through all of the files in both the W and L folders, just in case something was filed by first or last name. Finding nothing else, he pushed the drawer back, used his tools to reposition the lock, and then ran his flashlight around the room to see if anything else seemed odd or out of place. He was careful to keep the beam low and away from the direction of the window up front, even though it had curtains pulled across it. Seeing nothing more of interest, Luke turned off the copier before trying to find the man's home address. It was probably a bust, but you never know. People kept work at home all of the time.

He opened the top drawer of the desk, hoping to find a bill or invoice. There was a business envelope with a generic "sign up with us" message inside from a local cable provider. And lucky for Luke, the address appeared to be a residence not too far away. Next, something bright colored in the drawer caught his eye. It was a slip from a pink message tablet preprinted with spaces to fill in the date, time, caller, etc., which more often than not people flipped over to write unrestricted by lines. The note had a date on the back, followed by an address. Nothing that would initially raise any red flags, except for one thing. The date noted on the message was the same day that this man had been killed by a hit-and-run driver. Luke pocketed the pink sheet, looked around a bit more, and then left the office.

~

Scott leaned up against the headboard in his hotel room, a bit exhausted from the long day and groggy from the extra Vicodin he'd just taken. He had set his alarm for four a.m., although he usually woke up around that time regardless, which annoyed him but might come in handy tomorrow. He figured he'd get up well before the couple would leave so he could watch for them and follow them when they came out. At this point, chances were they were getting it on in their hotel room the rest of the night. After all, if he were in a room with a girl like that, he'd have her melting in his bed in less than five minutes.

CHAPTER FOURTEEN

"Two Locals Wanted for Questioning in Murder" was the front-page headline when Rachel quickly checked the news back home, complete with large pictures of them both. Luke was implicated as her accomplice, believed to be acting on her behalf. The photo they'd chosen for her had been taken at a city council meeting not long ago. Too curious not to read what was being said about her, Rachel skimmed through the article. It was short, and the reporter was careful never to accuse, although she knew that usually mattered little to readers. They were guilty until proven innocent. There were some politically correct quotes from Captain Taylor, but the implication was clear—they were suspects in the murder case, and fleeing the area seemed to be the final evidence of their guilt. Add to that vague references to Rachel's "run-ins with the law a few years ago" and even she would consider them guilty after reading the article. Knowing her friends and clients would be seeing this bothered her to no end, but she had to remind herself there was nothing she could do about it, at least right now. The truth would come out eventually, she hoped, and then they would be cleared—although this could very well tarnish her reputation forever, depending how things turned out.

"Well, I guess if I can't get environmental work, I could always go into pet sitting." She laughed with half resignation, reaching over to pet Bella. On the other hand, she thought of her family seeing this article. Luckily her parents had been camping for a few nights in a remote area in Arizona and two days ago had sent her a quick text to let her know they barely had a cell signal and would be in touch a week later when they drove back to Yuma. She was thankful they couldn't read the news or use the phone. Her brothers, well, she would just have to deal with them later.

"OK, Bella, let's see what we can find out about our friends at Row Environmental." Bella moved slightly at the mention of her name but otherwise was used to Rachel talking to herself. Or as Rachel liked to say, she didn't talk to herself, she just kept Bella well informed. The basics were: Row Environmental, owned by Michael Row, had two offices. The original office was located in Elko, Nevada. Makes sense, she thought, since a lot of mining occurred in that area. They opened a second office several years ago in Douglas County, where they began to take on some forestry projects in addition to mining. That seemed a bit backward since the mining industry continued to soar, economically, while government-funded projects like forest management competed for ever-dwindling funds.

"Very interesting. So, Mr. Row, why would you invest in a less profitable line of work?" she mused out loud. Using one of Luke's passwords and a financial site he'd noted, she looked up the records for the business. It was an odd trend. Row Environmental had been operating in the negative more and more each year. Yet infused by sporadic sums of income every few months, they'd stayed open with at least half a dozen staff for the last five years while projects began to die off and accounts trended downward. They also shifted toward doing more forestry and local development projects around the same time the mysterious infusions of funds began. Regardless of the boosts from what looked like some questionable deposits, how this business hadn't yet closed its doors was beyond her. She also noted a list of about twenty consultants and firms subcontracted for work within the last five years. Below the names, three laboratories were listed. Two of them she'd heard of. The third was called SST Laboratories. Usually Rachel would at least recognize the name after having reviewed so many environmental projects in the past ten years, including mining, but she'd never heard of this group. Thankful for Luke's small portable printer, she sent the financials and website information to the device.

Rachel couldn't find much more information about SST Laboratories. They had one of those short generic websites, covered with several pictures of beakers and other lab garb next to two short sentences about what they did, and then a "Contact Us" page. No phone number or address listed anywhere on the site. She always thought commercial companies with websites that didn't give a phone number or address, instead forcing you to fill in a contact form that they may or may not respond to, were a bit shady.

She let out a frustrated sigh and leaned back right before hearing the click of the keycard scanner. The room door opened, and she looked up to see a very excited Luke holding up some white and pink papers.

"We have some work to do."

"Yes, we do," she responded, holding up the papers she'd just printed out while trying to hide her immense relief to seeing him unharmed and not running from men in dark-blue uniforms flashing badges around. After swapping stories, they sat together in front of Luke's laptop. "So let's check out this address on the pink sheet," Luke said, typing it in.

"Wait, this looks like the intersection where Joe was killed."

"Yes, and don't you agree it's a bit odd that it's not in the police notes or even listed with the information about his death? I mean, if not for the reporter interviewing bystanders, there might have been no reference at all."

Rachel peered in, reading the smaller text in the article. "Yes, and look at what that guy's quoted as saying there." She pointed.

Luke read the quote the reporter had included from a neighbor he'd interviewed: "I've lived nearby for over fifteen years and nothing like this has ever happened. This has always been such a safe intersection." He looked back up at Rachel.

"I'm thinking it was a setup. Someone wanted to murder Joe, and they succeeded," Luke said, sitting back in his chair.

~

"What's going on, Mike?" Jerome asked, anger in his voice radiating through the phone line. "Someone's dead and now that couple is wanted by the police? I thought the idea was to stay *under* the radar?" he yelled, trying to sound solid and angry but knowing his fear was probably reflected in his voice.

"Don't worry, it's under control. Things didn't go as originally planned, but the good news is Plan B is actually going to work out even better. You'll have what you need in time for the board meeting next month."

"I'd better, or we are all going down on this deal. Got it?"

"Yes, but like I said, don't worry, Jerome. It's coming along just fine, and some of the biggest hurdles are being resolved as we speak. Look, all these years I've helped you. Never steered you wrong. Stop worrying."

"And you've been well-compensated for it. Don't forget that," Jerome snapped. Slamming the phone down, he stood up and stomped out of his home office, much like a child throwing a temper tantrum. He hadn't realized Diane was home already, and her presence in the kitchen surprised him. She had apparently heard him yelling behind the closed door and was staring at him when he entered the room, a shocked expression on her face. He attempted to smile at her but knew he failed, so he decided to head over and pour himself a drink for distraction. She didn't pry into his business.

"Want a drink, honey?" he asked, although most of the time she declined or failed to respond altogether. He knew she didn't approve of his drinking habit, but he didn't care anymore.

"No thanks, Jerome. Sorry if I startled you, the show ended a bit sooner than we thought." She resumed stirring a pan of boiling pasta on the stove. "Is . . . everything okay?" she asked, although he could tell she was hesitant. He couldn't blame her. Sometimes he started ranting about something and just got more worked up as he talked about it. He truly did love her when they met and really had hoped to provide her with a better life. He thought he still loved her now, but he wasn't sure anymore. He sometimes wondered why she stayed with him. Maybe she felt trapped or apathetic after all of these years? He did wonder if getting involved with Mike on these projects throughout the last few years had just made things worse. When the opportunity first came up to work on a project together, he'd actually thought it might help his marriage.

He poured the whiskey and managed to respond with more calmness than he felt. "Just your brother, being himself," he said, hoping it would end the discussion.

"Yeah, Mike can be a pain sometimes, for sure," she agreed. He nodded, turned, walked back to his office, and shut his door, all the while avoiding eye contact with her.

~

Luke and Rachel sat at the small round table, squeezed together as much as the cheap hotel chairs would allow, looking at the hard copies of the will in front of them that he'd brought back from Joe's office. Rachel leaned in next to him, and Luke couldn't help but notice the sweet smell of vanilla that always radiated from her. He shook his head and refocused.

"This looks like what Melanie and Janet were referring to. Spencer gets most of the liquid assets along with ownership of several properties, although it doesn't all take effect until he's twenty-five. The rest were to be donated to the public or various charities."

"Which, of course, Spencer was already well beyond that age when Lloyd died," Rachel noted.

"Doesn't seem to fly if someone altered the will. Why would they put that age clause in there?"

"You know, I've seen people do this before. People think if something looks too perfect, it probably won't be believed. So, they add something that would seem less desirable, thinking it will improve the lie. In this case, if Lloyd went from complaining about his grandson to suddenly giving him the full inheritance the moment he died, it might raise some questions. But add a few clauses that put some restrictions on it and maybe it seems a bit more legitimate. People accept the change without a lot of questions."

"Kind of makes sense . . . in a slightly twisted way." Luke nodded, adding, "How about we compare these two other pages?" They set the two duplicate pages next to each other and began comparing the language. The differences were obvious from the first line, which on the first wrinkled page began with the following:

> Spencer shall receive an annual salary beginning at $70,000 per year and increasing based on inflation, so long as he continues to work as a representative of the Wells' family interests for the first five years following my death. At this time, he will receive no more money from the Wells Family Trust, unless he has proven a valuable employee to the Board, at which time the Board may vote to hire him at their discretion.

"There's supposed to be a board set up for the estate?" he heard Rachel ask, partly to herself.

"Yeah, clearly different than the original, or rather the fake. It looks like Spencer was supposed to continue pursuing Lloyd's wishes."

After a brief description of what the position would entail, a new paragraph began:

> The estate's funds will continue to be administered
> by Mrs. Janet Fields, or her appointee, and approval
> of any purchases and donations will require the
> majority vote of the Board established by this will.

The document continued with more legal language that was too much for Luke. "OK, you spend your days buried in legal stuff kind of like this. Do you mind reading this last part and translating? My eyes are starting to get crossed."

"I'll try." She leaned in closer to read the remaining text on the page. He tried to continue looking at the documents, but he couldn't help himself. As she'd leaned forward, a strand of loose hair had fallen to the side of her cheek, and it took everything he had not to reach over and tuck it behind her ear. He'd noticed she didn't like loose hairs hanging in her face.

Luke may have lost his internal struggle and reached out had she not sat up a bit straighter and began to talk. "I'm no lawyer, but it looks like there's a list of properties that were supposed to be donated for public preservation. In cases where the agreements weren't finalized, the board was supposed to review the drafts and make sure the final transfers to public ownership occurred. No mention of Spencer at all."

"Well, I'm going to state the obvious here; I think we agree that someone swapped out the will. That might explain why it looked like the file cabinet had already been broken into before. And why the attorney was killed."

"So if Spencer received all of this money, since he was already over twenty-five when Lloyd died, why wasn't he off spending it in some spring-break town?"

"Good question. Maybe he was expecting a better payoff in

the future?" Luke speculated.

"OK, but then there's another thing that doesn't make sense. Whether Spencer came by his money legally or otherwise, either way, what benefit could it be to someone else if he's dead? He's not married, has no children, and no other family to speak of that I could find."

"Now that's a good question," Luke added. "But, at the moment, I'm so tired that I can't seem to concentrate anymore."

"I'm with you on that," Rachel yawned. He walked with her to take Bella out one last time before they each collapsed on the two beds. Yes, he was beat, but it didn't stop him from imagining her crawling into his bed next to him, that soft skin pressing against his. With that image in mind, Luke drifted to sleep, a smile on his lips.

CHAPTER FIFTEEN

It was early morning, and Ted sat in the small kitchen of his apartment, having opted for caffeinated tea, something he rarely drank. It had been a late night after the incident in the evidence room. Knowing the station was manned by one or two officers after hours, and unable to sleep until he'd looked around the evidence room at least once more, he'd gone back to the office. As expected, though, he found nothing.

Barely awake after just a few hours of sleep, with his green tea and a bowl of oatmeal, Ted spread out the pictures he'd taken of the blood smear and fingerprints across the table in front of him. Maybe with a fresh view he might notice something new. With the bright morning sun beaming on his small kitchen table, he saw it; rather, it was what he didn't see—dirt. When he'd found the body and the bloody rock next to it, the blood on the rock wasn't dirty. If someone had knocked this kid over the head with the rock, then tossed it down or dropped it, it should have rolled, causing the dirt to stick to the wet blood. But it was clean—as if someone had set the rock down strategically next to the body, bloody side up—which begged even more questions. How did Luke's print get on the rock, and, presuming his suspicions were correct, where was the rock that had actually been used to bash the victim's head?

Back at the office around nine a.m. he picked up the phone and dialed the ME. "Good morning, Jill. Guess who?" he teased. He'd been friends with Jillian since they were kids, so there were no formal greetings needed. He had also been repeatedly warned never to call her by her full first name. Apparently she'd been named after a great-grandmother who had not been the type of ancestor that inspired Jill.

"Teddy, hey. I wanted to talk to you the other day on that trail, but I was too busy training the new lab assistant."

Jill's new assistant, Tracy, a younger blonde woman with shoulder-length hair and zebra-colored eyeglass frames, was slow to pick things up. But Jill said she was smart, and once she learned something she quickly jumped in and did great work. "No problem. It was a long, crazy day. How late were you out there?"

"Well, we got back here around eight, I think."

"Not bad, all things considered. Do you have the kids this morning?"

"No, they spent last night with *their dad*." Jill said this last part as if spitting. Ted knew she was going through a pretty nasty divorce while trying to keep things easier on the kids. Unfortunately, it usually meant she went out of her way to accommodate the cheating bastard she'd married when he made spontaneous schedule changes or requests involving the kids.

"Yeah, how are they doing?"

"Okay, I guess. Apparently the new girlfriend has a small dog. I think they like the dog more than the girlfriend," she laughed. "So, calling to check in or need some actual work-related information?"

"How about both? But first, Jill, let me know if I can do anything. I know you're trying to keep things friendlier for the kids' sake, but he's taking advantage of that."

"I know . . . just not sure what's best yet. Thanks for the

offer. You said you had an official reason for calling?" He sensed she didn't want to talk about the soon-to-be ex anymore.

"Yes. I'll preface it by saying I know it may be a long shot, but I was wondering if I could send you some pictures of the rock we found with that kid's body and see if you see what I'm seeing."

"Sure, e-mail them over."

He clicked his mouse. "They are on the way as we speak."

"OK, here it is. Let me get these open. Hold on just a second."

As he imagined her peering closely at her two computer monitors, comparing several pictures at once, it occurred to him it might be a good idea to continue this conversation in a more private setting. He looked around and saw that Captain Taylor wasn't in yet, so he walked into his office and shut the door. He could still see the station through the large window in the office. Apparently even a captain couldn't get full privacy. He heard Jill moving around a bit, as if shifting the phone from one ear to another, then sigh and ask, "OK, what should I be seeing here?"

"How about this—if someone drops or throws a rock down after hitting someone with it hard enough to kill them, wouldn't you expect some dirt might get stuck to the fresh blood?"

"Hmm, very interesting. Let me zoom in a bit more."

As he waited, hearing the sounds of a mouse clicking, Ted glanced out the interior office window and saw Leona return to her desk. She looked around but didn't seem to notice he was in the captain's office. Instead of taking her sweater off and getting set up in her chair like she did every morning, she peered around the room again and walked to Ted's chair to look at his monitor. Then it hit him. In his haste to find an office, he hadn't cleared the "message sent" notice that had popped up after he'd e-mailed Jill. Unless Leona selected the message, it would only reveal whom he had e-mailed and a paper-clip icon noting there was an attachment. She stared at it a moment longer with a look of mild confusion, walked back around to her chair, and sat down. After the customary removal of the sweater, she began typing intently on her own keyboard.

"Ted? You still there?" He heard Jill's voice on the phone and realized he'd spaced out, intent on watching what Leona was doing.

"Oh, yes, sorry about that. I just noticed something that caught my attention for a few seconds. What were you saying?"

"That you had a good point. The blood in this picture does look too clean. Can you get me the rock for comparison before the afternoon?"

"Well, that's going to be a problem. It was removed from the evidence locker late yesterday, and I have no idea who did it."

"You mean someone broke in? How could they do that?"

"Actually they walked in the front door. I think they spiked the security kid's lunch with something, like a fast-acting laxative, and then took advantage of his mad dash to the bathroom."

"He didn't lock the door I take it? What about video?" Jill sounded exasperated.

"No, he didn't, and the camera was tampered with when the person came into the room," Ted sighed.

"My God. So what you're saying is . . . wow, I'm going to guess no one else knows what you've discovered about this blood smear?"

"No, and I think it's best to keep it that way for now."

"Understood. I've got something I can look at here on the body, so give me about five minutes and I'll call you back," she said.

"Thanks, Jill."

Not wanting to wait in the captain's office for what might look to an observer like snooping, he decided to go back to his desk until she called back. Just as he turned, something shiny on the captain's floor caught his eye, and he bent over to see what it was—a cuff link. But it seemed a bit fancy for the captain. Boasting his initials, it was obviously silver and lined with small stones he assumed were cubic zirconia—or maybe they were the real thing. Ted wouldn't know the difference. He looked at it one more time, thinking he'd never seen the captain wear cuff links that . . . *ritzy*, but then again, he never paid much attention when the man wore a suit. Setting it on the captain's mouse pad, he opened the door and headed back to his desk. Leona was still focused on her computer, but when she looked up, he had the feeling he'd startled her.

"Mornin'. Sorry if I snuck up on you—had a personal call, so I snuck into the cap's office."

"No problem. Everything okay?"

"Yes, fine. Thanks for asking. Hey, I'm going to hit the vending machine and grab a snack. Want anything?"

She nodded no, quickly focusing back on her screen. He walked into the back room and decided he'd better make his story real, so he pulled some change from his pocket and walked over to junk-food central. He noticed Shelby, talking with another officer nearby, Norton or Nolan, he couldn't quite remember. The guy had worked in a separate division and usually made no effort to communicate with anyone else, so it was curious to see him chatting up Shelby. It didn't look like they noticed him, and Ted walked out the back door, hoping to appear to any curious onlooker to be taking a quick break outside.

Right on time, his cell rang. "Hey, Ted," said Jill's voice on the other end in an odd tone. "Are we okay to talk freely?" she asked carefully.

"Yes, I decided to grab some fresh air out back."

She dropped to almost a whisper. "Good. I compared the rock's shape where the blood smear was to the wound on the victim's head. Although the shapes seem similar at first glance, when you look closer, there's a slight knob on the rock underneath the smear. With the strength and pressure that had to be behind this blow to the head, the impression of that knob should have been detectable in the kid's wound. It's not there. And when I zoomed into those pictures with a new program Tracy had us sign up for, I can see what looks like lines in the blood on the rock you found. Unfortunately, without the rock itself, I don't think I could say this definitively in court. It would be speculation at best." She paused. "Unless you could find the actual rock that was used."

He was already on the same page. "Thanks, Jill. I guess I'm looking at another hike. And Jill, I don't know what this is going to lead to, but I'll keep you out of it the best I can."

"Appreciate it. Oh, wait a minute. Actually, I have something else for you. I ran the kid's prints once we got him in here, and he wasn't showing up on any recent databases. But I know when I was a kid they had us printed in case we ever got kidnapped. So I started a search going back twenty or so years, and they matched a sealed juvie record. I don't have access to open it or get the name, but I have a file number if it helps."

"You, my friend, are a goddess. Yes, let me grab something to write on."

Ten minutes later, Ted had looked up an old friend's number and went out to his Explorer to make the call in private.

The line picked up after two rings. "Hey, Franklin—it's Ted. How's the wife?" he asked.

"Still living with me, unfortunately," Franklin chuckled. Ted knew that regardless of the wife jokes his old friend always threw out, the man loved his wife dearly and would do anything for her. "So, what can I do for you, my lucky single friend?"

"I've got a juvie file here that matches the prints we found on a murder victim. I was hoping you could check the system and get me a name so I can officially identify him."

"That shouldn't be a problem." After Ted read off the file name, he heard the sound of Franklin slowly tapping on the keyboard, one key at a time. He wasn't one of the world's fastest typists, but he was great at the part of his job that mattered—

helping troubled youth who had ended up tangling with the law. A moment later, Franklin said, "I've got a name. Just remind me that you know you didn't get it from me? I have a feeling looking this up may be a bit of a grey area."

"No problem."

"All right, the kid's name was Spencer Wells, Junior. Looks like he was born in 1979 and got into a few bad situations about the time he hit his teens."

Ted repeated the name as he wrote it down. "Franklin, man, I really appreciate it." Then he paused and added, "And tell that beautiful wife of yours I love her to death, but please no more matchmaking." He chuckled, thinking of the friend of a friend he'd been set up with who spent the entire dinner conversation talking about her ex-boyfriends.

Franklin laughed. "I'll try, but you know Ginny, she's determined. Anyway, good luck on that case, Ted." The call ended.

Ted redialed Jill and gave her Spencer's information. He tried the door to go back inside, but it had automatically locked when he'd closed it. He walked around the side of the building just in time to notice Captain Taylor finally arriving, parking in his assigned spot a few spaces away. Again driving the shiny, too-clean-for-the-mountains Lexus, it looked like he was in deep conversation with someone on his earpiece. Ron noticed Ted coming around the building and waved at him distractedly.

Returning to his desk, Ted waited ten minutes, but Ron had yet to come inside. So he stuck a short note on the man's monitor—leaving a note instead of sending an e-mail had been a very specific request from Captain Taylor to his staff. He was not fond of e-mails. Ted quickly scrawled that an emergency had come up and he might be out for the remainder of the afternoon. Signing with his apologies, he left the note and went back out to his SUV, glad he still had his hiking boots in back. As he quickly changed his shoes, he saw that the captain still sat in his car, head down, right arm shifting like he was writing something. This time, he didn't seem to notice Ted.

~

Ron finished his call and headed into the office building, holding a paper coffee cup in one hand and his bag in the other, still preoccupied by the phone call. Although he had noticed Ted leaving, he didn't think much of it.

"Hey, Ron." Chief Tim Parker's voice broke through his concentration. Apparently Ron had just brushed past Tim—he could never bring himself to call him TIP like the others—who was accompanied by the officer that seemed to be stuck to Tim's side lately. He stopped, feeling a bit embarrassed, and smiled back at the two.

"Oh, sorry about that, Tim. Got something on my mind."

Tim smiled, although the intent stare from the young rookie standing next to him gave Ron the spooks. "I just saw your guy Ted take off a few minutes ago. What's he working on these days?"

"Not quite sure why he left now, but chances are there's a note on my computer screen. He's good about that." The implication being not everyone else was. "It's probably related to the murder case. I gave him the okay to look at that rock evidence one more time. Something about it was bugging him, and his instincts are usually right on. I was out all afternoon yesterday, so I'm not sure if he found anything new. Now that I think about it, he was changing his shoes before he left."

"A bit early in the day for a lunch break, isn't it, Captain?" the smirking younger officer said, his tone and expression reminding Ron of his own son during his rude teenage years.

"Lenny, is it?" Ron turned to the young man.

"Leo*nard*," he said back, emphasizing the second syllable. Ron didn't know the kid very well but knew he'd been working in various capacities at the department for some time, although the recent attachment to the chief remained a mystery to them all.

Tim broke the awkward silence that followed, saying with what seemed to be fake lightheartedness, "I was just curious. OK, Leonard, time to hit the road again." He smiled, and the two walked away.

Ron strolled back toward his office, curious about the exchange, but quickly dismissing it. He looked at his screen, and sure enough there was Ted's note.

~

"One of the officers may be heading back out there," the voice said when Mike picked up the phone.

"Do you know why?"

"No, not even sure he's going there, but I thought I'd call, just in case."

Mike sighed, trying not to worry. "Can't imagine what would be left to find anyway. Well, thanks for the heads up." The call disconnected, and Mike sat for a moment, pondering what to do. But what could he do? He had no one he could send. Regardless, was he willing to take out a cop? No, that would probably create a mess he didn't need. Well, let the guy go fish around—there's nothing left to find. And if there was, he knew he could bury it.

~

"I'm not a fan of continental breakfasts," Rachel said as she stared at the selection of puffy doughnuts and other items that, to her, were just a big pile of colorful sugar and carbohydrates.

"Agreed."

As she reluctantly reached for a bowl of cereal off to the side, she asked, "Got enough caffeine in you yet?"

"It's five thirty in the morning. It's not possible to have enough coffee yet," Luke exclaimed.

"Good point."

"You seem to be handling the early hour well enough," Luke said. "Quite a change."

"No, I'm still struggling on the inside. So please keep your sentences short and easy. In fact, how about we take Bella out for a quick stroll? That will help wake us up."

"I walked right into that one, didn't I?" he laughed. She nodded, grabbing the box of cereal and container of soy milk, figuring it was the lesser of all evils.

"I'm still surprised Bella is allowed to walk with those stitches."

"Yes, I asked the vet before we left. She's a high-energy pup, and trying to completely contain her would be a nightmare. He said she's fine, just keep the walks mellow."

An hour later, they were strolling on a nearby paved path already crowded with people out getting their morning jog before rushing to work.

"So, if the will was changed illegally, with Joe dead, would there be a way to prove it? Find the original will?" Rachel asked.

"I've been wondering that myself. It seems like if he had set up some kind of board to oversee his estate, he'd have talked to some of those folks beforehand about it. It doesn't seem like something you'd spring on someone unexpectedly in your will."

"But would a board member have a copy of the will in advance, regardless?"

"Good point," Luke responded after taking another large gulp of coffee. "I wouldn't expect so. OK, let's suppose someone gets in there and changes the will. Joe's security was almost nonexistent, so that's not a stretch. But, before Joe can access the will to even notice it was changed, he gets a call that makes him rush to the address on the pink slip. He's dead, so someone else accesses his files to read Lloyd's will, never realizing it wasn't the original."

"You said earlier you thought he might have a copy of the original at home? Even if he did, would it still be there now?" she pondered.

"Chances are it's been cleared out and rented or sold by now, but it can't hurt to try. Especially considering his office hasn't been packed up yet after all of this time," Luke replied, taking another sip of coffee. "So, what do you think?"

"You got his home address?" Rachel perked up.

"Yes. Somewhere in Arvada."

"That's a suburb just north of here." She remembered the times she'd driven that way when she lived in the area, often heading up to play in the mountains off Highway 70 or up to Boulder. "We can take Wadsworth Avenue, which isn't too far."

"OK, I nominate you to drive then," he laughed. When they returned to the hotel, the parking lot was busy with people packing up to leave. This must be checkout rush hour, Rachel thought, thankful they'd already packed the truck before the walk so they were able to quickly leave without going back inside.

"I think that's the house," Luke said fifteen minutes later as Rachel drove by a medium-sized light-brown ranch-style home with a "For Sale" sign out front.

"Should I park here?"

"No, let's head up a block first and then pull off." He looked around as she drove slowly on by. "Actually, the for-sale sign works in our favor. There are two other homes for sale here."

"Park here?" she asked, and Luke nodded. "What are you thinking we should do now?"

"We can play a young couple looking for a home to buy. Although there aren't many people around, if we are seen peeking into backyards, looking in windows—that wouldn't seem too out of place, right?" He smiled, held up the small black case of his special tool kit, and tucked it into an inside pocket in the light jacket he was wearing.

"I'm supposed to pretend to be your wife? Not sure I can pull *that* one off," she said halfheartedly joking. Not only was it *Luke*, but she couldn't even imagine being someone's wife. She'd been alone for way too long and, especially after the ordeal with Matt, had been focusing on other things—although she always hoped one day she would meet Mr. Right—she was just in no hurry.

As Luke opened his door and stepped out, he responded,

"Actually, I think you could play the spoiled, ever-annoyed wife quite well, Ms. Independent." She looked at him, and he winked. Such an arrogant gesture but strangely affectionate, too. She climbed out, unable to come up with a witty response, try as she might to think of something. Instead she leashed Bella, helped her out of the truck, careful of the sutures, and came around the other side where Luke was waiting.

"OK, I'll follow your lead, *sweetheart*. Well, for now."

"Come on, *honey*." He smiled and grabbed her hand. She wasn't expecting that. His hand was warm. Soft but calloused. She wasn't sure what part of his job that would be from. Perhaps the biking. Her first instinct was to pull away, more so she wouldn't be thinking about that kiss the night before than because she wanted to make a point at the moment. She left her hand in his and fell in step beside him.

~

Scott had watched them finally emerge from the hotel earlier that morning, load their truck, and unexpectedly walk away. It took a moment to realize they were taking the dog for a walk. That would work quite well, he thought. Early morning jaunt along a discreet trail, easy approach, easy retreat. That was, until he saw the crowds of people on the trail. Instead, he fell in step about twenty feet or so behind them, trying to appear like just another casual morning walker, getting some fresh air before work. After a while, he watched as they stopped, briefly discussed something, then turned back around. That pause was just enough for him to lean over and pretend to tie his shoe. The dog was on a leash and as they walked by, the mutt had tried to pull toward him. He heard Rachel call out something, and although hesitant at first, the dog gave in and turned back to follow them. *Too damn close.* Scott wasn't sure if Rachel would recognize him after almost ten years, but best not take the chance. Well, only until he had them where he wanted them. Then he'd be glad to have a little reunion with Miss Winters.

Unfortunately, he never got the chance. He couldn't believe how many people were out that early in the morning, walking dogs or jogging. Back at the hotel, everyone apparently checked out at the same time, resulting in a busy parking lot. Too many potential witnesses meant he was now stuck following them north into suburbia. When they'd taken a few turns on residential streets and then parked, he'd hung back farther, stopping a couple of blocks away, watching.

CHAPTER SIXTEEN

Rachel followed Luke's lead as they walked up to the first house, looked in the windows, and walked around the sides. Repeat on house two. There didn't seem to be anyone around. Everyone must be at work or indoors.

"All right, still think you can handle a little breaking and entering? I know that goes against, well, *you*."

"Hey now, I've got a dangerous side," Rachel quipped. She saw him about to protest this statement and cut in. "But, OK, it's usually involving legal things."

"Uh-huh."

"Speaking of which, were you really a cop?" she asked sarcastically, as they moved to the side of the house and peered into another window, continuing their act for anyone who might be watching. There were quite a few large bushes and trees around these suburban houses, so she felt a bit more sheltered. Rachel had learned how much of a landscaping nightmare it could be when she lived here and had to care for the yard of the home she rented, but it was certainly great cover for them now. Joe's house had a solid wooden fence lining his property that looked about fifteen years old. The side fence was hanging open.

"Look at this backyard, honey," he said, a bit louder than

necessary, then added with a whisper, "Yes, I was a cop, and by the way, that's why so far I've been able to save your ass. You're welcome." His last two words were dripping with sarcasm as well. She had learned they shared a similar sense of humor—which she liked. Before she could respond, he abruptly stopped in front of her.

"Oh, crap!"

"What happened?" she said, concerned.

"Crap." He pointed down where he'd just stepped in a fresh pile of poop and began trying to slide his shoe on the nearby lawn.

"Oh."

As he continued trying to wipe off his shoe, she walked up the back porch, Bella in tow behind her. She was looking at a large sliding glass door. Usually there were extra locks up top or below, or the good old-fashioned wooden-stick-in-the-bottom-panel method. Luke came up next to her.

"This might be easier than I'd thought. See any security rods or anything?" he inquired, still bending over to check his tread.

"Nope," she said. Then, repeating the same thing she'd done when breaking into her parent's old place, she slipped the door up and over and casually walked inside. Luke was still clearing off his shoe when she called out over her shoulder as she walked. "Door's open if you wanted to come inside." A few seconds passed and she heard him laugh, but he didn't follow her in yet. She stopped to wait in what looked like the main family room. Bella remained next to her.

"Says the girl whose paranoid about anything remotely criminal, eh?" She turned back toward him and watched as he pulled a cloth from his back pocket and wiped away her prints. "*Amateurs*."

She couldn't help but smile. A moment later she looked around. "The house is completely empty."

"Well, you never know what we could find. Or where people

might hide things. He lived alone, and his death was obviously unexpected. Maybe he left something that no one knew about," Luke surmised.

"Do you really believe that?"

"Not really. But then I also didn't believe you'd come in here with me. So I'm thinking anything is possible right now." He smiled. "I say we fish around a bit. One thing to keep in mind is that the guy could have backup copies on paper, or they could be on a thumb drive. If it's the latter, it could be hidden just about anywhere. But, based on his office, I hold out hope he was a bit old-fashioned."

They checked the kitchen, living area, and bathroom and found nothing. "I'm going to look for a basement while you check those other bedrooms."

"I'll also look for a door to the garage," Luke said.

Rachel looked around for doors that might lead to a downstairs area. After opening what had first appeared to be another closet door, she saw a descending staircase and called out to Luke as she fished for a light switch and found one just inside the door.

"Found it." He joined her and they carefully walked down into the room, which appeared to be much like the basement-turned-bedroom she'd had in the place she rented in Littleton. Half of the walls had been covered in drywall, with the other half still showing the two-by-four frames. Even the walls around the staircase hadn't been completely paneled yet, although that might have been on purpose, to leave room for the storage area she noticed underneath the stairs. Bella had found the open spot and began sniffing, tail wagging.

"Hope she hasn't scented some mice."

Luke didn't respond right away, instead moving in to get a closer look inside the half-enclosed space. "You know what? I think this open space here should be larger." He crawled halfway inside, and Rachel kneeled nearby, pulling Bella back to give him more room. He felt around the walls inside the opening. "The texture is different here than the other sides." He seemed to be talking to himself, continuing to feel around and becoming more frustrated by the minute. Then he let slip a quiet "son of a . . ." as he kicked the wall in frustration, and they both stared for a moment at the half-inch gap that had just appeared on one side.

"How about that?" he laughed. She saw him look closely at the bottom of the door that had just moved, and he grabbed at something. "There's some kind of thin wire here, probably to pull it shut. I guess we figured out how to open it, although I bet it was much easier when he lived here."

As he pushed the door in all the way, Rachel squeezed herself into the spot next to him, curious to see what was inside. The small space looked to be roughly four feet wide and two feet tall, and it sloped down in back with the bottom of the staircase. The sides were lined with several white office boxes with letters hastily written on the sides. "Wow, he *was* old school."

"I know it's not good for the trees, but right now I'm loving the old days," Luke said, reaching for the first box. "OK, this one says A–F."

Rachel grabbed the next one, but, as suspected, it was the one tucked farthest back that had the Ws. She slid it out so she could see inside better, took the lid off, and began searching through the individual folders. A moment later, she struck gold. "And here it is—Wells, Lloyd." They examined it. "Well, it certainly doesn't match the will from the office folder," she noted, although two of the pages were familiar. "How can we prove this is the actual will?"

"They have ways of detecting alterations. I figure no one had any reason to look, but now they do. Or will, when we get this straightened out. I say we grab this and get going," Luke said. They put the other boxes away, used the wire to shut the storage bin, and crawled back into the main room. And that's when they heard it—the sound of a creaking floorboard overhead. Rachel's heart froze, and she looked at Luke, scared but focused enough to remember to put her hand in front of Bella's nose to signal no barking. She just hoped the pup obeyed. It was one of the commands they were still working on, so it was fifty-fifty that Bella would understand.

"Think it's a realtor? Prospective buyer?" she whispered.

Luke mouthed, "Too quiet." She watched him look around and stare for a second at the only window in the room. He leaned in closer toward her ear, and she felt his warm breath tickle her neck. "I think you and Bella can get through that window, but it's pretty rusty so it's going to make noise to get it open. I need you two to hide while I distract him, or them; then break that thing open and run."

"But what about you?"

"Remember—I was a cop; I can handle it," he smiled. She could tell he was nervous, too, but he was right. This was his job. "You and Bella get back inside that storage space, and I'll try to distract whoever it is. Give me about one minute, and then get yourselves up and out that window. Wait for me on the north side of the second house we looked at, OK? And . . . if I don't get the chance to distract him, stay in there. If realtors didn't find it, I doubt he would, so it's probably the safest place." She nodded, not wanting to think about what it meant if he "didn't get the chance," and went back into the crawl space and quietly pushed the door open. She squeezed herself and Bella inside, holding her breath as she pushed it closed. She tried not to panic. She had a big problem with small spaces. But, Rachel told herself, she had no choice but to deal with it; otherwise she could be dead. She had an even bigger problem with being dead.

~

His back and shoulder again throbbing from his recent fall, Scott had popped two pain pills and sat in his rental car, watching the couple park and get out of their truck, followed by that damn dog. The creature was probably treated better than most human kids he knew. Confused about what they were doing on this suburban side street, and certainly very curious, he had patiently watched them stroll down the sidewalk, hand in hand, looking like they didn't have a care in the world and peeking into several houses for sale. When they didn't return from snooping around the back of the third one, he knew something was up.

Scott looked around again and saw no signs of anyone else in the area. He casually walked toward the house and grabbed one of the brochures attached to the sign along the way. The front door was locked, as expected, so he'd slowly walked around the side and through the gate to the backyard. His movements were slow and quiet, in part because the dog might be loose back there somewhere and part because he didn't want to alert them to his presence. A few more steps and he noticed the fresh smeared footprints heading up the steps of the back porch, where a sliding glass door stood open just enough for him to slip inside without having to open it farther.

Once inside he'd heard the murmur of voices from somewhere down the hallway. Perfect. He couldn't have planned it any better. Poor couple on the run, breaking into a house up for sale so they could hide from the law, only to be killed by some anonymous squatter. Following the voices, he advanced carefully down the hallway. They were somewhere below his level. In a basement. Just a few more steps and he'd be by the open door ahead. But then, the board creaked under his foot. The voices stopped. The element of surprise was gone. But no reason to worry. He still had them right where he wanted them. Piece of cake.

~

Jack decided reviewing the sample results he'd run for David might help provide some clues about his whereabouts, so he sat down with the reports and carefully studied them. After some online searching, he'd already found that several environmental companies had hired David as an independent hydrologist over the years. But the chemistry in the water samples suggested they were from a pine forest, not the desert. So maybe he could rule out David's projects with the companies that dealt with mining. That left a few firms with projects in forested areas of the northern Sierra Nevada.

In the samples he'd run, half of them had too much suspended sediment to be natural. He'd tried to explain to his wife once that this was like "floating dirt," with some of the soil particles being so small you had to view them with special equipment. But too much "floating dirt" in the water and it could change the environment of downstream systems, such as lakes and ponds fed by streams and rivers. Something else he'd screened was also too high to be natural—the nitrogen in the water. This he had also explained to his wife once, comparing it to when humans get sick from taking too high a dose of certain vitamins. Some amount of nitrogen is natural, and high nitrogen concentrations aren't uncommon next to places like golf courses, where heavy amounts of fertilizer—which contains nitrogen—are used to provide the dense green lawns everyone loves so much. But this was like someone had literally stirred a bag of fertilizer into a bucket filled with water and collected the sample before anything could settle out. The other half of the samples measured far better. Not perfectly clean, but more like what you'd expect to see in a mountain stream or river affected by eroding hillsides or minor human disturbance. The high levels of sediment could create a lot of problems, both in natural settings and man-made systems, like facilities designed to help handle storm-water runoff. He knew in some areas—like Lake Tahoe, which wasn't far from where David lived—it was also a concern with regard to the clarity of lakes that just decades ago were so clear people could see deep down through the water. As more human development around lakes like Tahoe caused more sediment to enter the water bodies, that clarity had been lost.

Add too much nitrogen and it makes things that much worse,

leading to problems such as fish kills and bad odors, and it can destroy the natural processes that keep the environment in balance. Although a concern for outdoor enthusiasts and fishermen, the implications stretch well beyond the damaged bodies of water. When tasked with public presentations about his work in places well removed from forested lands, he always said, "Anyone who drinks or pays for water coming from the forest should definitely be concerned about what's going on in the forest, even if you never leave your home."

"What are you involved in, my friend?" he said out loud, although alone in the room. Next, Jack looked into the geology of the areas in the vicinity of where David lived and worked. The type of rocks and soil could help narrow the locations as well, and he was soon confident that the samples came from a forested area on the eastern side of the ridgeline of the Sierra Nevada. With this knowledge fresh in his mind, he plugged in the websites for the forest service office that managed the projects in those areas where David might have been working. There were two. One, the West Hills Erosion Control and Forest Recycling Project, had been started several years ago and appeared to be focused on reducing erosion using wood chips to improve water quality. The other project focused more on stabilizing the road cuts along some local highways.

If he had to select between the two, he thought to himself, he'd expect typical samples from a roadway runoff project to contain oil and other chemicals. They didn't. So the most likely source was the West Hills project, although he'd tell Officer Choe about both options just to be thorough. Maybe David was out collecting more samples and stumbled and broke his ankle. It would make sense. Cell service is poor in the mountains. That would also explain why no employer had reported him missing.

CHAPTER SEVENTEEN

Luke slowly made his way back up the steps, gun in hand. The person—he hoped it *was* just one—knew they were down there, and their silence would confirm they'd heard the intruder. Well, the *other* intruder. Given where it came from, the guy must be down the hallway, the same direction they'd come from. He knew the rest of the hallway was pale with half-filtered sunlight. Once he shut off the basement light, he'd be in the dark, and he'd have just a split second before the guy's eyes adjusted enough to make him out. Luke had to be smart and fast.

He quickly turned the light off and ducked low to the staircase. A gunshot rang out just as he heard the chipping sound of a bullet entering the wall inches above him. The guy knew how to aim. Still staying low, he immediately fired back in the direction of the shooter. His bullet hit low. Bending around the doorway made shooting from his position awkward. He felt relief as he heard a quick sound of pain and the man's form stumbled, dropping down on one knee. Eyes adjusted, Luke could make out that the man was tall, thin, and fairly young looking. In fact, his form reminded Luke of the man in the hoodie back on the trail. He could give that more thought later. It looked like Luke's shot had hit flesh—a good, painful wound but nothing that would kill the guy. There wouldn't be much time before the perp recovered enough to take aim again, and by now he could probably see Luke better.

"I'm aiming right at your head. I wouldn't try that again if I were you." Luke was bluffing. His position prevented him from getting a clear shot, but he hoped the man wouldn't figure that out right away. There was a tense moment of complete silence, broken by the slightest scraping sound resonating from the basement below. Rachel was opening the window—and the attacker had just figured that out. He raised his gun to shoot again in Luke's general direction, but Luke was faster. This time Luke's bullet grazed the man's wrist, causing him to drop his gun. The guy bolted up and stumbled as he attempted to run toward the back door. Luke was able to catch up to him just before he got there. Both men appeared to see, at the same time, that Rachel and Bella were running across the yard.

Fueled by anger, fear, and a strong protective instinct he'd never felt before, Luke slammed the handle of his gun down hard and with precision. The guy fell to the ground with a thud. He felt for the man's pulse. Slow but steady. With a shaky voice, still struggling to catch his breath, he called out as loud as he could.

"Rachel, it's clear."

"I know; you don't need to yell so loud." She was already entering through the open doorway. That was far too fast, he thought.

"Please tell me you are just a fast sprinter, because if not, I'd have to worry that you didn't listen to me and were coming back while I was still dealing with this idiot," he said with a mix of anger and fear. She didn't respond to that and instead looked at him with her own expression of concern.

"Are you hit?"

"No, the blood's all his," he sighed. No point in lecturing her now. She was safe; he was safe. "Bella?"

"She's fine. I told her to wait just to the side of the yard, and thankfully she listened." She turned around and called out, "Bella, come here girl." He noticed the shakiness in her voice. She was still scared but doing a great job of holding herself together.

"Good girl." Then Luke couldn't help himself—he had to say it. "You should take pointers from her." He wasn't sure if Rachel heard his teasing comment as she was leaning over to greet Bella at that moment. It was probably best to let it go. He spoke up again. "Look, I doubt we have much time now. The safest bet is to assume a neighbor heard the gunshots and has already called the cops. Grab his gun while I search him, and let's get out of here," he said, nodding in the direction of the gun lying on the floor.

One hand holding the papers they'd discovered downstairs, Rachel reached for it with her free hand, and he noticed a slight tremble in her hand. Then she paused. "You know I hate guns. Can you make sure the safety's on first? I don't want to trip and accidently shoot you. At least, not today." He was impressed. Here she was, standing there, smiling and joking, after what just happened.

"Rachel, you amaze me," he said under his breath. As he was reaching to slip the safety switch on the gun, she stared intently at the unconscious man on the floor.

"He kind of looks familiar, but I can't be sure. Does he have any ID?"

"No, and I didn't get the chance to ask him before he shot at me." If she was able to joke around, well, good. He would, too.

"Very funny. So, do your investigator thing—check his pockets or whatever." He gave her a wry smile, handed her the gun—handle first—then searched the guy's pockets.

"No ID. But there's a set of rental agency keys for a Camry, at least according to the tag."

"What should we do now?"

"Well, as much as I don't want to turn on my own phone, we need to get some pictures of this guy. I have a few friends who might be able to help us figure out who he is. Then again, I was more worried about the killer finding us by tracking our phones than the cops, and I guess that's pretty much irrelevant at this point." He turned on his cell phone as he stood up and took several pictures from a variety of angles while Rachel seemed to examine the gun. Finally, she stood still and gripped it carefully.

"All right, let's get out of here." Luke grabbed her hand again, this time without even thinking about it, and they walked toward the door and retraced their path back to the truck, Bella following at their heels. Pretending to be a calm couple was definitely out the window now. They both carried guns, although they were trying their best to shield them along their sides. Rachel opened the door for Bella to hop in back, helping her as she'd been doing since the dogfight. Then before he could offer to drive, she hopped into the driver's seat and started the ignition. Luke sighed. Why he thought she'd let him drive was beyond him. Instead, he climbed in, and she sped off.

"I don't hear sirens yet. I think if we can, let's see if we can find that Camry. It can't be too far."

"Got it," she said.

"There it is!" he exclaimed, pointing down the street. There sat an older green Camry with a small but obvious rental sticker on the bumper. "Pull up next to it, let me out, and then drive in front and park by the curb. I'll see what I can find." They both heard it—the sound of sirens drawing closer. The law enforcement vehicles were still off in the distance but would be there soon. Luke jumped out, keys in hand, and opened the driver's side door. He would have preferred to look in the trunk, but there was no time. Worse yet, the glove box required a key. He found a smaller key on the keychain and opened it, upset to lose the precious seconds it had taken. He grabbed anything that looked like paper and then, hearing the sirens much closer now, jumped out of the seat and ran up to get into Rachel's truck.

"Let's go!" Luke said excitedly, adrenaline pumping through

his veins. About a minute later, he realized he'd made one mistake, although there was nothing they could do about it now. He'd left the keys stuck in the lock for the glove box. Hopefully, the guy wouldn't have the chance to use them again.

Once they were clear of the area, Luke looked over at Rachel. She was smiling. He couldn't tell if it was a good smile or a scared-shitless smile. She answered that thought a second later when she let out a huge breath and spoke excitedly. "Wow, I was scared out of my mind, but that was kind of a rush, too." And then to his astonishment, she laughed.

"You have got to be kidding me," Luke exclaimed. Probably just her nervous energy, he thought to himself, but then again, it certainly didn't sound like hysterical laughter. Go figure. He started laughing with her, too, and turned around to rub Bella, thanking her for behaving so well.

"So what did you get from the car?" she asked, once they had quieted.

"Basically . . . the car rental agreement." He looked over the folded documents. "Unfortunately, someone at the rental agency is a complete moron. Want to guess what name he gave?"

"George Bush?" she said.

"Very funny. Although I believe they both are criminals."

"I'm kind of surprised you just said that."

"Well, I'll tell you this now. I won't talk politics. But I will talk crime. Anyhow, *James Smith.*"

She paused. "Seriously? Someone believed that?"

"Or they just didn't care."

"Well, guess the car search was a bust then?" she sighed.

"Probably, but you have to admit it was kind of fun, right?"

"Maybe a little," she said with a smirk.

~

It was almost noon, and after a fast-paced hike up the trail, Ted scoured every inch of ground within a thirty-foot radius of where the body had been found. Nothing. Not surprising. Someone had prepared the scene to set up Luke, so of course they wouldn't leave the real evidence nearby. Ted needed to follow their path—chances were they'd chucked the rock some distance from the body. Given Rachel's description of what had happened with body number one, he'd guess the killer must have come up from the less used southern trailhead. Time to explore some new territory, he thought, as he started to walk down the path, intently scanning the sides of the trail as he went.

There were quite a few baseball-sized rocks scattered here and there along this side of the Sierra Nevada; however, pinecones and brush outnumbered the loose rocks. He was about to give up hope when he saw something that didn't look right: a *pile* of rocks stacked too high and too symmetrical to look natural. He put his gloves on and carefully began removing one at a time, inspecting each one for blood. He found it on the fifth rock he examined. After taking several pictures, Ted placed it in an evidence bag and checked for anything else in the area. He didn't see anything suspicious, and having found what he came for he began walking back. He couldn't help but let out a short laugh. If the perp had just tossed it to the side instead of trying so hard to bury it, it was likely he'd never have found it.

Just over an hour later—it was so much faster hiking downhill—Ted was at his Explorer, glad to see he finally had enough of a cell signal to put a call through. The signal strength was never consistent out here. "Jill, it's me."

"Teddy. So, do you have something for me?" He could hear the smile in her voice.

"I sure do. I'll bring it down right now."

~

Scott had just started coming to at about the time that jerk was going through his pockets. *Pervert.* He was still too dizzy and foggy to do more, and it wasn't worth trying to take them down half awake, so he stayed where he was, playing possum. He heard the faint clicks of a cell-phone camera, followed by Luke saying something about the Camry. After they left he sat up, letting pain and nausea wash over him before trying to stand. Then Scott heard the approaching sirens—time to get out of there. He managed to rise to his knees and eventually stand, suffering through one more wave of nausea. His wrist and leg ached, and there were two pools of his blood on the wooden floor. Nothing he could do to clean it up now. He stumbled toward the open back door, using the walls to support himself, and felt his strength returning as he climbed off the back porch. He came around the side of the yard just as Rachel's truck pulled up to the Camry. He watched Luke jump into the Camry and was sure they hadn't seen him.

Scott had parked closer to the house so he didn't have as far to get to his car. The sirens were getting louder. He took his eyes off of the couple for a moment so he could step around some bushes. When he looked back, Luke was climbing back into the passenger side of the truck as it took off, heading right on the next street. With a strength fueled by rage he managed to get to the passenger side of the car, crouching down to hide behind the vehicle as the police cars rushed by. Once the first round of responders had turned down the next street, he reached for the handle. It was unlocked. Even better, he thought, when he opened the door and saw the set of keys dangling right in front of him from an open glove box, just waiting for his return. Although the rental agent had said there was another ignition key under the floor mat, this was much faster. He grabbed the keys, climbed into to the driver's side, and took off in the direction the truck had gone.

Once he saw them in the distance ahead, he called Mike to check in. "It's me," he said, a bit out of breath.

"Where have you been?" Mike yelled.

"Things are taking a bit longer than expected out here. Are we secure?" If Mike was at the office, people might be close enough to hear them. Alternatively, if Mike wasn't at the office, chances were he was with one of his many female companions.

"Yes. Now tell me what the hell's going on!"

"They got away, but I'm following them on the highway, heading north out of town."

After a few moments of Mike yelling various curses into the phone, he finally took a calm breath and asked Scott for details.

"I had to wait this morning because there were too many people around the hotel, so I followed them when they left. Strangest thing—they drove over to some empty house in Arvada and broke in. When they didn't come out right away, I followed them in, but, uh, the guy got the drop on me and they got away. But I promise you I'm behind them right now, and I'll get them next time." He stuttered a bit on the last few words, in part due to the pain in his leg and in part because of his nervousness at having to tell Mike he'd been duped.

"Did you say a house in Arvada?"

"Pretty sure that's the suburb name. I didn't pay attention to street names, but I know we turned off of Wadsworth and passed a park . . ."

"This is not good," Mike said, although what Arvada meant to Mike, Scott had no idea. "OK, you need to catch up to them, and take them out the moment you get the chance. And don't screw up this time!" he yelled before Scott heard the click of the phone disconnecting.

A moment later, his cell phone rang again. Mike was calling back. "Yeah?"

"However you do it, you need to make sure nothing in that truck can be recovered. I mean nothing, Scott," he emphasized. "You know as well as I do how important this all is. Remember the girls."

Scott paused, said he understood, and disconnected.

~

Jill finished her examination of the rock Ted had brought in and looked up at him.

"Shape matches almost perfectly."

"Could we get any prints from it?"

"I don't think so. The guy was probably wearing gloves." Jill looked back down at the rock.

"Figured that." Ted looked at his notebook. He had the victim's name, and he knew who *didn't* kill him. Luke and Rachel were probably on the run, hiding somewhere after guessing someone in the department was working against them, and Ted didn't blame them. Normally he's the kind of cop who would always follow the rules, and if you are innocent, let it be proven in a court of law. But that only works when you are given a fair trial and with evidence that hasn't been tampered with.

"OK, Jill, here's what I'm thinking. If you don't mind, I'd like to see what else I can find out about our victim. Got a free computer?" She nodded in the direction of one just outside her office door. It appeared to be a shared station used by lab technicians. "Great. Second, it's a long shot, but I'm going to try to get in touch with Luke. Chances are they've both turned their phones off by now or they are somewhere without a signal, but it's worth a shot. Luke was always determined to solve cases when he worked for us, and frankly he was very good at it. No doubt he's trying to figure this one out, too."

"Sounds good. And please, let me know if you need anything. I've got some reports to file, so I'll be stuck here for a little while at least."

He thanked her again and then walked out to the computer. Ted sent a text, figuring Luke was more apt to see the message immediately versus having to dial in to his voicemail, presuming he had his phone, and turned it on. "LUKE. IT'S TED. KNOW U HAVE BEEN SET UP. DO NOT CONTACT STATION. I CAN HELP. PLS CALL ME @ THIS #. LINE SECURE. TED."

Now all he could do was wait. In the meantime, he was going to find out more about this murder victim. At least the second one. Of course, with all that had happened now, he fully believed Rachel's report about the first body. But someone had done a great job of cleaning it up before they could get back out there. Even so, he still wondered how they could miss something—anything. Sure, there had been a major thunderstorm in between Rachel's discovery and their trip out there, but was it enough to erase all evidence? Or could his fellow officer that day have had something to do with it?

CHAPTER EIGHTEEN

Around three thirty in the afternoon, Mike and Jerome sat at a small conference table, facing six other people. Mike knew three of the others had been at the meeting with Jerome the other night.

"Hello everyone. I appreciate you taking time out of your busy schedules to come today. We have some information we need to share with you that demands immediate attention," Jerome said, doing his best to be cordial and appreciative, although Mike knew he was a bundle of nerves on the inside. He gestured to Mike sitting next to him. "Although most of us have met, I think it would be good to do quick introductions. This is Michael Row, president of Row Environmental, and the principal investigator on the project." Mike stood up, shaking the hands of those he hadn't met before, although given his lead role, he was heavily involved in most aspects of the project. "And . . . he's also my brother-in-law," he added with an attempted lighthearted laugh that probably didn't fool anyone. Playing along, a few people chuckled, probably hoping to ease the tension that penetrated the room.

"On my other side is Lexy Gaines, from SST Lab. She's been the primary person running the water samples for the project."

The young woman nodded but made no attempts to shake hands and didn't say anything. She stood about five feet tall at best, her hair trimmed well above her shoulders and interspersed with purple highlights. Mike had been working with her for years and she had always been abrasive and unfriendly, frequently reminding him that she wasn't happy to be in this situation. It was no surprise that after he'd picked her up that morning from the airport in Reno not one word was spoken during the entire ninety-minute drive to South Lake Tahoe. "All right, I'll let the rest of you speak for yourselves then," he said, looking at the man sitting next to Lexy.

"Thanks, Jerome. Well, it's pretty obvious I'm here on behalf of the forest service," the man said, bringing attention to the uniform he was wearing. "My name is Chuck Stanton. I've been the primary representative for the planning part of the project." He was young, in his mid- to late twenties, and, with his baby-faced smile, looked as innocent as Mike knew he was in this matter. He wore a gold band on his left hand, had a smear of dried food on the back of his right shoulder, and had thick dark circles under his eyes. Mike had been told he married last winter and they'd had a baby soon after.

Next to Chuck was a woman who looked around fifty years old, with dark-brown and grey shoulder-length hair, wearing a three-piece business suit and displaying an air of arrogance unlike the employee next to her. "I'm Kathryn Jones, forest service supervisor. I have been personally overseeing this project and the contract with Row Environmental," she boasted, shaking hands around the room. "With the assistance of Chuck here and a staff member who couldn't make it today, we helped apply for the federal grants that have paid for the work thus far."

As she sat back down, a much older and heavier woman next to her brushed her gray hair back, revealing large dangling diamond earrings, and spoke in a monotonous tone, obviously not happy to be there either. "Monica Jameson, Alpine County

Planning Commission." Like Lexy, she remained sitting, quickly looking for the man next to her to take his turn. The message was clear: she didn't have a lot of time for pretense.

"Garrett Mathem, executive director, Tahoe Regional Planning." Garrett paused, readjusted his glasses, and then awkwardly smiled as if to appear friendly without taking the time to shake hands.

The final attendee announced himself. "Ron Taylor . . . *Senior*," he added almost as an afterthought. Mike knew there had been some issues with his son on the force years ago. "Alpine County Board of Supervisors," Ron Sr. added.

Monica jumped in before Ron could continue. "Enough socializing—let's get on with it. What's this all about?" she demanded impatiently. Mike was aware that Monica knew full well what this was about, but they had to put on a show for those few who didn't.

"I've got some bad news about the project's results so far," Jerome said. "However, before I go into details, know that we may have a solution. Obviously it will be up to the planning commission and board to make the final call, but we wanted to have this meeting with you today to explain what's going on." He nodded to Mike to explain further.

"I've asked Lexy to be here to answer any questions about the water-quality results. Thanks again, Lexy." Mike nodded her way. She curled one corner of her mouth up as if attempting a pleasantry but not able to bring herself to follow through. "As you know, this project was based on the use of innovative techniques—that is, new, improved ways of doing things. It was a bit of a science experiment in itself, with the goal being to see a major reduction in suspended sediment in the West Carson River and other water bodies in the watershed as well as to lower levels of nutrients like nitrogen and phosphorus. However, keep in mind we were trying something completely *new*. The first year after we applied the wood chips, we focused most of our monitoring on making sure that the sloped areas were holding and the chips weren't getting washed away. We expected to see a temporary increase in the sediment and nutrients due to the ground disturbance from implementing the project. In the second year, things were about the same. But, the last full year's results show a strange *increase* in sediment and nutrient levels. We've done a few more collections this past spring, and things continue to get worse. We've been trying to figure out what's going on. In fact, Kathryn has accompanied us on a few visits to the project site to investigate." He looked her way and smiled a professional yet slightly friendly smile, unlike the smile he'd given her in bed early that morning. "Although it's just a theory, we're thinking that there may be an unexpected chemical reaction going on with the wood chips that's causing more pollution. Unfortunately, we can't just go out and scrape off the top foot or two of the surface that we mixed them into." To make his point, he passed around packets to each attendee, filled with graphic displays and charts, illustrating what he'd described.

Mike watched as Chuck examined the papers carefully. The kid hadn't been directly involved in this project since they'd physically done the work; his part mostly ended after the planning documents were approved. Further, Kathryn had taken a primary role on behalf of her agency, explaining to her staff members that she wanted to maintain some on-the-ground work so she wasn't stuck in her office all day. Mike knew she'd since been keeping Chuck busy with the planning documents and public meetings for other projects.

Kathryn, on the other hand, was not in the dark, at least on this part of the project. Mike had told her what they'd found some time ago, assuring her he was working hard to find out what was going wrong. In fact, they'd been seeing each other off and on for the duration of the project. He'd asked her out for drinks after the second meeting they'd attended, and that had led to one dinner, then another, and so on. He had suggested they keep their affair private, at least until the project was over. He didn't want any potential conflicts of interest to arise that could threaten her career. Kathryn had agreed, appreciative of his consideration. Mike had let her see him struggle with the results, his frustration and disappointment compelling him to work harder to find out the cause. Over the previous year or so as the numbers went up, he'd asked her not to say anything to her staff until he had more information to give. She'd readily agreed.

"You have got to be kidding me?" Garrett said, full of righteous indignation. "We stuck our necks out to help you get the money for this project based on the assurance that we'd be kept in the loop. And yet you're just telling us now?" he said. Quite the actor, Mike thought. Garrett also knew full well what had been going on. In fact, they all did, except for the forest service employees. Lexy knew just enough to help with the results, and so long as she was bound by their arrangement she didn't raise questions.

"Just hold on there, Garrett," Mike said, raising his hand. "Like I said, we wanted to figure out why this was happening first, in the hope we could fix it or at least present you with a solution. And you know there's a lag time between collecting the water samples and getting the lab results as well. We didn't know about this until months after it started happening."

"OK, everyone just calm down," Jerome said, playing the helpful facilitator. "Mike explained all of the details to me yesterday, and we'd be happy to run through them all now if you'd prefer. But we have a mess on our hands here. Not only environmentally, but the water districts down the line were relying on this to help reduce the cost of treating the water for their customers. A few have pitched in some man-hours and even matched some of the funding. We need to do something."

"And what do you propose?" Ron Sr. said pointedly. "After all, the federal grant is used up. There's no more money."

Mike sat back, looked at Jerome, and responded. "Well, that's true. There are no more *public* dollars. But the private owner of the two hundred acres within the project area may be able to help." He pointed at the colored box on one of the maps he'd handed out with the sample results, noting where the private parcel was. "When we began this project, we were working on an agreement with Mr. Lloyd Wells, the owner, who wanted to donate the property to the public for natural management by the US Forest Service. But he was waiting for the project to be completed first. Early on he'd mentioned a few 'bad experiences with public land managers,' as he put it. So there were some trust issues about following through. He put his grandson, Spencer, in charge of overseeing their involvement. Unfortunately, Lloyd passed away about six months ago, but I've been working with Spencer for quite some time, and he is willing to reconsider his grandfather's original agreement, which hadn't yet been finalized, if it will help pay to treat the runoff." Mike realized he'd come far too close to saying *was*, as no one officially knew Spencer was dead. "One of the reasons we'd hoped these new techniques would work is because, if successful, it would cost far less to treat this water on the hill than it does to clean it up downstream using conventional treatment systems. So even though that part didn't work, we can still clean it up downstream. It's just going to be far more . . . costly."

Everyone was leaning forward, all but the two forest service representatives, feigning curiosity for this solution. Mike had told Kathryn that Spencer was willing to help with a solution but hadn't told her the details, again using the excuse of protecting her career and avoiding conflicts. She'd trusted him hook, line, and sinker.

As he passed out some additional handouts, Mike thought about the years and political will it had taken to get this moving, especially to get participation from the water districts down the line. A lot of heads would roll, including that of the forest service, if in the end, they'd just made it worse. So he had relied on the knowledge that there would be a lot of motivation to find ways to clean up the water, just about any way possible.

~

Ted stood up to stretch, having become so deeply involved in his search that he sat in the uncomfortable chair for too long. But his time hadn't been wasted. He'd found that Spencer Wells was the grandson of a wealthy and charitable man in Denver. But there wasn't much else to find. That was odd. You'd expect families like that to have more media coverage, although he'd only started looking at the more basic Internet search sites.

As Ted began walking around to get blood flow back into his legs, he noticed a bulletin board in one corner where employees typically posted notices or other information. He walked closer and saw that just below the board was a fax machine. The last fax received still sat, print side up, on top of the device. Something about it made him take a second look. It was a missing persons report. MP reports were not uncommon to see here, since they were often sent to police stations, hospitals, morgues, and, of course, medical examiners. But something about this man's picture was almost . . . familiar. He pulled his notebook from his pocket and began flipping back pages to the date when he'd first spoken with Rachel Winters. She had provided a rough sketch at the time. It wasn't very good, but it had enough to be useful. The hard copy was up at his office, but he thought he still had a scanned version attached to an e-mail he'd forwarded to Captain Taylor. Back on the computer, he retrieved the e-mail, selected the attachment, and watched the image pop up on the screen. Oh yes, he was pretty dang sure it was the same guy.

He peeked his head into Jill's office, where she still sat at her desk working on some paperwork. "Jill, I think I've identified the first victim." She looked up at him excitedly as he told her about his find.

"I'm going to call Brian Choe, the officer on the report, and let Luke and Rachel know."

"Good news, I suppose. But now I've got to hide two IDs? You, my friend, are going to take me and the kids out for some pizza after all of this." Jill smiled.

A minute later, Ted sent his second text to Luke's phone. "FIRST VICTIM ID'D. DAVID PAYTON. KEEP UNDER RADAR. CALL ME ASAP."

CHAPTER NINETEEN

Luke knew exactly who he could trust to help identify the man. An old friend of his and his first mentor on the force, John Myers, had retired years ago and moved to Arizona, where his wife's family lived. His friend was fed up with snow removal and tourist season, but he hadn't wanted to admit it to his wife. Luke supposed he got more sympathy points if it looked like he selflessly moved down there solely for her sake. Retired or not, John always kept a few fingers in the pie to "keep from getting too bored."

"John wouldn't doubt me for a minute. And he's completely trustworthy. When my first partner was killed in the line of duty, John was like a brother to me," Luke explained to Rachel as he turned his phone on to get John's number. He mumbled as he waited for it to power up, "Problem is, I don't remember any phone numbers. They're all stored in this thing."

Rachel had been quiet for a moment, waiting to respond to his first statement. "I'm sorry about your partner, Luke. I had no idea."

"Yeah, he was about my age, and this stupid kid had—" He stopped, hearing beeps indicating he had messages.

"Luke, everything okay?"

"Sorry, it's just . . . I've got some text messages." The first was from a friend back in town, asking what the heck was going on—clearly he'd seen the papers. The next was from his accountant, raising similar questions and fretting over how to handle bills if he was going to stay "on the run," as she'd put it. The last two caught his interest the most. Ted Benson, one of his old coworkers, had sent him two texts that day. He read through them, partly relieved.

"I've got some good news and some bad news. Which do you want first?" he said, knowing she'd been anxiously waiting for him to explain the texts he'd been intently reading.

"Just spill it!" she said.

He read the text messages to her and saw her body relax slightly. "What's the bad news?"

"His ability to help may be limited due to the unknown dirty cop, as you put it."

"Well, it's better than nothing," she said as he put the disposable phone on speaker and called the number Ted had used. The call was answered on the second ring by Ted, who sounded a bit hesitant. It was probably the unknown number on his caller ID.

"Hello?"

"Ted, it's Luke and Rachel. We got your messages." He heard Ted exhale a sigh of relief.

"I was afraid you'd turned your phone off for good but thought it was worth a shot. Here, give me a minute to . . . relocate." They heard the sound of a door closing, and then Ted asked, "First, are you both okay? And the dog?"

"Yes, we're both fine, so far. Bella has a few sutures from an unrelated incident but is doing fine. Not that someone hasn't been trying to take us out, though. In fact, that's why I turned my cell on."

"Good. I mean the fact that you are all okay. So, I think it's time we swapped some information," Ted said. "I won't ask for specifics, but whereabouts are you guys?"

"Colorado, for now," Luke said.

Ted chuckled. "I figured you were on the case. So let me guess—something to do with a Mr. Spencer Wells?"

"Yes, and apparently we've found out something that someone doesn't want us to know. Just not sure which part of it they are worried about."

"All right. How about I start. Can Rachel hear me?"

"Yes, I'm here," she said.

"Good. First, sorry for thinking you were, well, a bit off your rocker, Rachel. Second, as my text said, I believe the guy you found is a Dr. David Payton. He's a hydrologist." Ted relayed the details of his conversation with Brian Choe in missing persons, including what David's friend Jack had suggested about the water samples and the two projects.

"Great finds. OK, our turn," Luke said, smiling. He explained what they'd found regarding the will and the private property in the West Hills project.

"So, let's review," Ted said. Luke remembered that Ted had always been a checklist kind of guy. "First—victim number one. David Payton, independent hydrologist collecting samples for the West Hills project, shot in the head roughly three weeks ago north of the project area not long after his buddy Jack confirms, unofficially, that something's not right with the water samples. For some reason the killer chooses that location to kill him but didn't want him to be found. Rachel and Bella happened to hike the trail on the wrong day, interrupting the killer's plan and seeing the body."

Rachel chimed in, excitedly. "In terms of the location, given David's line of work, he might have been out collecting water samples upstream of the project area. Typically they'd test the water in the stream above where the project was to compare it to the water quality after it's passed through the project area. Maybe the killer snuck up on him. He'd be concentrating on recording everything in log books and labeling each sample."

"That makes sense. But what if the killer was actually helping David collect the samples? Would he typically take someone along? Are the samples pretty heavy?" Ted brainstormed.

"Good point. I don't think he would need someone to help if he had the right backpack, but it can get to be a bit of a load, depending on how many he was collecting and how much ice he brought to keep the samples cold. So, no, I guess it wouldn't be strange to bring someone along."

Luke chimed in. "Either way, someone kills him, sticks around to remove the body and all evidence, but yet doesn't seem to worry about having a witness?"

"Well, maybe he or she knew their friend at the station would help clean up any discoveries. Or maybe they got lucky with the thunderstorms. Either way, I honestly didn't find anything suspicious there, as you know, Rachel. Although I'm not a forensic expert, I'd like to think I have a good eye for things," Ted said. "Moving on to our next fact here, we know the name of victim number two, thanks to the help of a friendly medical examiner who understands the nature of the situation."

"Would that ME by chance be Jill?" Luke asked. He remembered her as always smiling even when you could tell she had the weight of the world on her shoulders.

"Yes, and she's withholding the ID for now. Both of them."

"Please give her our thanks," Luke said. He then continued Ted's line of thought. "Spencer was assigned to be involved in this project by his grandfather, who hoped earning his keep would help shape the kid up. The kid worked with the agencies and consultants for years. Then Grandpa Lloyd died of a heart attack, whether it was natural or someone helped him, I'd say it's too late to find out now. The body was cremated according to Lloyd's wishes."

"Now that we know the will was swapped, maybe that was part of the cover up," Rachel said.

"That's true," Luke agreed. "So as a result of Lloyd's death, Spencer inherits some land, including the two-hundred-acre parcel in the West Hills project area, based on a will that was faked after Lloyd's death. And before the attorney can follow up on what he knew or would know to be a forgery, he's set up and killed by a hit-and-run driver, leaving no one who could do much about the strange change of heart Lloyd's *new* will exhibited toward Spencer," Luke paused. "I've seen the guy's office—it wasn't that hard for someone to break into it."

"I won't ask, Luke, how you would know such a thing," Ted chuckled.

"So why kill Spencer and then set us up to take the blame?" Rachel pondered.

"Good question. Opportunity maybe? Or a combination of both?" Ted said. "Either way, the next question is, who gets the property now?"

"The killer? Or whoever he's working for?" Luke guessed.

"I agree. Then again, this clearly reaches far beyond one or two people. There's got to be more going on than just inheriting some land someone could build a house on," Ted responded. "On that note, I bet when the guy realized he couldn't kill you both, he decided to frame you instead. If you're arrested, your credibility is gone. Of course you'll say anything to avoid going to prison. But then someone finds out I'm going to take another look at the evidence and makes sure it disappears before I can get to it."

"So Luke's been tied to the murder now, guilty before proven innocent. Even if they can't convict him without the evidence, no one will believe him regardless," Rachel concluded.

"Not bad for a civilian," Ted responded kindly.

For a brief second, Luke felt an unexpected pulse of jealousy run through him when Ted's friendly tone with Rachel bothered him. Well, the time to analyze that reaction was definitely not now. Then something Ted had just said finally registered. "Wait a minute . . . someone removed the evidence? How did no one see that?" Security wasn't perfect, but it seemed tight enough to prevent someone from walking in off the street and accessing locked evidence. Then the revelation. "The inside cop."

"Yes, that's what I'm thinking. But he or she made sure no one could identify them from video or otherwise," Ted responded.

"If the guy killed Spencer, he must have known whatever they are trying to do, and they no longer need Spencer to do it then, right?" Rachel asked. "Which brings us back to who gets the property now. If Spencer's part of the plan, why risk killing him?"

"Maybe so the killer didn't have to split the profits? You never know. Criminals do stupid things."

"Not just criminals," she added. Luke smiled.

"And confirm this if I'm right, Rachel: it's just a forest on that parcel, right? No homes, no buildings, or anything like that?" Ted asked a moment later.

"Nothing yet, and, at first glance, they couldn't do much based on the current zoning. But there are always loopholes. I'll look through the regulations next chance we get."

"Sounds good. I'll keep the IDs under wraps for now and see what I can find out about who benefits from Spencer's death."

Luke jumped in. "How about I focus on the second part? Your actions might be traceable at the station."

"All right, you do that—but I don't know anything about it. I'll focus on checking into some of my fellow officers, though I still can't believe anyone here would be involved in this."

"I know what you mean," Luke said. "And one last thing. I was just about to call an old friend to help identify this guy who tried to kill us this morning. I'm pretty sure he can find a way to run a facial recognition scan under the radar—unless you have a better idea?"

"No, that's probably best. But Luke . . . there isn't a body somewhere in Colorado that I should know about, right?"

"No, I got his leg and then knocked him out before we had to run. Neighbors must have called after the gunshots because the cops didn't take long. Hopefully, he's locked away in the local station, crying like a baby and asking for his attorney."

"That I can find out easily enough, if you feel safe telling me where."

"It's fine, we're not *there* anymore. It was in Denver. Specifically a place in Arvada—some kind of suburb of Denver. How about we touch base in a few hours and see what we've found?"

"Talk to you then. You both keep safe!" Ted said before disconnecting.

Luke looked over at Rachel. "Well, at least we have some help."

"Yep, he seems pretty trustworthy. He was pretty friendly in my dealings with him, although he did a good job of hiding his opinion about my relative level of sanity."

"Well, you kind of are a bit off kilter sometimes," he joked, wanting to see that I'm-pretending-to-be-angry-with-you-but-you-have-a-point-too expression he'd learned to like. He got his wish.

~

"Leona, where's your partner?" Captain Taylor asked. Ted had been gone for several hours now, and he hadn't heard from him.

She looked up, as usual having been totally focused on her computer. "Oh, sorry, sir. He called a bit ago and said some kind of emergency with a friend came up and he needed to use comp time off this afternoon. He promised to check in as soon as he had more information. He sounded pretty worried."

"Yes, he left me a note earlier, but he didn't know if it would be all day at that point I guess. Well, please let me know when you hear from him again," Captain Taylor said. He turned and briskly walked back into his office, closing the door behind him and reaching for his phone the minute he sat down. Ron Junior, as his friends used to call him, had another important call to make. Once that was done, he called the chief.

"Just checking in, since you wanted to be kept in the loop. Ted's away helping a friend this afternoon on some emergency, so I'm not sure if he found anything more yet. I'll keep trying his cell, but depending on where he's at the signal could be spotty."

He heard the chief sigh and sensed some nervous energy in his voice when he responded. "OK, thanks for the update."

~

That was odd, Leona thought. The captain was usually so laid back about things, so why the noted concern about Ted? Then she thought about that new Lexus he'd been driving, and although she knew it was perhaps juvenile, it angered her. Here she was struggling to pay for a lifesaving treatment for her little boy and her captain's buying an expensive new car. Even so, she was sure she'd be judged harshly if anyone found out what she'd been doing to earn a bit of extra cash to help pay down those debts.

Leona's cell phone began ringing, and according to the caller ID it was Shelby. Her friend had been quite reserved when they first met, but after a couple of years they'd started to become closer and catch a few movies here and there or grab a quick lunch. She hadn't told Shelby about what she was dealing with at home, but maybe it was time. She could use another woman to confide in. She answered the phone, "Hey, Shelby, what's up?"

"Long day. I was thinking of a coffee run; our place around the corner this time?" Leona wasn't surprised. The woman could drink a quadruple espresso then go to bed an hour later and sleep just fine.

"I'll meet you in five."

~

Chief Tim Parker was counting the days until his retirement. He was looking forward to the joy of traveling around the country in his fifth-wheel trailer with his wife and their two small dogs. He was just over a year away from being able to retire, but he was exhausted. Decades of seeing the worst side of people had worn on him. When he'd started, it seemed like the bad guys would be obvious—easy enough, arrest the criminals, and save the innocent. Unfortunately, it didn't take long before Tim realized too many criminals wore business suits and often got away with bad things, thanks to family money and lawyers who twisted the truth and because jurors missed their families and only wanted to get home—as anyone would. Meanwhile, some poor kid who grew up in foster homes was tossed out on the street at eighteen and falls into a bad crowd, and now he's serving twenty to life for robbery. So why shouldn't the chief try to retire early? Unknown to his wife, he'd made a little *investment*.

But he'd just received a message that had his guts twisting inside out. Everything he'd done could be for nothing, and he could lose what he'd invested so far, including some of his retirement. The chief had an errand that couldn't wait.

"Leonard, can you please come in here?" The tall slightly awkward man stood up from his desk not far outside the chief's office and came to the door. He had a look of annoyance as he walked in, and, as usual, he wasn't concerned about hiding it.

"Thanks. I need to head out for an hour or so. I want you to monitor my phone line, and if you see a call coming from Captain Taylor, Ted Benson, or my wife, answer it and have them call my cell. If it's any other number, let it go to voicemail."

Leonard nodded and briskly walked back to his desk. Tim sighed. The kid had the physical skills and seemed to have a pretty good head on his shoulders, when he used it, but his attitude was going to get in the way of any advancement if he didn't figure out how to stop being such an ass.

CHAPTER TWENTY

"John's going to run the pictures through a friend's program and get back to us as soon as he finds anything . . . if he finds anything," Luke said after hanging up his call.

"Great. How long does something like that take?" Rachel asked.

"Hours, minutes, it all depends. But he's on it. He feels bad he didn't get my message right away, so he said he'd work as quickly as possible."

"Nice guy. And yes, minutes would be great," she said. They were driving west on Interstate 80 toward Elko. There hadn't been a lot of traffic on the interstate given the time of day, mostly cross-country travelers and a few vehicles associated with the oil and gas industry, a big player in this part of the country. She'd noticed the fast approaching car in her rearview mirror but, due to the sun's angle, hadn't been able to make out the color or other features. She expected the car to move over and pass any moment, yet it kept advancing, coming closer behind them.

"This idiot behind me is coming up fast and it doesn't look like he intends to go around us. Think I should pull off or what?" She was nervous, more because she had been rear-ended twice before and had a huge problem with tailgaters.

Luke turned around and looked out the back window. "Damn. I think it's the guy from Joe's house."

"What?" she cried. Fear was quickly replaced with adrenaline as the Camry closed the last few inches between them and rammed into her bumper. The car was much smaller and lighter than her Tacoma. Rachel held steadily to the steering wheel, unsure whether to slow down or speed up. "Is he trying to run us off the road?" She was gripping the wheel so tight her knuckles turned white.

"Keep going; maintain your speed. He's smaller, so he probably figures he can rattle you enough to cause you to do something stupid. But keep in mind, he doesn't have his gun; we do." As he said this Luke began digging through the bag he'd placed the gun in, although his own gun was still resting in the holster attached to his belt.

"But couldn't he have another one?" she asked nervously.

"Let's hope not," Luke responded, his hands still shuffling through the bag.

"What about your gun?"

"His has better range. Will Bella freak out and jump around if she hears a shot this close?" he asked.

"I don't think so. First day I had her she stood right next to me while I hammered on the fence in the backyard. She didn't even flinch." Too much information, Rachel knew, but she talked excessively when she was nervous.

"OK. I'm going to edge out the window and take aim. I need you to maintain your speed but move left into the next lane. Right now, your camper shell is in the way. Hopefully he won't move with you right away and I'll have him in my sight just long enough." She heard the sound of Luke unlatching his seat belt. He shifted in his seat to face the rear of the truck. Rachel tried to focus straight ahead, but it was difficult. Even more so when Luke started climbing halfway out his window. She couldn't help but visualize hitting a bump and causing him to fall out—tossed onto the interstate at eighty miles an hour. "Rachel, you can do this," she said to herself and carefully began moving her pickup left.

As Luke had hoped, the lane change gave him the opportunity he needed. Luke got off a shot, and Rachel looked in the rearview mirror as the car behind them shifted and swerved, but the driver was able to correct it. Another shot, a quick moment of dread, and then relief as Rachel saw the car disappear from the rearview mirror followed by Luke's return to his seat.

"I could only get his tire—looks like it was enough. He lost control and went off the side into the muddy ditch."

"What now?"

"Just keep going. And by the way, good driving," he said and reached over to gently squeeze her bare knee. It was an intimate gesture, probably unexpected by both of them.

"Good shooting. Think he'll catch up anytime soon?"

"He's got to figure out how to get that car out of the ditch and then change the tire. By then, we'll be cozying up in some hotel room . . . sipping wine." This made her glance at him, and he winked.

"Men," she sighed. But she had to admit she was still thinking about that kiss they'd shared as well. Next time, she wanted to be perfectly sober to really enjoy every single minute. Wait, next time? There couldn't be a next time.

"Thinking about that kiss?" he asked casually. She could hear the knowing tone in his voice.

"Are you?" she countered. Then, thankfully, Bella broke the moment, sticking her head through the gap between the front seats, licking Luke right across the cheek.

"Wow, Bella, that was a bit . . . my God, girl, you have a huge tongue," Luke said, wiping his cheek with his sleeve but laughing at the same time. Rachel smiled, repeatedly looking in the rearview mirror as they continued down the highway.

~

Eventually, a highway patrol officer noticed Scott's predicament and pulled up alongside to ask if he needed help. The cop appeared to be a younger guy, probably a rookie stuck with the thankless job of writing tickets for speeders. He had the typical army brush cut and wore the dark uniform of traffic cops.

"Why sure, that would be great. Guess I hit something on the highway and it took my tire out." Scott laughed, trying to sound slightly frazzled.

"Yes, not surprising. Unfortunately a lot of things can fall off of vehicles or vibrate out of truck beds and land on the highway, screwing up the next guy who comes along." He smiled, coming around to the passenger side to view the damage. The cop leaned down to look at the tire, which was not only flat but stuck in about three inches of mud. Scott came from behind and hit the man hard with the tire iron he'd pulled out of the trunk earlier. The cop toppled to the muddy ground.

Scott grabbed his gun, his baton, and—what the heck?—his badge and ran to the black-and-white car and quickly jumped inside, smiling when he saw the poor trusting cop had left the keys in the ignition. He heard the sounds of voices coming across the radio, so he found the power knob and shut them off. He stepped on the gas, turned on the siren and lights, and focused on finding that damn Tacoma as he sped down the highway, pushing over a hundred miles per hour.

~

Mike left the meeting an hour later, feeling better about his plan. There had been some hiccups, but things were still going to work out. The couple would be taken care of. Even better, they were hundreds of miles away, and, afterward, no one would look very hard for them. They were, after all, considered fugitives on the run. He walked out of the meeting next to Kathryn, giving her a wink when no one was looking, then they casually walked to separate parts of the parking lot. Just as he climbed inside his

Hummer, his phone rang.

"Yes?" he said, answering quickly, assuming it was Scott.

"A missing persons report has been filed on our first trail victim." He paused slightly, registering who the caller was and then the information about the MP report.

"How did that happen? He had no family or friends in the area."

"Looks like some friend from up north called it in earlier. According to the time stamp, it was faxed yesterday afternoon."

"OK. Let me know if someone responds," he said curtly and then added a quick "thanks" before hanging up. Mike did not need this trouble. Especially when everything was just starting to come together so that he could reclaim his daughter soon. Then he thought back to his fruitless search in David's office. He redialed the number, asking, "Who is the contact for the MP case?"

"Brian Choe, Douglas County Sheriff's Department. Want his info?"

"Yes, thanks." Mike wrote it down and hung up again, wondering how to go about getting this information without giving anything away. He could try searching David's place again, but chances were the cops had already been there or could be there right now. He hadn't worn gloves the day he looked through it, but he had hired the guy, so his fingerprints in David's office wouldn't be unexpected and it was much easier to look through papers with bare hands. Well, now what?

He needed to access to David's phone records. It could raise red flags if he had his insider do the search on their system, especially so soon after looking into Rachel's records for Scott, so he needed to get someone else with computer skills to find out for him. Someone who would keep his or her mouth shut. Like Lexy. He picked up his phone and dialed her number. She had just left the lot in her rental car, heading back to the hotel room she'd rented for the night. She didn't hide her anger at his intrusion into her one evening in this town but agreed to get the information when she was back in her room with her computer. After all, she didn't have much choice.

~

"How about this rest stop here?" Rachel asked, needing to get out and stretch.

"Sounds good," Luke said. "There are quite a few truckers there."

"I suppose that's the main reason for this rest stop. Looks like we need to squeeze in behind them." After parking in the area designated for autos, Rachel stepped out of the pickup, a bit shaky on the first few steps. The rush had passed, and although she hadn't fallen apart, the danger they just faced had her nerves a bit riled. She reached in and leashed Bella, planning to take her to the nearby pet area, or so it was labeled. In reality, it was five square feet of grass surrounded by dirt.

"Well now, that's the first highway patrol I've seen or heard today. Yet isn't this one of the most traveled highways?" Luke asked as they heard the sound of a siren speed by, although Rachel couldn't see it because of the four semis between them and the highway.

"I'm not sure if I'd rather have seen more or am glad we didn't." She began walking toward the pet area when she heard Luke's disposable phone ring. She stopped and walked back to stand next to him.

Luke answered and said Ted's name, putting the phone on speaker mode so she could hear.

"How are you all doing?" Ted asked.

"Still alive, man."

"Always a good thing. OK, first, no one has been found or arrested in that area of Colorado," Ted said.

"Unfortunately we figured that one out about an hour ago when he tried to run us off the road." Luke explained what happened.

"Do you think you've lost him for now?" Ted's concern was obvious.

"I think so. He wasn't getting that car out of the mud anytime soon."

"I'm glad you're both okay. The other thing I want to tell you is that I've been doing some digging into some of my coworkers, much as I still hate to think about it, but I haven't found anything that jumps out at me yet, just a few officers who are in debt and might be open for a payoff, I suppose. My captain has come into some extra money lately, but he comes from a rich family, so I'm thinking he made up with the father he hasn't spoken with for years. I'll keep looking. Anything else new? That is besides the car chase and second near-death experience?"

"Not yet," Luke responded.

"OK. Be safe." They disconnected the call, and Luke began to walk back toward the truck.

"I think we should get going, just in case he did get that car out somehow." Rachel nodded then quickly walked Bella to the pet area. A minute later they returned, and Luke asked, "Want me to drive?"

"I'm totally and completely fine with that idea right now," she said, handing him the keys. He took them from her, held her hand an instant longer than necessary, and looked her straight in the eyes.

"You are taking this all very well. I just wanted to let you know I admire that."

"Thanks. So are you. I know it's your line of work, but I doubt this happens every day."

"No, just every other day," he laughed.

"Thank you. For everything. I know I'm not very good at relying on someone else, and I, uh, have some stubborn moments . . ."

He moved closer, gently placing his other hand on her cheek, tucking some loose hair behind her ear. "Not at all. I knew you were strong and independent the moment I met you. Admittedly, it wasn't my first instinct to *like* that, but I guess you've begun to grow on me. Honestly, you just continue to amaze me."

Rachel was taken aback by his declaration as well as his touch, and they stood like that, bodies close, hands together, gazes locked, for what seemed like hours. Then she felt him draw the slightest bit closer to her, and excitement surged through her body. She didn't want to resist it, even though her mind told her she should. She closed her eyes, and when their lips met it was as if they were starved for each other and couldn't get enough. If not for Bella, gently tugging on the leash in Rachel's hand, they may have stood there tightly embraced and tasting each other's lips for who knows how long. Yet they both knew they needed to get going, and soon. Rachel stepped back, lips swollen from the kiss. Luke appeared confused at first, but once he noticed that Bella was the reason for the abrupt ending, he laughed.

"Bella, you're the most wonderful dog I've ever met. But your timing stinks," he said, laughing. "But, much as I want to stay here and keep doing that, Bella's got a point. Can I ask for a rain check?" He winked.

"Depends on how you behave."

"Do you prefer naughty or nice?"

"A bit of both," she said, letting Bella in the truck and then getting into the passenger seat.

CHAPTER TWENTY-ONE

Chuck Stanton hadn't liked the proposal. He sensed his boss, Kathryn, hadn't been very excited about it either. It wasn't public land. They couldn't force the kid to sell it or donate it. So much was riding on getting the water coming out of that area cleaned up that he could see the other side of the issue, especially during such bad economic times. The proposed agreement Mike and Jerome explained was above both of their heads in terms of who would make the decisions, and he knew Kathryn was the unlucky one who would be discussing it with her superiors. However, the planning commission and board members seemed fully supportive, and usually that meant his "powers that be" would most likely go along with their decision, presuming the regulations allowed for such an arrangement. From what had been presented today, it did appear the development could be permitted, more because there were no regulations to specifically prohibit it than because anything said it was allowed.

On the way out Chuck cautiously asked Kathryn, "So, what do you think, really?"

She sighed like someone resigned to do something they weren't happy about. "Personally, I'm not too excited about it—

but professionally, I don't know what else to do. Mike's a good guy, and I can see he's struggling with this, too."

"Do you know him very well?" Chuck asked, wondering about the familiarity in her voice when she spoke his name.

"I've gotten to know him a bit after working on this project, had a couple of discussions over drinks, that sort of thing."

"Oh, OK," he said, suspecting that she knew him a lot better than that. Whether it mattered in terms of the project, he didn't know. But either way, what would he do about it? He was about three rungs down the ladder from her, and he certainly couldn't do anything that could jeopardize his job. He had a family now, and they relied on his paycheck and health benefits.

"No, I definitely don't like the idea. It's not appropriate for that area. Those ridiculous railroad laws . . . but I guess the end game is all about improving the water quality, right?"

"I guess. But I still don't understand what happened. The treatment should have worked." Chuck shook his head.

"I know. Well, I'll take this to the top and see what they say." Kathryn sighed, and they rode the rest of the way back to the office in complete silence.

~

After Mike, Lexy, and the two forest service staff left, Jerome sat at the conference table facing the others. "I think that went pretty well. How about you all?" Jerome said, sitting back in a relaxed position.

"I agree. Presuming there are no unexpected . . . *problems* . . . I think we can get enough political support to make this happen," Garrett said. Jerome knew he was hinting that he was still concerned about some of the rumors he'd been hearing.

"Don't worry about it. We're fine. Mike always follows through on his jobs. Plus, he's got plenty to gain when this all goes through," Jerome said, reassuring them. Mike had confessed to Jerome once about having a daughter and his intentions to unite with her once he had increased his financial resources.

There were no better motivators than family and greed, as far as Jerome was concerned. After all, weren't those basically his motivations in all this?

"Think this kid, Spencer, will agree to it?" Monica asked.

"Mike has assured me that won't be a problem," Jerome answered. He didn't know the details of everything Mike had done or planned to do and frankly didn't want to. He'd always had the feeling Mike was the kind of guy who would do extreme things to get what he wanted. And when Rachel Winters had reported the dead body a few weeks ago, Jerome didn't have to ask. He was pretty sure he knew who was responsible based on what Mike had told him earlier that morning about the hydrologist's concerns. Regardless, he found it odd that Spencer wasn't with Mike at the meeting, but he'd been pretty quiet the few times Jerome had met him, so maybe he'd chosen not to come.

~

"Well, I guess this will work. I'm glad they had a room with parking right in front. I always hate having to carry luggage up and down stairs and long hallways," Rachel said as they entered the small hotel room in Rawlins, Wyoming. It was a fairly inexpensive chain motel offering the basics like wireless and, as Luke had immediately confirmed, coffeemakers in each room.

"OK, I see the extras for Bella, but I don't see you with a huge amount of luggage when you travel."

"Well, when I'm not running from murderers and law enforcement, I like to bring a few . . . comforts. My pillows. Food." She ended there, deciding that was enough information. She knew she brought a bit more than the typical person, but she had a pickup. She could fit it all in, so why not?

"And that's it?"

"Of course," she fibbed before rushing out of the room mumbling, "I need to grab a few more things to get Bella set up."

When they came back in, Luke was already sitting at the table, laptop set up in front of him and powering on. She prepared Bella's food and water, setting it on the floor, then sat on her bed, laptop resting in front of her, also getting back to work.

About twenty minutes later, Rachel interrupted the sounds of Bella's quiet snoring and the tapping on two keyboards. "Well, I do believe there's a money motive. Got a second to hear me out?" she asked, knowing she'd interrupted whatever he was concentrating on.

"Yes, please share." He smiled, leaning back.

"OK. Yes, there appears to be an old remnant zoning law that could allow the property to be subdivided into ten separate twenty-acre parcels. That's likely, on its own, profitable enough; but add to that another one of these remnant two-step subdivision approaches and it's possible, with the right political clout and a lot of nasty backroom dealings, it could actually be subdivided even more than that—making a lot of money for whoever owns the property and anyone who invests in it."

"What's a two-step approach?"

"It's a loophole that allows subdivisions of land that wouldn't otherwise be allowed. Basically, they . . ."

"OK, that's good enough," he said, laughing, hand raised in a stop gesture. "So, isn't it surrounded by public land on all sides? How would people access it?"

"That's the other thing. There's an old set of federal regulations that refer to having to approve linear rights-of-way under certain circumstances, such that they have to allow a driveway across federal land to access private property. I'm not certain, but based on my experience with policy and regulations it looks possible. And it would make sense."

"And the forest service would have to approve it?"

"They might. There are a lot of times their hands are tied, like with old mining laws. The public may own the top of the land, but a private party may have rights to the minerals underneath. Ever look at a map of old mining claims?"

Luke nodded. "First, I think I'll take criminal law over environmental law any day. Second, yes, I guess I'd call that a money motive. All right, my turn."

"Go ahead," Rachel said, anxious to hear what he found.

"Well, unlike good old Lloyd Wells, Spencer liked everything electronic. Strangely he did not hire an attorney to create a will but instead went through one of those online deals a few months ago and paid for the packet to create one. He then made it official. Guess who the lucky winner is?" he asked.

"I'm never good at this sort of thing. Just tell me."

"Our friendly consultant, Mr. Michael Row, who, as the will reads, was the—and I quote—'father Spencer never had.'"

"Seriously? How convenient," she said, sitting up a bit more. "Think Spencer even knew he had a will?"

"Good question."

"Either way, it just seems like it would take a lot of political will to get such a project passed in that area. If they just implemented an erosion control project with public tax dollars to clean up the water, it seems like it would be political suicide to support private development that is just going to make it worse again." She was thinking out loud, and then it clicked. "Unless, of course, they were supporting the wonderful new trend in public–private partnerships!"

"What?" Luke looked confused. Yet Rachel was so caught up in figuring it out in her head, she ignored his question and kept on talking.

"Someone would have been watching the results of water samples during and after the project. I would think flags would have been raised quite some time ago had things not been getting any better, unless someone was messing with the results. Hey, didn't Ted say David's friend who called in the report mentioned something about running water samples?"

"Yes, some guy up in Oregon. He works for a lab but apparently ran them on his own at David's request so there would be no official record." He still looked confused, but she was on a roll now and didn't want to stop.

"OK, I need to talk to that guy. Think Ted could get you his contact info?" she asked.

"I would expect so."

Rachel smiled. She knew she was probably frustrating Luke by pursuing this without explanation, but he apparently decided to let her see it through and wait for answers. He dialed Ted's number.

~

Scott sat in the cop car, wondering how he could have lost them. He'd been driving fast enough to catch up to them miles ago. Even considering they might stop for gas, he'd checked around the stations as he drove. There weren't that many stations to check. He looked at his watch. Chances were they'd have found a motel room somewhere to hide out for the night. Although math hadn't been one of his best subjects, he tried to sketch out the distance they could have gone in the last few hours and compared that to the larger towns that might have rooms. He felt pretty certain there was no way they went past Rock Springs. He could drive around for a bit, looking for their truck. Although there were a lot of Tacomas out this way, most didn't have camper shells with ski resort and paw-print bumper stickers on the back. Her truck would be easy to distinguish. If he couldn't, he'd find the next roadside rest off I-80 and look for them as soon as the sun came up. He could not mess up this time. Not just because he was afraid of what Mike might do—being related didn't mean much to Mike when things didn't go his way—but also because it would ruin Scott's own plans to find her and make her pay.

In the meantime, he had to take care of the throbbing in his head and dull ache from the bullet wound in his leg. After purchasing some bandages at a local pharmacy and swallowing a few more narcotic painkillers, he began driving around the main streets in Rock Springs, looking at the parking lots of each motel. At the same time, he dialed Mike's number, knowing he should report in but hoping he wouldn't answer. Scott didn't want to have to say he'd lost them again. He got lucky; it went straight to voicemail. At that point, he decided to just hang up. Better to report in tomorrow when he had good news to share.

~

"Got it." Mike hung up after writing down the Oregon phone number that had been listed on David's cell phone records three times in the month before his death. He grabbed his disposable phone and dialed the number. After two rings, he heard an anxious man answer, "Hello?"

Mike used a high-pitched voice, trying to sound casual at the same time. "Yeah, I was calling for Jack?"

"That's me. Who is this?" The uncertainty in the man's voice was obvious.

"Hi Jack. My name's Roy, and I'm an old coworker of David's. I heard you were the one who filed the missing persons report on him," he said, trying to sound like a nervous, caring friend.

The man hesitated, responding with obvious suspicion in his voice. "He's mentioned some of the people he's worked with over the years, but never anyone named Roy. Which projects were you involved in together?"

Mike hung up. He'd already learned what he needed to know. This was the man who had filed the MP report, which meant he had to be the person who ran the extra water samples for David. Now the question was—what to do with this information.

CHAPTER TWENTY-TWO

Rachel thanked Ted again then passed the phone to Luke so they could touch base while she retrieved the ice chest from the truck. At least they had some leftovers they could munch on. She opted to let Luke relay the basics to her. Not only was she was getting a bit tired of the speaker-phone conversations, but she felt the need to move. She was restless. As she unpacked a few items into the room's small refrigerator, she heard Luke sign off on his call with Ted.

"OK, Ted's found out a few other things, but I have a feeling you would prefer to follow up on your deal first?" he asked.

"Thanks, although I do have to wait a bit, so maybe you can tell me what you know. Ted got us the friend's name, but said he'd call Officer Choe first so he could get in touch with the guy in Oregon to give him a heads up about my call."

"Good. So, what's the cover?"

"It's a partial truth. I'm a local environmental scientist who Ted asked to review the samples so I could relay what it might mean in nontechnical terms. Which I *am*, and I *will* do for Ted . . . so it's not really lying, right?"

He laughed. "You and your guilt. You Catholic or something?"

"No. Heredity, I guess," she smiled. "So tell me what Ted found out."

"Well, he's still trying to uncover the insider. His captain recently came into some money, although he's the son of a big political powerhouse—Ron Taylor *Senior*—in the area. But they haven't talked for years. Apparently there had been some kind of scandal regarding development approvals and payoffs where Ron Senior was suspected of involvement, and after that Ron Junior cut all ties, including financial."

"I remember hearing a bit about that, but it wasn't local, so I didn't get directly involved. But Ron Senior was never convicted of anything, right?" Then as an afterthought, she added, "Lying slime."

"No. Ted said it was obvious the guy was involved, but there wasn't enough strong evidence to win in court. And no one would testify against him. Bad enough, I know, but a few years passed and this guy ran for office again, playing the poor, innocent, angry victim. Voters sucked it right up, and now he's currently on the board of supervisors for Alpine County. Ted said Ron Junior has since refused to talk to him."

"Why am I not surprised?" Rachel said. "Well, so, where did the money come from then?"

"Apparently Ron Junior's wife recently inherited money from a distant relative who just passed away."

"Poor relative, lucky wife," she mused.

"Lucky husband, too."

"Well, a bit longer and I'll call Mr. Stine," Rachel said, looking at her watch.

Twenty-five minutes later, she was listening to a man's voice answer. "Hello?" It only rang twice. His voice seemed anxious yet hesitant.

"Hi, is this Dr. Jack Stine?"

"Oh, this must be Rachel?" he said, breathing a sigh of relief.

"Yes. Officer Choe was able to get in touch with you then?"

"About ten minutes ago. I was a bit nervous because just before that a man called claiming to be a former coworker of David's named Roy. It seemed odd, and when I tried to ask him for more details he hung up. Choe suggested I take my family to visit friends for a few days." He must have agreed; she could hear the sounds of packing in the background.

"That is a good idea. Is Choe going to be able to look into the caller?"

"He's going to try, but it's an unknown number. Probably a disposable cell," he said. "So what can I do for you?"

"I hate to keep you, but the officers feel that perhaps if you could explain to me more about the samples, it might help us figure out what's going on." She bit her lip to prevent saying she was sorry about his friend, knowing he hadn't been told yet.

"Sure, no, I've got time. My wife is packing up the kids' stuff, and that always takes a while," he laughed nervously. "Unfortunately David didn't tell me specifics, but he said some results from another lab didn't make a lot of sense, and he wanted me to run a set of samples myself. He sent eight different bottles, and I screened them for the usual's, but with emphasis on the suspended sediment and nutrient concentrations. Three samples were extremely high, while three others were very low—in fact, well below the standards. The last two were fairly clean, like you'd expect in an undisturbed watershed."

Like the open forest above the project area where the hiking trail goes, Rachel surmised. She asked him a few more technical questions then asked if he'd be able to e-mail her the files. "Sure. Brian said maybe you could look them over, and it might help them find David. I really appreciate it," Jack said hopefully.

She gave him one of her e-mail addresses, and he promised to send them immediately. Rachel thanked him again, hung up, and signed into the e-mail account. She looked over to Luke, who'd stopped typing and was listening to her call intently. "He's going to e-mail me the detailed files right now."

"Good. And Rachel, stop feeling guilty about not telling him yet. You have no choice right now."

My God, could he read her mind? Rachel nodded, embarrassed at being such an open book, then looked back at her in-box. Less than a minute had passed when an e-mail showed up with an icon noting an attachment. Jack must have been right in front of his computer, she thought. She opened the file and began looking over the data. Jack had summed up the basics. A few things she noted included statistics from David's field notes, which it appeared he'd scanned in and sent electronically to Jack. Other notes included typical scrawled information like ambient air temperature, the water temperature at time of collection, and a few other measurements. He also noted some kind of "distance from WF CR," obviously from the West Fork Carson River. As she scrolled further down she reached the last page of his handwritten notes, and there it was: a cartoon-looking map that he'd drawn, noting the names of the samples and where they'd been collected. Dr. Payton was certainly no artist, but since she already knew the area, his sketches were good enough for her to understand where the samples were from. Luke heard her shifting around and looked over.

"Find something?"

"Yes, although it doesn't make sense. The sample results that were reported from SST Lab make it look like the wood chips had made no difference and the water from where the treatments were applied is just as dirty as it was before, if not worse. David's samples start very clean upstream, but it's well below the project area that the pollution in the water samples suddenly spikes."

"Which means . . . ?"

"I think someone was purposely polluting the water below the slopes they'd added the wood chips to, although the wood-chip treatment itself was working."

Luke paused, looking a bit confused. "How could something like that go unnoticed? Aren't the federal agencies out there taking regular samples?"

"Well, typically a lot of projects are monitored *visually*, meaning someone basically goes out and looks to make sure things are still in place. Although, in the case of a special project like this, regular water samples should have to be collected. But I suspect someone at SST was messing with the results, and unfortunately due to budget cuts and pretty lax federal monitoring requirements from the Bush era, the forest service was probably relying mostly on the lab reports."

"Can you explain to me a bit more about this dumping thing?" he asked.

"Let me pull this satellite image up first . . . OK, got it." She zoomed in closer, following the image of the forested area from where the main stream entered the Carson River and then followed that stream north to where it eventually ran through the project area. "I can see a small footpath that ends right around where it looks like sample four was taken. So . . . if someone were physically dumping bad water into the stream, they were probably too lazy to go beyond the end of the existing path, meaning they'd have to dump it in right there; let me check David's files again for something."

"I still can't believe this hasn't been detected sooner by the feds or someone." Luke came over and sat next to her again as she looked between the map image and David's scanned notes.

"Yep, I'm pretty certain someone was dumping polluted water or liquids into the water at the end of the path."

"Why even do that at all? Why not just have the lab results reflect what they want, especially if they are already messing with them?"

Rachel thought about that for a moment.

"Maybe another agency is performing more regular monitoring around where the stream enters the Carson River. Possibly the US Geological Survey—they do a lot of regular sampling like that. In which case, the water would have to truly be polluted. Actually I can look that up right now." She went to the USGS website and quickly found their monitoring pages for the area; as expected, there had been ongoing monitoring around where the stream entered the river. "Yep, it shows they have been monitoring, but there's quite a lag in time between the last results they posted and now, which might explain why no one else blew the whistle."

"So I think I follow, but what's the deal with the public–private thing, or whatever it was you said?"

"Oh, yeah. Sorry, I didn't explain earlier. Prepare for a bit of preaching, but this really ticks me off," she laughed. "I think the reason they'd want to show the project isn't working is so they can propose a public–private partnership that will get them the support they need to develop the property and basically . . . make a hefty profit. A little background might help: because the government is so broke, agencies have tried this concept of rewarding developers by permitting them to build more than zoning rules allow, so long as they build or contribute to some kind of environmental improvement, usually on their own property or nearby."

"Um, example please, for the rest of us?"

"Ha ha. All right, something basic. Say there's an area where there are miles of old paved roads that haven't been maintained well. Keep in mind that there is a lot of polluted runoff from paved roads, even worse during storms, and before we knew better, a lot of roads were built. Now, decades later, these roads are causing major pollution problems, but the government doesn't have enough money to repair the infrastructure, nor the money or political will to actually remove the pavement and restore or build wetlands—which is really the best way to clean up the water. Frankly, millions of our tax dollars have been wasted on projects that didn't do much. But, I digress." She smiled and then continued. "As part of one of these partnerships, the public agency might allow someone to build forty condos instead of just ten if they pay half the cost of storm-water treatment for county or state-owned roads in the same area. Hence a public–private partnership."

"So if I understand correctly, you're thinking that Row is going to use the dirty runoff to bargain for more development rights?"

"That's my best guess. And that would take some serious political support and probably some major financial investments from other people as well, because based on Row's financial records his company couldn't pay the upfront costs on its own."

"Do these partnerships really work?"

"That, Mr. Reed, is a loaded question. Everyone has their own opinion, and I'll first say I know the concept might work in some areas. But barring that, in my own opinion—which, OK, I don't know everything, but I have been working with this stuff for years—in reality, I haven't yet seen any scientific evidence that it's possible to build on unspoiled land and have zero impact, no matter what type of building you create. As to whether a developer can pay toward systems off-site to help clean up existing water-quality problems to create a net reduction in pollution, I can tell you that so far, the engineered technology they have been relying on in lieu of natural wetlands doesn't stop the pollutants it needs to. At least in Lake Tahoe."

"Is that why the water along the South Shore and up by Tahoe City isn't very clear anymore?" he asked. She nodded.

"It may be existing development that's caused the biggest problem, but the solutions aren't working to clean it up. I'll warn you not to let me get up on my high horse over that whole situation. I'll never shut up."

"Noted," Luke smiled.

"So, the question is at what point does solving one problem not come at the cost of creating far more? I know it's not a one-size-fits-all deal, but I've been discouraged by a lot of the projects I've seen that have just caused more pollution. I'll leave it at that.

Obviously there are those that take advantage of this public–private concept because it can be very profitable. Plus, it's a great way to sell the approval of something otherwise distasteful to the public. After all, who wouldn't want to see the river cleaned up?" She finished with a cautious smile. The room went silent for a moment.

"You *chose* this career path? Really?" Luke asked.

"I ask myself the same question sometimes," she laughed. "But, in all seriousness, I think it originally chose me. It's definitely depressing sometimes. Hard, too, but rewarding all the same. Part of the problem is we think we know something and try to do the right thing, but then we learn more, and it turns out we just made it worse. A lot of people are simply trying to do their jobs and figure out solutions. But clearly I have a *big* problem with politicians and greedy developers who'll manipulate things for their own profit." She ended with an exasperated exhale.

"I can see your blood pressure rising the more questions I ask. I say we take a break from Environmental Politics 101 and grab some food." Although she thought Luke might have been frustrated because she rambled on so long, when she looked over at him, his smile was sincere enough.

"Sounds good." Then she yawned and looked over at Bella peacefully sleeping on her dog bed, a chew toy hanging halfway out of her mouth.

"Damn that girl is cute," she said. Luke hadn't moved yet, nor did he respond, so she looked over at him and saw a strange look on his face. He was staring at *her*.

"Yes, she sure is." Their eyes met and that's all it took. He leaned toward her, his hand curving around her cheek, and pulled her to him. Then all she could think about was the feel of his lips on hers and the soft caress of his hand on her cheek. They slowly fell back onto the pile of pillows, and she sank down with Luke poised over her. Rachel felt the warm trail as his lips moved toward her ear, sending goose bumps throughout her body. At the same time, his hand was reaching, seeking hers out. When they connected, he gently wrapped his fingers in hers as his other hand removed the tie from her braid. Luke slowly loosened her hair on the pillows beneath her and brushed his fingers through her strands. "So beautiful," he whispered into her ear. Then she felt his lips touch crook of her neck. Sending her body into a paroxysm of pleasure, the only thing in her world at that moment was the warmth of his body next to hers, along with the overwhelming need to feel his bare skin as soon as possible. He continued sending shivers through her entire body as his lips traced her collarbone. When he slowly pulled her loose shirt to the side, brushing his lips across the shoulder he'd exposed, she moaned. Without thinking about it, her free hand reached out and began tugging up on his shirt.

A moment later her wish was granted as she finally felt his bare skin. She instinctively ran both hands over his chest, then down his back, pulling his body closer to hers. The only distance between them now was that of the few clothes they still wore. Luke fell over to her side so that they were facing each other, heads resting on the pillows, eye contact intense. There was no question—he wanted her as much as she wanted him. She sat up just enough to get her own shirt off and quickly initiated another kiss. They took turns removing each other's clothes in between smoldering flashes of kissing and touching, until finally there was nothing between them but the shared longing for each other.

~

Mike had debated about how to handle Mr. Jack Stine. But what could he do at this point? He had no contacts in the area the man lived. Chances were the guy had the results on his computer, so making him disappear like David wasn't an option. But maybe that wasn't necessary. Perhaps he could "convince" the man to delete the files and even claim his buddy David came by for a visit, nullifying the need for an MP report. After all, blackmail was proving to be a very helpful strategy with many of Mike's contacts—speaking of which, one of them might be able to get him what he needed now.

He dialed Lexy's number, and again she made no attempt to hide her anger at the late interruption.

"I need you to dig into phone records one more time." He heard her sigh then begin to tell him to call back in the morning. Mike cut her off. "*Now.*" He didn't have to remind her what would happen if she didn't do what he asked.

"Fine, fine," she muttered, sounding as if she'd been half asleep. As he heard the sounds of her laptop booting up, he thought about how beneficial her cooperation had been. He'd met her through work for the mining industry. Eventually the day came when he needed someone to adjust monitoring results to ensure one of his biggest clients wasn't going to be slapped with huge fines. So, as he'd done before, he did a little digging and found out Ms. Lexy had a few of her own skeletons. Turns out, she'd been part of a complex bank heist years before that had required some notable hacking skills. Her partner had been shot during the escape, but the FBI could never directly tie her to the crime.

They had questioned Lexy when they determined it was her boyfriend who had been killed trying to rob the bank. She had convinced them she was merely a sad, grieving victim. The cops had left her alone then, but soon after she was enrolled in college with her tuition fully paid. The financial trend continued until she earned her science degree and eventually got a job with SST Laboratories. Mike had simply connected the dots and suggested there might be some evidence that could tie her back to the bank robbery. However, he'd make sure that didn't happen as long as she helped him with a few projects. That was years ago, and he knew she was upset for still being tethered to him. *Too bad.* Lexy could have done the right thing and turned herself in years ago. Now she gets to pay the price for her freedom.

"OK, what's the number you want me to check?" she spat into the phone.

He read off Jack's home number, deciding not to remind her she'd been the one who had retrieved it for him in the first place. "I want to see the list of all of his incoming and outgoing calls for the last year through today. I need to learn a bit more about this man."

"So you can screw him over like you've been doing to me?" she blurted out.

"Trust me, Lexy, I have no interest in screwing you. E-mail me the records when you get them."

"It's going to take a few minutes. Up until the last bill will be easy enough, but tracking the recent calls is a bit more tricky."

"Fine, just get it done." Mike abruptly ended the call and sat, anger boiling up with each passing minute waiting for a new message to arrive in his e-mail's in-box. Finally, there it was. He opened the file she'd attached, looking at the most recent calls and location—and then he saw it. Not long ago, Mr. Stine had received a call from an unknown number just ten minutes after an incoming call from the Douglas County Sheriff's Department. Mike called Lexy back.

"Got it. Now I need to know the location the last call came from." He heard a few more clicks and sat waiting for what felt like an hour but turned out to be several minutes.

"It looks like it bounced off cell towers somewhere in Wyoming . . . Rawlins? Never heard of it."

But Mike had. He'd done a few jobs the oil and gas industry earlier in his career and spent a good deal of time up that way. Realizing he hadn't heard from Scott in a while, he said, "I have another number I need you to track for the last twenty-four hours." He read off Scott's current number.

After a few more clicks she said, "Last tower registered it in Rock Springs, Wyoming. Before that it looks like it bounced off towers between there and Denver."

Son of a bitch! Scott hadn't been able to get his prey after he'd called earlier and must be following them back home. Although why would they be coming home only to be arrested when they arrived? Something was going on. He couldn't figure out why else they'd be heading west on I-80. Given the officer had called Jack Stine ten minutes before that party from Rawlins did, it made sense it had to be the couple. Probably that damn enviro bitch, trying to find out about the results.

"Anything else? I'd like to actually get some sleep before my flight," Lexy said, annoyance clear in her voice.

"I'll let you know. Keep your ringer on." Hanging up again, he immediate dialed Scott's number and fumed when it went straight to voicemail. If they were in Rawlins and he was in Rock Springs, somehow he'd passed them up and probably didn't know where they were. When the phone beeped, signaling the caller to leave a message, he shouted, "They are in Rawlins. Get your worthless ass back there and take care of them. Now!" He knew Rawlins was a small town. It wouldn't take long to cruise the streets and check motel parking lots. He called the number again, leaving another message. "And call me immediately!"

Mike couldn't believe what was happening. Years of delicate work, ongoing payoffs, blackmail, all for his daughter, Lori. He'd had to stay away during her childhood but always hoped to be able to someday claim what was his. Her cheating mother had made sure he had to wait. He was poor back then, barely scraping by, and she'd convinced him that her lover, who had a home, a stable job, the works, would make a better father for the girl. Add to that the restraining order, and she made clear any attempts would end in legal troubles for Mike. He'd stopped himself so many times over the years from approaching Lori to tell her who he was. He instead waited, getting his ducks in a row first so he'd have the resources needed to disappear with her. Lori's mother would never be able to find them, for that matter. Especially after this deal went through.

One night while he was watching Lori through her apartment window, he had been shocked to see Spencer in the apartment, clearly more than friends with his twenty-year-old daughter— Spencer, the kid he'd treated like a son all these years. Spencer knew he had a daughter. After a few beers, he'd confided in the younger man about a year ago. Although Mike knew he had never said her name or described her, it didn't matter. Spencer was over ten years older than Lori, and there he was with his hands all over Mike's innocent little girl. That's when Mike's fatherly concern for Spencer ran out, and soon after he was reconsidering his plan. In fact, it was also ironic that around the same time Scott showed up, dealing with some similar familial issues. But, unlike Spencer, Scott didn't hesitate at anything Mike asked him to do, although he'd never been so incompetent as he was with this current situation.

Now it could all come unraveled because of one woman. Or rather, a freakin' dog. But, if Scott could take care of them tonight, there's still a chance to make it work, he mused. The tests David had taken weren't official. No one could confirm they'd actually been collected where he said. He could tell them to look at the USGS data for confirmation of SST's results and offer to pay for additional samples to be run. David's body hadn't been found and never would be. Spencer hadn't been identified yet, and thanks to some work by Scott and Lexy on their computers it would take some time to figure that out. This could be resolved. Add the political backing of Jerome and the others, and things would work out.

CHAPTER TWENTY-THREE

Something was making noise, trying to break into Luke's half-asleep brain. The first thing he registered was the feel of Rachel's naked body wrapped in his arms, their legs tangled together. The fruity scent of her hair. Then the obtrusive noise again. It was his cell phone. He quickly looked at Rachel, who briefly stirred. Bella was curled up in the space next to their feet. The pup had apparently jumped up on the bed at some point after they'd drifted off. He reached over to the nightstand out of habit but realized it was across the room on the table. Damn.

Then she opened her eyes, smiling at him, and said groggily, "Probably should get that."

"I know. I'm just so comfortable here." With obvious reluctance he detangled his arms and legs from hers and got up to retrieve the phone. Answering it, he walked back over and lay down next to her. With a smile he reached over and ran his fingers across the side of her neck. He realized that he was falling for her, and it surprised him. The voice on the phone brought him out of his reverie.

"Luke? Rachel?" It was Ted, sounding slightly confused from the silence on the line.

"Ted, hey. Sorry about that. We figured we wouldn't hear

from you until the morning." He paused, waiting to see if Ted would say any more.

"Yes, sorry to . . . interrupt, but I'm fully loaded with caffeine and adrenaline." He laughed. Then after a moment of awkward silence, he asked, "You two good?" There was a slight inflection in how he said *you two* and *good*. Ted was a detective after all, so no surprise there.

"Yes, we're fine. We found a good place to bunk for the night. I think we're off the beaten track enough so that the guy won't find us, at least not for a while."

"Good. In fact, that's one reason I called. I've been paying attention to news out your way, and it turns out a highway patrol reported having stopped to assist a man who'd slid off the road. When he turned to help inspect the tire, the man knocked him out and took his car. Apparently it was almost an hour before a trucker saw the stranded car and stopped, and when he found the officer he called 9-1-1. The highway patrol officer is okay, and several police and highway patrols are out looking for the stolen car now, but at this point they figure he could be anywhere within several hundred miles of the area."

"I guess I'm not surprised," Luke sighed.

"Thought I'd warn you in case you found yourselves being pulled over by a patrol car. In other words—be careful and don't speed."

"Thanks for the heads up. Also—Rachel talked to the hydrologist up in Oregon, and she thinks she may have figured something out. But I'll let her explain it." He laughed, handing her the phone and putting it on speaker.

She summarized what she'd learned, and when she was done, they heard a slight pause on Ted's end. "Rachel . . . did you say *Mike Row*?" he asked excitedly.

"Yes, Mike's the main lead on the project as well as the owner of that parcel. Well, that is, once Spencer's death is officially acknowledged and someone looks up the convenient will that leaves it to Mike. We were going to his office in Elko tomorrow before we knew we were being followed. Not sure what the plan is now."

"I've heard that name somewhere," Ted said quietly. They waited and then heard an intake of breath, "Oh boy. Diane—*Mike's sister*—is married to Jerome Baxter, our esteemed county supervisor."

"I know that jerk!" Rachel exclaimed. "In fact, I've challenged him at several board meetings. He's an arrogant ass but has a great way of twisting things to make them look good for the community. Somehow he manages to keep going."

"This goes a lot higher up the food chain than we thought, I take it?" Luke asked, getting a sinking feeling in the pit of his stomach.

"Unfortunately I think so," Ted said. "I would recommend you steer clear of coming home just yet. I've still got to figure out who I can trust to help us with this."

"Agreed," Luke said. "I'll let you know when I learn the identity of our mystery killer. And if you'd like, I can do a little extra fishing around on some of your coworkers, if you give me some names." Luke sensed Ted's hesitation. "Well, you think it over, and we'll touch base with you in the morning. I guess we'll hang around here until we figure more out."

"All right, I'll do some brainstorming," Ted said, sounding miles away. After they ended the call, Luke noticed his phone was showing a voicemail. He dialed in and they listened to the message, unmoving.

"Hey, it's John. Looks like your guy might be someone named Scott Baxter. Around forty years old, currently registered as a resident of New Mexico. If you need more, give me a call back. Otherwise, good luck, buddy." Luke looked at Rachel after the message ended, an intent look on her face.

"That's Jerome Baxter's son. And Mike Row's nephew," she said with a grimace. "I knew there was something familiar about him. I may have seen his picture before, but I've never met him, well, before today. I've heard Jerome's wife talk about her two kids, both now moved away with their own families. She was complaining to a friend once that they never called her. Poor woman married to that slug and then her kids go and desert her."

"So Scott's working for his uncle and his own mother doesn't know?" Luke wondered.

"Well, you mentioned you'd cut ties with your family, right? Maybe he'd done the same and she has no idea he's living just a couple of mountain ranges over. If his license is from New Mexico, she might think he's still there. Or she's a good liar and has known all along, but I just don't get that vibe."

"I have to say I trust your instincts on that. Let me call Ted back. This can't wait."

~

Scott shut his cell phone off after attempting to call his uncle. He was afraid Mike would call him back and he'd have to tell him the truth. He spent another good hour or more looking for the woman's truck, but it was completely dark, and traffic in the town was almost nonexistent. He knew he would start to look suspicious at some point. Plus, the fewer the cars, the more his stood out. And by now, someone would have stopped and found the officer. He hadn't hit him hard enough to kill him. That was extra heat he did *not* need. So the smart thing now would be to find another vehicle.

He remembered a great place to look. Scott had passed a popular bar not long ago, where the parking lot was full but very dark. After parking the patrol car a couple of blocks away, wiping everywhere he'd touched by habit, he walked quietly over to the lot and began searching cars. He found an older style passenger car that was unlocked. No keys, but it was easy enough to hot-wire one of these classics.

He drove the car up the highway to an area of dense trees he'd noticed before and backed in, tucking the car so it wouldn't be noticed, at least in the dark. He'd set his watch alarm to wake up before the sun came up so he could keep watch but had at that point become so tired and in pain that he never thought to check his cell phone before nodding off.

~

Jerome awoke with a start. He drank more last night than he'd intended to, trying to forget his worries about the threats to the deal. He hadn't heard from Mike since midday yesterday, and had learned the cop who'd gone looking back up the trail had apparently taken the afternoon off to help some friend. But something seemed off, the timing just a bit too coincidental. He tried calling his son later in the evening and was frustrated when the call went to Scott's voicemail. He knew his son worked for Mike, and although he'd never asked either of them directly, he had an idea of the types of things Scott did for him. Regardless, the three men had kept it all from Diane. As far as she knew, Scott was happily married down in New Mexico.

Jerome worried about his son, but it was too late to change the course of his life. When Scott had first gone off to college, Jerome had been the typical proud father. His son had selected a school about a thousand miles away and rarely came home to visit. Over time, he called less often, and Jerome and Diane both worried something bad was going on in his life. Posed with this question during a quick weekend visit, Scott had assured them things were great. In fact, he'd met a woman, and they were going to get married. Although happy to hear the good news, when they expressed some concerns about the quick wedding, Scott just laughed and said it was love at first sight. Jerome hadn't been surprised to hear that just a few months after eloping he had a new grandchild.

In today's world, having children out of wedlock was not uncommon and usually wouldn't end a political career. However, Jerome had swayed a significant number of voters his way when he'd attacked the other candidate running against him for having a daughter who had been a prostitute. The girl had cleaned up when she got pregnant at seventeen, but Jerome had used this to boost his own platform, implying his fellow candidate was a bad parent and therefore couldn't be trusted to represent the public.

With another election coming up soon, Jerome and Diane tried to hide their son's situation and succeeded quite well, at least around the communities Jerome worked in. He'd then discouraged any visits for a while, to let things die down so when Scott eventually came back with family in tow no one would care enough to look into the matter. But then they didn't see their son for over a year. It broke his heart to hear Diane on the phone begging her son to come visit so she could meet her new granddaughter, but Scott always had some reason that the timing was bad, and he promised to set something up soon. If not for Jerome's job as a County Supervisor putting the actions of him and his wife in the public eye, they might have just flown out to see Scott at that point—forget waiting for an invitation. But they didn't, and after another year passed Jerome received a curt e-mail from Scott. His wife had left him and taken the baby.

It wasn't long before Jerome had learned what really happened. His son had developed a drug habit, and when he was high he used his wife as a punching bag. She hadn't filed any reports, though, until the night he'd gone too far. The wife later told the police that she was with him in their car, their baby girl in the backseat, when he said he needed to make one quick stop. Scott pulled up in front of a run-down motel, left the car running, and went inside. A minute later, she heard a gunshot, and he came bursting out of the building with a pistol in hand. He jumped in the car and peeled out of the lot, breathing hard. She'd seen spots of blood on his cheek and knew. That night, after another round of punches, she'd slipped a sleeping pill into his beer, and when he was knocked out she packed up their daughter and headed straight to the nearest twenty-four-hour police station. Her directions led the cops to the dead body of a prominent businessman, and soon after the wife agreed to testify against Scott if she and her daughter were placed in witness protection. Assigned new identities and moved God knows where, they disappeared, and Scott was arrested. Of course Jerome wasn't going let his son go to jail. But he also couldn't let Diane know what had really happened.

Jerome made the excuse of a business trip and drove the thousand-mile distance to the police station, calling several well-placed friends along the way. The next day the evidence was conveniently misplaced, leaving only the wife's testimony to make a case. Thankfully, she hadn't actually *seen* the shooting, and the defense attorney could easily explain that for all the woman knew, her husband was the target and was merely holding the gun to defend himself. In the end, the prosecutor reluctantly dropped all charges, and Jerome convinced his son to come back with him and just leave his wife and daughter in the program. Jerome loved his son, and he'd done a lot of bad things in his own life, but he would never condone what his son had done, and he felt the wife and daughter were probably best left alone.

By that time his brother-in-law's business had taken off, and Mike was willing to hire the kid—off the books, of course, to avoid the issues that might interfere with Jerome's political career. It also made it far easier to keep Diane from knowing what had happened. Better she think of her son and his family off living happily somewhere far away than know the truth. That's when Jerome found himself drinking more.

The shrill ringing of his phone brought him back from his memories.

"I need to meet with you," Mike said quickly when he answered.

"The office?" Jerome said groggily.

"Yes. I'm heading straight there."

After they hung up, Jerome's nausea from the hangover got worse. He didn't know what was going on, but Mike's call added to the sinking feeling that had already formed in his gut. The payoff when this deal went through would be huge. The problem was getting everything set up had been a long, delicate process, and they were only partway there. Once things were set in order, even when they had the personal approval of the right players, there were still laws requiring lengthy environmental reviews that often took months, if not years, to complete, and only then could they go to the appropriate governing bodies for approval. They expected they could easily expedite this process by showing the public and decision makers big, colorful charts illustrating the pollution that was entering their water source, coupled with high numbers from SST Lab. Hence their plan was the only way to fix it, and the sooner, the better for the environment and citizens who relied on the water. Projects with overwhelming public support were easier, and faster, to get approved. As for lawsuits that could be filed, what group would want to stop a project that would provide such great water-quality benefits?

Jerome slowly got up and walked to his room. He grabbed a fresh set of clothes and went to take a quick shower, letting the hot water ease his nerves.

~

Scott's watch beeped at four a.m., and as he slowly woke up the pain in his head and leg almost overwhelmed him. He had to take a few deep breaths to keep his focus. He took four more pain pills—after all, he couldn't afford to be slowed down at this point. After stepping out to relieve himself, he stretched a bit, limping around behind the car. As his mind grew more aware, he remembered the cell phone. Better turn it on now. Sure enough, he had a voicemail from Mike. But the numbers on his phone also served to remind him it was also an hour later here now than back home; he had forgotten about the time difference when he set his watch. Scott listened to the message, angry at the revelation he'd passed them. He remembered seeing Rawlins. He'd pulled through looking at gas stations the day before. How he'd missed them he couldn't figure out, but now he knew where they were.

He was back on the highway heading east a few minutes later. He was already motivated before this all started, but killing them had become personal and would be much more satisfying. Once he got his payoff from Mike, he could afford to grease the right palms and do some searching. He had told his father over a year ago that he'd just let it be, but he had no intention of letting his bitch of a wife run away with his daughter. He'd find them both, and Mommy would regret what she did—at least for the minute she'd have to think about it before her last breath. Of course this last part he'd kept from Uncle Mike, instead only sharing his plan to reunite with his daughter when he could afford to locate her.

~

Kathryn hadn't slept very well the night before. The proposal from Jerome and Mike had upset her, and it only became worse as the day went on. Upon returning to their office, she immediately reported the problems with the project, followed by the proposed solution. Her regional boss, who was disappointed the project was failing, was pleased to hear there still might be a way to address the water-quality issue.

"I'm just concerned about allowing new development on that two-hundred-acre parcel. It's right in the middle of an open forest and totally inappropriate for the area," Kathryn asserted.

"I agree with you, Kathryn, but it's not our job to regulate private land, so it's going to be up to the locals. As for the driveway access, I think our hands may be tied on that deal as well. In any case, I'll run this by our legal staff tomorrow morning. Before we go any further, we need to meet with this Spencer Wells and make sure he's still on board."

"Mike said he is."

"Yeah, well, I want to hear it directly from him before we go upsetting any more people."

"OK, I'll work on it." Kathryn had actually met Spencer

several times when she was with Mike, although she wasn't about to tell this to her boss, of course. The kid had always come off as a bit shy and reserved. He also hadn't seemed too happy about being involved in the project at first, but over time she'd noticed he'd become more active in their planning sessions. He even showed some enthusiasm at the last two meetings.

After the conversation with her boss, Kathryn checked into her e-mails and calls and headed out. She was looking forward to dinner with Mike, which often included a steamy sex session afterward. Their relationship had been welcome after years of marriage to a man who wouldn't even touch her. Mike had a way of making her forget her worries when they were together. They'd discussed meeting for dinner when parting ways early that morning, but when she called him after leaving the office around five p.m. his line went straight to voicemail. She tried an hour later with the same outcome. This wasn't uncommon, since he traveled around a lot for his job and signals went in and out in this area. But Mike usually called her back within an hour or two. When midnight came and went with no response, she began to worry. He'd always been very attentive to her and rarely canceled any plans they'd made; although he had always been strategic in planning things in advance, too.

Kathryn sat at work the next morning half asleep and still no call from Mike. Personally, she was ticked; professionally, she was stuck. She had intended to talk to him before trying to get a hold of Spencer directly but couldn't wait any longer. Finally, she called their Elko office, where she knew Mike currently had a full-time receptionist.

"Hello, Row Environmental," a woman's tired voice answered.

"Hi, this is Kathryn Jones. I'm the forest supervisor near your Carson office."

"Oh yes, Kathryn, hi. This is Joyce. I think I've met you before at a company event."

"Great," she said, although she had no clue what this woman looked like. "Well, I can't get in touch with Mike, and I need to talk to Spencer about something my boss has requested regarding one of our projects here. I don't have his cell number. Do you by chance have that information?"

"Sure, give me just a second here." Kathryn heard some typing and soon the woman spoke again. "OK, here's the number."

Kathryn wrote it down, thanked the woman, hung up, and immediately dialed Spencer's line. She wasn't surprised when it too went to voicemail. She decided to try again later.

CHAPTER TWENTY-FOUR

Bella stirred, waking up Rachel. It was around sunrise, although the room remained fairly dark thanks to the thick motel drapes. Bella likely needed to go outside. Rachel quietly put on some clothes and took the pup out back. They returned a few minutes later, and she decided to hop into the shower to let Luke sleep a bit longer.

When she emerged from the shower, hair wet and wearing a fresh set of clothes, she found Luke next to the motel coffeemaker, dark-brown liquid half brewed. His laptop was on the nearby table, already showing signs of various searches. He turned to her, raised one eyebrow, and said, "I was hoping to help you get dressed this morning."

"Well, maybe you can help me get undressed later," she smiled a mischievous grin. The thought of another night like last night turned her on in a flash. No one had ever made her feel so good. This man was amazing.

"I'll remember that." He winked. "Ted called and asked me to look into a few people," he waved at the computer. "Coffee?"

"Are there fifteen containers of creamer to make it tolerable?"

"No, just five. Although I didn't expect you to even consider my question."

"Extreme circumstances."

"Got it."

Rachel thanked him, grabbed the other mug on the counter, and poured coffee into it. As she reached for the creamers, Luke came up behind her, gently moving her damp hair to the side. He softly placed his lips on the back of her shoulder, giving her a gentle kiss. Just one. But that was enough to make her almost melt into a puddle of bliss on the floor. Rachel couldn't help but let out a small moan of pleasure. She heard him chuckle as he headed straight into the bathroom to take a shower. Oh no, she thought, I am so hooked on this guy. She couldn't remember the last time she'd wanted someone so completely.

Bringing her mind back to the task at hand, Rachel began packing things back into their bags, although unsure when or where they were headed. She set out Spencer's cell phone and hit the power button. Luke had suggested they periodically check it to see if anyone had tried to call. So far nothing. A minute later the bathroom door opened as Luke walked out, his hair wet and mussed, a towel wrapped around his waist. Beads of water still dripped down his chest. It took a lot of willpower on Rachel's part not to just jump the man then and there. But the cell phone she'd just powered up started beeping. She walked over to it and looked at the display.

"Missed call," she said to Luke. Then she checked the number that had called, and was so surprised she had to look again.

"What is it, Rachel?" Luke said anxiously, walking over to her.

"I'm having *your* déjà vu . . . the missed call—I know the number." He looked at her anxiously. "Kathryn Jones, forest service supervisor. And she's using her personal cell phone." Rachel had worked with her a few times, and the woman's cell number had been one that was easy to remember.

~

Jill promised Ted she'd keep a lid on the official identification for twenty-four hours, longer if possible, but that was already pushing it. He also knew Brian Choe's hands were tied. The officer couldn't justify waiting much beyond the twenty-four-hour window before notifying others of the information about David. So all told Ted expected the shit to hit the fan sometime today. He had called Luke earlier, hesitant but knowing if he wanted to try to find out more about his coworkers, chances were Luke could find out faster and more discreetly than he could. Ted was limited by the computer access he had available at the station and the possibility that someone now watched his every move.

His cell phone rang. "Ted, it's Luke again."

"Hey, Luke. So did you find anything?" He was hoping Luke would say no, yet obviously someone he worked with couldn't be trusted.

"I'll get to that in a minute. First, an interesting connection popped up earlier. Rachel turned on the kid's phone to see if anyone had called and there's a missed call from the personal cell of Kathryn Jones, our forest service supervisor."

"Interesting. Wonder what she's involved in, although I guess if she knew he was dead, she probably wouldn't be calling his phone. I'll check into it. Also, so you know, I expect Jill's going to have to officially identify the kid, and Brian needs to report what he knows about David Payton by the end of the day, if not sooner. They've both already bent the rules holding onto both IDs for this long."

"Yes, figured that," Luke responded.

"Find out anything else?"

"A few things. Are you taking notes?"

"Yes, go ahead."

"OK, Officer Nolan Ramos had a little gambling problem. He is about ten thousand dollars in debt at the moment," Luke relayed.

"He's been on vacation for the last several days, so he has an alibi. But dumb kid is vacationing in Vegas. Doubt that's going to help his debt," Ted said.

"Sounds like great financial planning. All right, next guy: Officer Leonard Barry. Looks like good old Lenny got in a bit of trouble with a local prostitute about a month or so ago. His father, apparently a well-known businessman, conveniently went to high school with your chief. Looks like Lenny's record was kept clear, but you'd mentioned this morning that he'd been glued to the chief's side lately. My guess is he's doing penance for his crime, serving as the chief's lackey. But I don't see anything that suggests he's our guy." That might explain the bad attitude, Ted thought.

"Next, your chief. Now I know you left his name off the list and said he has a good, honest rep, but I checked it regardless. Looks like he's probably a good year away from retirement, but he took a bit of a hit with some investments over the past year or so, and he's recently moved some money around again. But the strange part is that the source of the funds for some of his more recent investments isn't clear. It didn't seem to come from any of his bank accounts."

"Oh great, just what I need—the chief as a suspect," Ted sighed, taking notes as Luke continued.

"Hopefully it's something like Captain Taylor—an innocent inheritance. Next: Caroline Johnson." She'd been on the force for some time but was usually out patrolling streets or running up calls, so she didn't spend as much time in the office, and as a result Ted didn't know her all that well. He thought she was about thirty-five-years old, divorced or widowed, no kids.

"She's extremely wealthy, but the source is clear. Her husband helped start up a company that manufactured a popular computer gadget, and when shares went public he sold his portion and made millions. He died about a year ago from an aneurism. I don't see any motives there," Luke suggested.

"I agree," Ted replied.

"Next: Shelby Coats. You said she's been there a few years

now and seemed to do well enough. I looked into her financials, too, and she lives alone in a small place that belonged to her parents who died a few years ago. Her car is maybe ten years old, and I found a few articles that talk about her volunteering for some local women's charities or something. Seems benign."

"True. But know what—she was just showing off a rather large engagement ring," Ted mused.

"Do you know who it's from?" Luke asked.

"No, in fact I've never even heard her mention a relationship before. And she can be a bit . . . moody, to say it nicely. I was surprised to hear someone would want to actually marry her, horrible as that sounds. That guy is going to be on his tiptoes for half his life."

"Well, I think it would be good if we can find out who the mystery fiancé is. And the last person, your partner—Leona." Luke paused.

"Yes?" Ted asked anxiously. He'd hesitantly explained her family's situation to Luke earlier, knowing that would help him with where to look.

"I know this isn't news to you—she really needs money. Big time. They are over one hundred thousand dollars upside down on their mortgage, the husband is unemployed, and the medical expenses for their kid's treatments have reached six figures. Poor kid. I hate to say it, but there are a few red flags."

"Like what?"

"There were two recent deposits in the amount of $9,999 each into their bank account," Luke replied.

"Below the federal reporting limit," Ted acknowledged.

"Yes. And I imagine a parent would do just about anything for their child . . . not that I would condone helping a murderer out, of course. But she's got a pretty strong motive."

"Damn," Ted said. "Anything else?"

"No, I'll call if we find out more."

"All right, thanks Luke. You guys take care. Oh, you probably would have already thought of this, but they haven't found the patrol officer's car out there yet, and I imagine Scott probably went looking for a new one by now."

"Yes, I had the same thought. Thanks."

They disconnected, and Ted looked at his notes, thinking. Unfortunately it looked like there were several people that could have a financial motive if someone were looking to hire an informant. And what was the forest service supervisor doing calling Spencer directly? He sat for a moment, reviewing the notes he'd just taken, when his phone rang again.

"Ted here," he answered absently.

"Hey, it's Brian. I've done what I can, but unfortunately I need to release the information about David Payton by one p.m. today. Sorry I can't wait any longer."

"Got it. Hey, man, I appreciate you holding on to it this long. I know it put you in a bit of a vulnerable spot with your superiors. If they have an issue, please have them call me directly."

"Sure, thanks. And good luck."

They disconnected, and Ted looked around for the chief and his partner, now curious to get a sense of what they were doing. He also hoped to see how they reacted when the news came about Dr. Payton. He was so distracted he almost jumped when Captain Taylor passed by.

"Ted, good to see you. How's your friend doing?"

"Oh, that. Yeah, thanks, Ron. I have a feeling she's going to be okay," he said, hoping *she* was. "Thanks for asking."

"Sure. Let me know if I can help," he said, gently patting Ted on the shoulder then heading into his office. Ted had been very relieved to learn about the source of the captain's recent windfall. He had an enormous amount of respect for him and couldn't imagine Ron doing anything underhanded, no matter the reason.

He didn't see Leona anywhere, so took a few minutes to sit at his desk and outline what else he needed to do. One—get in touch with Kathryn. But he might not have time to go in person, although he never liked questioning someone over the phone. He wanted to see her reaction face-to-face. Two—well, that depended on the release of the IDs. He wrote down some questions for Kathryn and eventually he heard the ring of the fax machine.

Ted walked over to it, and, as expected, it was Brian's updated MP report. Casually picking up the fax, he feigned curiosity at first then surprise, just in case he had an audience somewhere. He made a copy and walked over to the captain's office, lightly knocking on his glass window. Ron signaled him to come him, so he opened the door and handed him the copy. "We just got this fax. The body Ms. Winters described was likely that of this guy, Dr. David Payton." Ron took the report, carefully scrutinizing it.

"Well I'll be damned," he said. He looked back up at Ted. "Anyone else know about this yet around the office?"

"Fax just arrived, so I'm not sure. I know they also e-mail these out."

"Let's keep it under wraps for just a bit longer. Give me time to check into a few things." Ted nodded and left the office, closing the door behind him. That was a bit odd, he thought. Leona was at her desk when he returned, strangely intent on her own computer screen for someone who had just arrived. Ted had inadvertently left the original report face up on his desk. Although she didn't look like she'd seen it, he carefully filed it in his drawer.

"Hey, Leona, I think I'm going to go grab some lunch. Want anything?"

"No, but thanks for offering. I brought some snacks from home again." she said half distracted. "In fact, oops, I promised to meet the girls in the lunchroom about now." She looked at her watch, stood up, and grabbed her purse on her way out.

~

Jerome walked into Mike's office and found him holding his phone with one hand, his other bunched into a tight fist.

"OK, why am I here?" Jerome demanded.

Mike paused then spoke through gritted teeth. "I was going to relay some new information regarding the hitch in our plans and your son's complete inadequacy to you. But I just got a call that demands a bit more attention," he said, strained. "Someone has officially matched the sketch of the body that woman saw to David. Word is out that he's presumed dead."

Jerome paled. This was not good news. So long as people had thought Rachel was a mental case, and she and her lover were on the run from the law, Jerome, Mike, and Scott could continue as planned. But now with the confirmation that she really did see a body, coupled with a man reported missing in the same time frame, her story was credible. It also pretty much proved her innocence in Spencer's death. They were screwed.

"Can your friend take care of this?" Jerome asked, referring to Mike's contact in the police department. Mike had never said anything directly, but it had been obvious he was getting information from someone on the inside. Jerome had no idea who it was, and frankly he didn't want to know. Mike had either blackmailed someone into helping him or found someone in need of some cash—that's how he typically worked.

"I don't think so. The reports are out of a different department, and word's been spread to everyone contacted yesterday with the original MP report."

"OK, we'll figure this out. There's always a way," Jerome said, trying to convince himself as well as Mike. "First, tell me about the original reason you called. And by the way . . . how's Scott doing? You haven't mentioned him in a while, and Lord knows he never calls me."

Mike explained about his call to Oregon and his resulting suspicions that Rachel had talked with Mr. Stine directly.

"As for your son, he's still out of town dealing with a business matter that was taking longer than expected, and he messed it up. But he's going to fix it. He's fine."

Jerome paused, hesitant, but also feeling like he had nothing to lose now. Time to know the truth. "Mike, did you send my son to kill those two people?"

"Do you really want to know?"

"I suppose that answers it. Just . . . please keep an eye on him," Jerome mumbled. He then turned and left the office, shoulders sagging.

~

Kathryn was feeling more and more uneasy with every minute that passed. Mike had still not returned her call. Plus she'd called Spencer's number three times, and it continued to go directly to voicemail. Add to that her regional manager had called around noon, asking if she'd received confirmation from Mr. Wells yet. Needless to say she was stressed. She sat at her desk for what seemed like a long time, waging an internal war on what to do next, and was startled when her cell phone rang. Hoping it was Mike or Spencer, she quickly answered, failing to look at the caller ID first.

"Hello, is this Ms. Kathyrn Jones?" a man's voice asked.

"Yes, and who is this?"

"Detective Ted Benson from the South Lake Tahoe Police Department. I need a few moments of your time, Ms. Jones."

She paused. This couldn't be good. She pulled the phone away long enough to glimpse the number and write it down on a piece of notepaper. "Give me just a moment, please." Feeling unnerved, she quickly opened her drawer and removed the paper phone book that she'd been teased about several times. But she liked the ease of going right to where she needed. She checked the number for the police station and it matched her caller. "OK, sorry about that. What can I do for you, detective?"

"Well, Ms. Jones, I'm not sure if you'd heard about that

unidentified man we found murdered on the Yova-Pioneer Trail recently?" Of course she'd heard. The whole town knew about it—that and how two locals had skipped town afterward and were suspected of foul play in the matter.

"Yes . . . it's been all over the papers."

"Well, we just received the victim's identification this afternoon from the ME's office. His name is a Mr. Spencer Wells. According to his cell phone, you're the last person to call him."

Spencer was dead? Since days before the meeting? What?

"Ms. Jones, you still with me?" Detective Benson asked after several moments of silence. She stuttered a quick yes and waited for him to speak again. "May I ask why you were calling him?"

"Um, yes." She looked around her office, for something, although not sure what. Probably just anything that would indicate this wasn't actually happening. "He's been involved in an erosion control project we've been coordinating on that incorporates some private land, and he's the owner of the property. We discussed some options with the PI—principal investigator—on the case, and I called to confirm his agreement to the terms."

"When was the last time you actually saw or spoke to Mr. Wells?" The man's voice was steady and official. She paused again. The image of a stern-looking short-haired police officer came to mind, probably from a TV show. Her visual included him waiting for her response, phone against his ear, lined notepad in front, pencil at the ready.

"I guess it's been a few weeks or so. But the PI on the project has been in touch with him since. I got the idea they'd just spoken a couple of days ago about the proposal."

She knew she'd stuttered a bit when referring to the PI, and chances were the officer had noticed. He finally responded. "Ms. Jones, the PI for this project is Mr. Michael Row, correct?"

Kathryn wondered how he could know that already. "Yes.

Row Environmental."

"And can you please tell me the nature of your relationship with Mr. Row?"

"Now wait just a minute," she said, indignation flowing through her words.

The detective cut her off. "Now, I'm sorry, ma'am. I realize this is personal. You can tell me you want a lawyer and end this conversation right now, but there are some innocent people out there who may be running for their lives, and your answers might be what help us save them."

She had already started thinking about the name of the attorney who helped a friend of hers a year back. But then the detective's words seemed to penetrate her line of thought. The recent images of the couple in the papers flashed through her head. And the dog one of the reporters had decided to include as well. Then she recalled what Mike had told her yesterday—that he'd just spoken with Spencer. But if the kid had been dead for several days . . . she let out a huge sigh, as someone does when deciding to let go of a long-held secret. "Let me shut my door." Kathryn got up, quietly closed her office door, and sat back down, dreading what was coming next.

"We've been having an affair for some time. But I assure you he's a stand-up man, and we have kept our professional and work lives separate." She added this last part unconvincingly, no longer believing it herself.

"I appreciate your candor, and I'll do my best to keep you out of anything as much as I can," the detective replied. "But I think you may know more than you realize, and I'd like to ask if you could come over to the station and talk with me some more." He sounded sincere, but she was still nervous about getting involved.

"I've got a lot of work to do," she started to say.

"Kathryn, I hope you don't mind me calling you that." He paused, continuing when she raised no objections. "I'm going to be honest with you. I think you are involved in something way over your head, and if you don't come clean now, you may be left holding the bag from someone else's mess."

"But Mike's a good guy. He wouldn't be involved in anything illegal . . ."

"If I tell you something, I need you to promise you will not make any calls and please come directly to the station. For your own safety as well. Can you do that for me?"

Fear starting to creep into her voice, she responded, "Yes."

"Good. I'm going to trust you to do the right thing here. We suspect there's a financial motive for Spencer's murder having to do with the private property he owns and that project you are involved with. His will leaves the property to Michael Row."

She couldn't believe it. That lying, manipulative son of a bitch! She stood up, reaching for her purse. "I'll be right over." She walked quickly out of the building, heading straight to her car. What had she gotten tangled up in? If Mike would really kill Spencer for money, then would he kill her, too, to protect it?

Twenty minutes and several stoplights later, she arrived at the station asking immediately for Detective Ted Benson. She was escorted into a small conference room, asked if she needed anything, and told he'd be with her shortly. About five minutes later, a tall, handsome man appearing to be around forty came into the room, thanking her for coming.

"I know it wasn't easy, Ms. Jones, and it won't be easy until this is all resolved. However, I think you are really going to help us out here. I'm going to do my best to protect you, OK?"

Kathryn nodded and without further prompting she proceeded to tell him the entire story of the West Hills project, including the meeting yesterday and what was discussed. "The proposal was to build several units on the private property that would use a forest service access road for the driveway, and as part of this investment the owner would pay for additional storm-water treatment down the line. Without the private dollars, we don't have the money to clean up that water now. It's already been spent, and it didn't work."

"Thank you, Kathryn. I want you to know that you've helped enormously. Now, I'm going to need you to write all of this down for me." He placed a large yellow lined notepad and pen in front of her. "But I also think you should know that the project did work. Someone has been dumping polluted water into the stream below the project area, so the measurements downstream would be bad, and adjusting the upstream reports to make it look consistent. With no more dumping we expect that water's going to eventually clear up."

"My God! I don't know what to say." She was relieved to hear the project worked but all the more angry to think of everything Mike had done. She didn't know him at all. How could she be so easily fooled?

"Before you get started, can you please write a separate list of the names of everyone at that meeting yesterday?"

She agreed, but as she started to write, the enormity of this list hit her. She heard the officer's reference to her being stuck holding the bag. It might be good to get that lawyer. Not because of the cops but because these men and women were not the kind to mess around with.

"I admit I'm a bit nervous about the people on this list. I think I should get that attorney now."

Ted nodded then sat down next to her. "I won't promise anything, but I do know without your help they are more likely to get away with what they've done. But if you're not comfortable giving me that list before calling an attorney, I'll understand."

She looked back down at the paper, thinking about the murders. The poor couple on the run. She began slowly writing down the names. When she'd finished, she handed him the paper. "My employee Chuck Stanton had no idea about anything. I've pretty much kept him away from the project since it began, and he was out for paternity leave last fall."

"I'll make sure everyone knows that."

"Can I call my attorney now?"

"Of course. Also you are free to go, but if you are willing I'd like to have you stay here for a while so I can arrange for some protection for you. You can stay here or in our break room, if you'd like."

She stood up. "Yes, I think I could use some refreshments." She followed him as he led her across the office to the small room, still struggling to piece together how much she'd been fooled.

CHAPTER TWENTY-FIVE

"Luke, Rachel, Ted again."

"Yes. Got some news for us?" Luke asked.

"I just spoke with Kathryn Jones." He relayed her statement and heard Rachel's voice the background.

"Those worthless, greedy bast—"

"Ted, thanks for the info, man." Luke cut in, and Ted could tell he was on the verge of laughter, a needed break to the tension of the afternoon.

"I'll keep you two informed, but for now don't go anywhere just yet. I think we'll be able to get you home soon, safe and sound." Rachel hadn't resumed her volley of curses. Instead he suddenly heard her voice closer to the phone.

"Any word on Scott?"

"No, not yet. But I expect we'll be talking with his father very soon," Ted replied.

"OK, good." Then, her voice distant again, he heard, "That slimy, no good—"

"Thanks, Ted. From both of us," Luke again intervened.

"No problem. Good luck, Luke," Ted said, chuckling. After disconnecting, Ted did his best not to be charmed by Rachel's little cursing fits as he walked back to his office. He saw Leona in her seat, looking confused.

"Ted, what's going on? Some woman is in our break room, and I hear she's a murder witness or something? Also there's been some talk about bodies, and that Rachel woman?"

Ted looked at her, remembering what Luke had found out about her. He wanted to trust her, but until he knew for sure he still had to be careful. "They've identified the person who was killed with a rock. Also someone filed an MP report yesterday, and it turns out it matches the description Ms. Winters had provided of the dead man she saw several weeks ago."

He watched her reaction closely, and she seemed truly surprised as she blurted out, "Holy shit."

~

Not long after Jerome had left his office, Mike's phone rang—it was his connection in the police station. "They've identified the second body. There's apparently a witness related to the case in the office right now, although no one is saying how she's involved." His caller had an accusatory tone. Just what he needed.

"OK, *she*? Can you describe her?" Mike asked impatiently.

"Around fifty, dark-brown and grey hair, maybe five feet six inches tall or so. She's wearing one of those tacky women's business suits," the caller's feminine voice said.

Mike's face drained of color. Having described Kathryn, he wondered what she was doing there. How much could she know? He thought he'd done a good job of playing the innocent consultant, surprised by the failing project and seeking a worthwhile solution. But she could tie them together at that meeting, if it came up. Then another line of thought occurred to him. Worse yet, what if the two women got to talking . . . ? He sighed, and her voice cut into his reverie.

"Mike, who is she? And how is *she* involved?" his fiancée, Shelby, asked.

"Don't worry, honey. We'll sort this out later. I need to go."

He hung up abruptly, barely hearing her gear up to argue. He ran out front and saw that Jerome hadn't left yet. Instead he was just sitting there in the driver's seat. As Mike approached, he saw why. Jerome had a small flask in one hand, keys in the other. He didn't seem to notice Mike until he tapped on the window, and Jerome abruptly shook before looking up at him.

"Sorry, I . . . ," he said, rolling the window down.

"Jerome, we've got a major problem. You need to get back inside. Feel free to bring your poison with you. I have a feeling you'll think better drunk than sober at this point." They walked back into Mike's office and shut the door. Jerome sat in the visitor's chair, taking another long sip from the silver container.

"Our problems just got a lot worse. I suggest you notify the others to cover their tracks."

"What? Why?" snorted Jerome.

Mike gave a shortened version of what he'd found out about the body identifications and Kathryn's statement as he handed Jerome a disposable phone. He sat down, watching Jerome withdraw a small list he kept in his wallet and begin dialing. How Jerome could be so old school when it came to electronics versus paper and still get as far as he had in his career was beyond Mike's comprehension.

As he listened to Jerome's first conversation, he tried to figure out what he should do now. It didn't seem possible that after everything he'd done it could all be coming down around him. There had to be a way he could come out the innocent party. Maybe he could still sell the property off as the one-unit estate. It could easily be permitted for sale that way. The subdivided units would have brought in more money than he could ever spend, although he had intended to move far away. That was after, of course, retrieving his daughter. But subdivisions would require the full environmental review, public meetings, and numerous approvals by the county, and that clearly wasn't going to happen now. Yet maybe Mike could sell it as is and cover his expenses for a while. The question was how to make sure he wasn't connected to Spencer's death. The rest Mike could blame on everyone else. He'd have to play dumb, really dumb, but he could do it.

After a heated exchange, Jerome hung up and began dialing the next number. Mike knew Jerome's career would be over, for sure. Lexy's doctoring of the SST Lab results would be exposed and she'd probably lose her job. She'd also helped them select what to dump in the stream in the first place. The woman had been so angry, so distasteful to work with, it would serve her right if she got arrested. The question was what would she be more afraid of? Would she protect Mike's involvement in order to prevent her own crime with her boyfriend from coming out? Although, if she did tell the truth, how reliable was a witness who had participated in such a crime?

Spencer and Scott were responsible for the actual dumping, and clearly Spencer wouldn't be testifying. As for Scott, he was the only one who could tie Mike to Spencer's death. But Mike could easily deny that, saying Scott was acting on his own. Why would he want to kill the boy who'd been like the son he never had? Add to that Scott's reputation for losing his temper. He may not have been convicted of a crime, but there would be arrest records from the predicament Daddy had saved him from. Easy enough to sell that story.

Mike stood up, waiting for a pause in Jerome's conversation. As someone on the other end of the line yelled a string of various curses, Jerome looked up at Mike, moving the phone a bit away from his ear.

"I'm going to make a quick call in the other room," Mike said, excusing himself to go dial Scott's number again.

~

Shelby was angry. Mike's reaction suggested he knew this female witness *very well*. She walked back toward the main office from the closet she'd used for her call, her mind running through all of the late business meetings he'd claimed. Then just when she was about fed up—an apology and a huge ring. She had fallen for it and gladly continued to provide him the extra information that he promised would support their wonderful future together. As she entered the main office she saw Ted and Leona in excited conversation. Shelby tried to act casual as she strolled over to them.

"What's going on? Seems to be some excitement around here, and I'm hearing something about a woman giving a statement?"

"We've got identifications for the two murder victims from that trail," Ted responded, providing no additional details.

"Two?" She did her best to sound surprised. Ted nodded, naming the men.

"Wow. I guess Ms. Winters was telling the truth then, huh? So, who's the female witness?"

She saw Ted hesitate before responding. "She appears to be an innocent player in a situation I don't think she fully comprehends. She's a forest service supervisor who has been dating one of the consultants involved in the matter."

Shelby paused for a moment, an irate look coming over her features as her suspicions were confirmed. "One of the consultants? Would that be Mr. Mike Row?" she said angrily, fidgeting nervously at the engagement ring on her hand. Then it occurred to her she'd given herself away as she saw the look of anger flash over Ted's features. He knew.

"You're their insider, aren't you, Shelby?" Ted said matter-of-factly.

She was caught in his stare like a deer in headlights, and she knew there was no getting out of this one. Shelby physically sagged, took the ring off, and threw it across the room. "That cheating bastard has been lying to me from the start! I swear I had no idea just how far he was taking all of this."

"Shelby, I need your badge and gun. Then you need to go wait in that interview room." He held out his hand as she slowly set them on his palm. Trying to maintain what dignity she could muster, she stood up straight, walked slowly to the room he'd noted, and calmly sat in the chair behind the table.

She heard Leona's shocked voice behind her ask Ted, "What was that all about?"

"A woman scorned," he responded. From the chair in the room, Shelby watched Ted make a phone call, grab his notebook, and begin walking in her direction. She hoped she could at least make a deal to testify against the jerk.

~

Luke and Rachel had been waiting to hear back from Ted before deciding what to do. Check out time was ten a.m.—long passed by now—so they'd paid for another night at the hotel. Rachel was restless. She had packed everything up, including the food, thinking they would be leaving. As time passed, she unpacked some snacks. She did more searches online but wasn't focused and frankly unsure of what to look up at this point. Luke seemed to be looking for stuff to do, too. It hadn't been an awkward morning. In fact it had been strangely . . . easy, she thought. The problem was every time she looked at him she wanted a repeat of the night before. But that's why they missed a call last night, and they had to be ready to answer when Ted called now. A repeat would have to wait.

Finally Rachel spoke up. "OK, this isn't working, and Bella is going to need a good walk soon or she'll start chewing up the pillows. I'm so anxious I might join her. There's a path going up that hill behind the parking lot. What do you say? I would assume we'd still get cell reception if he calls."

Luke responded so fast it was as if he'd just been waiting for someone to solve the problem of his own restlessness. "Sounds great—I'll grab a few things and change into my boots." Then he paused and added, "But keep in mind, we need to be careful about Scott. Don't let your guard down at all." After that, she saw him grab his gun and put it in the holster attached to his belt.

"I wish you'd be willing to take Scott's gun, but then again, I guess you *have* warned me that you might shoot me."

"And that still stands. Although the first time I warned you, it may not have bothered me so much."

"Oh, and now?" he asked, with a sexy look on his face as he closed the distance between them.

"I might feel *just a bit* upset," she said coyly.

"Just a bit, huh?" he asked then quickly pulled her lips to his. She could feel the slight pressure of his hands on the back of her neck as the kiss grew deeper. Again she felt chills rush from her head to her toes. If she didn't stop this now, Bella wasn't going to get her walk, so she slowly placed her hand on his waist, lightly pushing back.

"Much as I'd love to continue, I think we'd better get going. So we can be ready for Ted's call, too."

"Sometimes, Rachel, you can be so damn . . . sensible," he said teasingly. "All right, let's go. I'll grab the room key."

She grabbed the small hip pack she used for shorter walks. It held a small bottle of water, a dish for Bella, and a few other items. It took them about ten minutes to reach the top of the hill. There weren't any trees in the area, and this part of Wyoming looked similar to the desert areas in Nevada or southern Oregon—dirt with large sagebrush, scattered among a few rocks here and there. She looked around in the distance and saw a few areas where it looked like flash floods had recently caused small fissures in the land. She also heard the chirps of birds, but otherwise there wasn't much around.

"That was a bit steeper than I'd realized," Luke said, cresting the hill just a few seconds behind her. She turned around to look at him and saw that he was staring at his phone. A moment later he said, "It's a bit hard to see, but I do have a signal, so we should be good to stay here for a while."

"Good. I was feeling pretty cooped up in there," she said, enjoying the breeze.

~

It had taken longer than he'd hoped, but Scott found their hotel. Sure, they had parked the truck around the back, but he'd driven through the parking lot of every hotel he came across, and finally there it was. As he was parking off to the side, he happened to notice movement on a hill behind the motel. He looked up, and there they were, casually strolling up with that damn mutt next to them. Well, chances were there was no one else out there. The downside was his throbbing leg; having taken a few more pills about fifteen minutes ago he could now feel them finally putting a mild dent in the pain. Either way, he had to just push through it. He quietly climbed out of the car and looked around but didn't notice anyone else. There was only one other car in the parking lot besides Rachel's pickup. The first part of the path ran through some tall bushes, and by the time he was out and walking up the bottom part of the path he couldn't see them anymore. They had gone over the hill. *Good. Guaranteed privacy. Even better.*

~

It was just after she tossed a small branch and watched Bella race off after it that Rachel heard it—the faint sound of a cell phone ringing. She looked at Luke; it wasn't his phone. He'd heard it, too, and pointed back down the hill, saying nothing. She understood and nodded. She looked over at Bella, who was running back to her again, carrying the stick, tail wagging. When Bella arrived, Rachel took hold of her collar, rubbing her while using the "don't speak" command, hoping Bella would listen again. Luke walked over and whispered in her ear.

"I think you two could fit behind that washout over there." He pointed to what resembled a small sunken fault line. If they climbed into it, the sides would be about a foot over her head.

Once again in survival mode, not thinking about the bigger picture, she readily agreed. "Bella, come," she whispered. They walked over to the washout, slowly climbing down the steep loose dirt, with Luke behind them. After she'd positioned herself and Bella in the crevice, she looked back at Luke. He'd remained on the edge above them, bending over to talk.

"Rachel, don't argue with me. Please take my gun. You won't shoot me. I promise."

"But what about you?" She was scared for Bella and herself, but the fear that Luke could get hurt, or worse, overwhelmed her.

"I'm just going to take a look. Maybe it's just another hotel guest taking a walk." She knew even as he said it Luke didn't believe that either. Before she could protest, he gently touched her cheek. "Either way, I think it's better for you to have this. Besides, I've got a forty-foot weapon of my own, thanks to you." He patted the other side of his belt, where he'd hung her can of bear spray. It was the one thing that didn't fit in her small pack, and she hadn't picked it up in the room before because they weren't in bear country. She looked at him questioningly.

"Well, I don't know this area. I thought maybe there were wolves or something." With a sly grin on his face, he handed her the gun, stood up, and began advancing toward the hillside.

~

The ringing stopped by the time Luke had returned to where he had first heard it. There were no voices, so he assumed the person hadn't answered the call. Make that *Scott* hadn't answered the call. He looked over the crest and down the path they'd just walked up, seeing no one. Carefully, he ducked for cover, at the same time searching each side for dense brush or washouts large enough to conceal him. A movement about ten feet away caught his attention, but when he focused on it he saw that several birds were flying away from a bush. Then Luke felt a searing pain run through his upper right chest, and the breath was knocked out of him. He wavered, lost his balance, and fell to the ground. He did his best to maintain focus as the throbbing pain threatened to take away his consciousness. With his left hand he pulled the bear spray can from his belt and held it firmly. Luke hoped Rachel would stay put; but she was too stubborn, and he assumed he didn't have a lot of time before either she came over to check on him or he passed out. So he tried to draw Scott out, taking a deep breath and doing his best to speak.

"Come out, Scott, you coward." Chances were Scott had the cop's gun and probably plenty of bullets left. In other words, he was the better-armed man here and had no reason not to simply wait. But Luke was also familiar with pride, and many criminals were smug. They didn't believe they'd get caught, and when they did they still didn't expect to fail. Calling that out would either give Scott the location he needed to shoot again or prompt him to make a mistake. Luke hoped for the latter. If it worked he might have, at best, a moment or two before Scott would aim for the second, and probably final, shot. "Typical loser doing someone else's dirty work for them. Getting paid well by Uncle Mike, are you? Couldn't make it on your own?"

It worked. He saw the tall man stand up, apparently having found shelter in another washout. Scott began moving a few steps toward him, gun in hand. "Oh no, Luke, this is all for *me* now," he said, raising the gun with a victorious smile on his face.

Scott had done exactly what Luke had been hoping for, giving him the time and the target. He aimed the bear spray and pulled the nozzle. Flaming hot peppered liquid shot out at the man, drenching his eyes, nostrils, and mouth with the burning substance. He fell back and dropped his gun, instinctively scratching at his eyes and nose. Luke could hear the man struggling to breathe. Then Luke's world went black.

~

Rachel couldn't see Luke once he'd stepped down the trail, and when she heard the gunshot ring out, fear and adrenaline shot through her. She wanted to jump up and run toward Luke, but she'd promised him she'd stay hidden. Then again, she couldn't just sit there either, especially if Luke was hurt. It was a struggle, and when silence followed after the gunshot, she knew she couldn't remain any longer. She commanded Bella to stay while she slowly crawled out of the crevice, keeping low to the ground as she moved. She looked back, thankful to see Bella was staying put.

Hunched down just a few feet shy of the hill's crest, Rachel heard Luke calling out to the man. She thanked God he was still alive. She crawled forward a few more feet and got a visual. Holding Luke's gun in her right hand, she expected it to be shaking, but her grip was steady. She looked at Scott just in time to watch the stream of bear spray hit him, covering his face and upper body. He'd fallen and dropped his gun on the way down but was still conscious. Rachel glanced quickly over at Luke, who was lying flat on his back, not moving, a huge bloodstain soaking through the chest of his shirt. Her heart sank. She ran to him, instantly relieved he was still breathing, and let out the breath she hadn't realized she'd been holding. Not a shot to the heart—he'll be okay. He has to be. She saw a quick movement to her side, and when she looked in that direction she saw that Scott was struggling to crawl on all fours, feeling for the gun he'd dropped but couldn't see.

"Oh no you don't, you pathetic little shit," she yelled. Without hesitation, she stood up and walked toward the struggling man. To his detriment, at that moment he represented all of the Matts, the Mikes, and the Scotts in the world, and that's why she felt so . . . confident. He was still about ten feet away from her and roughly four feet from his own gun. When Rachel heard herself speaking in a voice so firm, it even scared her.

"Scott, are you ready to die for your dear uncle?" He paused, stopped moving, and raised his hands as if in surrender. She took a few steps toward him, watching him carefully, hoping the emotional surge allowing her to do this would persist. Suddenly he rolled over making a quick leaping maneuver toward his gun, closing the distance in a second. Without thinking, Rachel aimed and fired, catching sight of a burst of red on the right back pocket of his pants. *She had shot him in the ass.*

Either he hadn't been able to grasp his gun fast enough or he'd let it go; she couldn't tell. The gun was tossed in the dirt a foot away from him, and he now lay on his side, cradling his newest bullet wound with one hand, the other rubbing at his stinging eyes again. All she wanted was to get back to Luke, but she couldn't risk leaving Scott lying there. She wondered how to contain him. Then it hit her: Bella's leash. She reached into her waist pack and pulled the six-foot leather leash out as she walked to him.

"You are not getting out of this one," Rachel declared, grabbing Scott's arms with all her strength. She wrapped the leash around his wrists and ankles, tying the best knot she could. He would probably get out of the restraint soon enough, but clearly he was too caught up in the pain of his new injuries to try anytime soon. Satisfied that he was secure for a while, she picked up the gun he dropped and turned around to get back to Luke, a gun in each hand. If only her brothers could see her now. She'd never hear the end of it.

Bella came running over the crest of the hill and approached Luke carefully, tail in air but not wagging, waiting to see whether she could celebrate. Rachel dropped to her knees next to Luke, setting the guns aside. Tears were streaming down her face, and she could barely see through them. She was just praying he would be okay. Rachel looked for something to put over his wound. She could use her T-shirt, but it would take a minute to undo the belt pack; then she realized she had her convertible hiking pants on. She quickly unzipped one leg and used it to press over the bullet wound.

"Please, please, please be okay. You can't leave me now, Luke!" she yelled desperately. Reaching into her back pocket for her phone, she fumbled as she dialed 9-1-1. When the operator answered, she told herself to calm down and speak slowly. Her heart was racing a hundred miles per minute. She explained their location and situation, trying to remain calm and patient when the operator asked her to repeat everything. Finally she set the phone down and, ignoring the operator's repetitive questions, left it on speaker so she could focus, hands free, on Luke.

"Just send an ambulance now!" she yelled at the phone. With one hand still pressing on the wound, she began running her fingers through his hair, like one might do to comfort a child. She leaned over and gently kissed his forehead, then his cheek, and then his lips. When she heard the welcome sounds of sirens in the distance and looked up to see where they were, she heard another sound that was far more welcome.

From just a few inches away, a scratchy, whispering voice said, "Not right now, mountaingirl, but I'll definitely take a rain check." She looked back down at him and saw his eyes were half open, looking up at her. Luke was actually grinning, but then his features shifted to concern. "Where is Scott?"

"He's not a problem at the moment." She glanced over, briefly noting the man lying in obvious agony, unable to do more than squirm. Then she grinned, looking immediately back down at Luke.

"As for that rain check, cowboy, I'll give you that and then some." She leaned over and kissed him again. A moment later a huge wet tongue ran across both of their faces. Bella had joined the celebration.

~

Mike was in a panic—Scott still hadn't answered his phone. Jerome had finished his calls in the other room and gone back to nursing his flask like a baby bottle. Something just wasn't right. It was time to bail. He began packing a few things into a duffle bag, including two guns, another disposable cell phone, ten thousand dollars in cash he kept in a wall safe, and two passports—one with his name and picture, the other with his image but someone else's name, just in case. He called out to Jerome, "I'll be back shortly," not caring if the man heard him as he ran out the front door and jumped into his Hummer. He started the engine and began backing out when he heard the high-pitched wails of police sirens. A moment later, blue and red lights approached from the other end of the short dirt driveway. There was nowhere to hide. He stopped his car and sat there as the officers approached his driver's side door.

"Mr. Michael Row, I presume," one of the officers said. Mike looked over and saw a man in plain clothes, aiming at gun at his head. He noted the man was a bit younger than David, but they looked alike—athletic and youthful, freckled by time spent in the sun. Then he wondered why such a thought would run through his mind right now. Mike nodded and raised his hands above his head. The officer reached out and pulled the door open.

"Mr. Row, my name is Detective Ted Benson, and you are under arrest," he said as he pulled Mike out of the car, flipped him around, and clasped handcuffs on his wrists.

EPILOGUE

Luke and Rachel sat with Ted, Brian Choe, and Jill, enjoying dinner at one of their favorite local restaurants situated in Hope Valley. It had impressive views, good food, and a dog-friendly policy on the outdoor patio. Bella was patiently lying at Rachel's feet, gnawing on a fresh elk antler. The restaurant was also a good 'middle ground' place to meet Brian and Jill, who both lived in the Carson Valley.

"And there goes another beautiful Sierra sunset," she said as they all paused to look at the sun setting behind the now purple mountains, rays of color surrounding it caught in the high, wispy clouds.

"Can't ask for more," Ted chimed in, raising his wine glass. "All right, just wanted to toast to everyone here. It's been a rough few months, and although I wished we'd all met under better circumstances, I'm glad to know each of you." He raised his glass, and everyone followed suit.

"Dude, that was . . . corny," Brian laughed.

"Well, I had to say something. You were all staring at the sunset. It was too damn quiet. Also I wanted an excuse to drink more without being rude."

"*Uh-huh*," Jill quipped sarcastically, nudging Ted's arm, then looking over at Brian who sat on her other side, with a look Rachel had come to know well lately. Something was brewing there, she was pretty sure.

"Yes, a bit lame, but true all the same," Luke said, raising the arm that was now free of the sling he'd had to wear until a week ago. "And if you ever want to leave the force, I'd say you could come work for me. But frankly I hope you don't. I like the idea of having a friend still working there."

"First, I assume you meant work *with* you, not for you," Ted corrected. "And by the way . . . how is your shoulder doing?"

"Pretty well. Even better at the moment thanks to this wine," he laughed. Luke had been airlifted to Salt Lake City where he underwent emergency surgery, but no major organs had been struck, and the doctors expected a full recovery. He was able to return home a week later, promising to be careful, to check in with his doctor daily, and to wear the arm sling for as long as his doctor ordered. Rachel had been by his side nonstop, to the frustration of many nurses.

"Just the wine, eh?" Rachel asked, winking at him. It was two weeks after the shooting that she'd made good on her promise of a rain check, not that either of them wanted to wait that long. Doctor's orders. Sure, even then, it was a bit more . . . adventurous . . . working around the arm and shoulder deal. But they were motivated to figure it out.

"Definitely not just the wine," he said, with the tone a guy takes when he's catering to his woman in front of the guys. Rachel rolled her eyes.

"So, I hear Scott's being transferred to Vegas until the trial," Ted said.

"Yes, he's been in our jail since he was released from the prison hospital, but now the waiting game begins," Brian commented. "The guys in Rock Springs said he flipped on his uncle and father so fast they didn't even have to ask."

"I heard Diane filed for divorce the next day. Good, she

deserves better," Rachel said. "It still irritates me that Monica, Ron Senior, and Garrett are probably going to escape legal action." The prosecutor had explained that given their positions in the community, they needed to have more than the word of Jerome and Mike, both charged with numerous crimes, to convict "a planning commissioner, a county supervisor, and an executive director of the regional planning agency." No physical evidence linking them to the crimes or any insider meetings could be found.

"At least two of them lost their jobs and reputations. Maybe for people like that it's as good as prison," Jill added.

"Maybe. But I have a feeling they'll cower away for a while then come back with some new spin to get everyone to overlook those 'horrible rumors from a few years ago that were absolutely not true.' But I'm even more upset that Garrett Mathem not only escaped conviction but got to keep his job. He's just as guilty as the rest them. Meanwhile a huge part of my job is reviewing decisions made by his board," Rachel paused, knowing she could get worked up over the outcome again easily, opting instead to sip her wine.

"I can't believe he had the audacity to not only pretend he had no idea about any of this but then to actually publicly accuse the forest service of failing to monitor the project properly, blaming *them* for letting it happen," Jill remarked, exasperation in her voice.

"At least Mike's not going anywhere, ever. Scott also told us about Mike's daughter, Lori. I'm so thankful the poor girl has remained completely in the dark on that family tie," Luke added.

"Whatever happened to that girl who doctored the results? Lexy?" Jill asked, turning toward Ted.

"Oh, get this! After she was fired and still refused to talk about any of it, she disappeared. You know what I just found out yesterday? She's apparently been hired by the government to help locate hackers. She's probably getting paid more than I am."

"Seriously? Hmm, can I withhold paying my taxes, please?" Jill said.

"I know what you mean," Brian agreed.

Rachel looked toward the southwest, her mind drifting as the conversations continued around her. It was almost dark now, but she could still picture the forest that remained there, untouched. With the original will they'd found having been certified through all legal channels, Janet had been placed in charge of Lloyd's estate as he'd intended and operated with the help of the board his will had created. They'd donated the two hundred acres to the forest service with the agreement it would remain as is. As expected, without the addition of the polluted water, the stream cleared up and the project was considered a success.

~

An hour later, Rachel pulled her pickup into her short driveway, but she and Luke didn't get out right away.

"Well, I guess I'd better get started reviewing those documents I mentioned." She had to review yet another frustrating proposal, at least as far as she was concerned. At first glance it appeared to be more spin on finding ways to make money, lacking any concern for environmental protection or maintaining the rural nature of the small community nearby. Yes, she was biased, and she knew it. But she felt she'd earned the right.

"Let me guess. Is it being pushed by our dear friend, Mr. Garrett Mathem?" Luke said.

"Yes, of course." She had confessed she was worried that Garrett would make her job more difficult after all that had happened. This was the first project she was hired to review that had come from the planning agency he directed. She was nervous but knew she had to get back in the game sometime.

"But you know what? Let him make it harder. And I'll just push back that much more," she said, defiance in her voice. "In fact, he knows I know he was involved. Maybe he'll watch his step a bit more." A second later they both looked at each other with "yeah, right" expressions on their faces. Bella, of course, chose that moment to again lick them each on the cheek from the backseat of the truck.

"Have I said before that girl has a hell of a tongue?" Luke laughed. Rachel reached back and rubbed her, and in a few minutes they walked through her front door, Bella and her huge tongue trailing behind.

"So did you notice the sparks between Brian and Jill tonight?" Rachel chuckled. Luke gave her a look.

"Honey, I'm a guy. I don't notice things like sparks unless they're coming from an engine or a firecracker," he teased.

"Oh really," she said, treating it like the challenge it was. She dropped her purse, closed the door behind them, reached behind his head, and pulled his lips to hers aggressively. She kissed him hard while simultaneously tossing the antler she'd carried in from the truck, knowing it would occupy Bella for some time.

Luke responded to her need and quickly embraced her with both arms, kissing her fiercely. With the small amount of control she had left, she reached over and pulled his shirt off, throwing it aside so she could quickly be near him again. He reached for hers with the same plan, but she stopped him.

"Let me do that for you, cowboy." She walked backward toward her bedroom, slowly removing her own shirt and tossing it on the floor next to his.

"No problem, mountaingirl," he said, desire on his face. He followed her into the bedroom, and as she gazed at him, her eyes caught the scar from the bullet that had almost taken this amazing man from her life. She moved closer to him, softly placing her lips against the discolored skin. She felt him shiver and stopped, looking back up into his bright blue eyes. She smiled and then pulled him onto the bed with her. That night, she did her best to make sure he knew all about sparks.

Later, after drifting off to sleep in each other's arms, Rachel woke up, just enough to hear the dog tags enter the room. A moment later, she felt the pressure of Bella's weight as the pup curled up at their feet.

"Bella, my sweet girl," she said, moving just enough to rub Bella's ears without disturbing Luke. "Good night."

ABOUT THE AUTHOR

Jennifer Quashnick holds a master's degree in environmental science and health and has spent over fifteen years advocating for scientifically supported policy-making to protect Lake Tahoe's environment and rural communities. She also makes a point to spend regular time hiking with her dog, Bella, refreshed by the beauty of the Sierra Nevada and the joy of being outdoors.

Jennifer's creative side emerged when she adopted Bella and became inspired by the dog's antics. The Mountaingirl Mysteries series is a result of regular time outdoors; years of hard work in environmental science, planning, and politics; and a dog named Bella.

Raised on a small ranch in northern California, Jennifer's childhood revolved around an outdoor lifestyle with weekends and summers spent in the mountains. Jennifer loves all that the Sierra Nevada have to offer, although she is most fond of hiking, snowshoeing, and downhill skiing, and is typically accompanied by Bella—the true star of her books.

83650504R00157

Made in the USA
San Bernardino, CA
29 July 2018